'Impeccable'
Sunday Times

'Superbly creepy modern horror story'
Book of the Week, *Sunday Mirror*

'This novel from the brilliant Peter James had
the hairs standing up on our arms from the first page'
Book of the Week, *Heat*

'James is a compelling storyteller and he ratchets up
the tension in increments, so that his readers will be
suitably terrified. By the time you want to scream
."Look behind you!", it's already too late'
Daily Mail

'James plays with your expectations – creating
a convincing and genuinely terrifying tale that, in the
best old-fashioned tradition, will frighten the wits
out of you in a most enjoyable way'
Irish Sunday Mirror

'A great piece of escapism that will have you
looking over your shoulder'
Scotsman

THE HOUSE ON COLD HILL

Peter James was educated at Charterhouse, then at film school. He lived in North America for a number of years, working as a screenwriter and film producer before returning to England. His novels, including the *Sunday Times* number one bestselling Roy Grace series, have been translated into thirty-six languages, with worldwide sales of sixteen million copies. Three books have been filmed. He has also written a short-story collection, A *Twist of the Knife*. All his books reflect his deep interest in the world of the police, with whom he does in-depth research, as well as his fascination with science, medicine and the paranormal. He has also produced numerous films, including *The Merchant of Venice*, starring Al Pacino, Jeremy Irons and Joseph Fiennes. He divides his time between his homes in Notting Hill, London, and near Brighton in Sussex.

Visit his website at www.peterjames.com

Or follow him on Twitter @peterjamesuk

Or Facebook: facebook.com/peterjames.roygrace

THE HOUSE ON COLD HILL

PETER JAMES

PAN BOOKS

First published 2015 by Macmillan

This edition published in paperback 2016 by Pan Books
an imprint of Pan Macmillan
20 New Wharf Road, London N1 9RR
Associated companies throughout the world
www.panmacmillan.com

ISBN 978-1-4472-5594-9

1 3 5 7 9 8 6 4 2

A CIP catalogue record for this book is available from the British Library.

FOR LINDA BUCKLEY –

MY TIRELESSLY WONDERFUL ASSISTANT

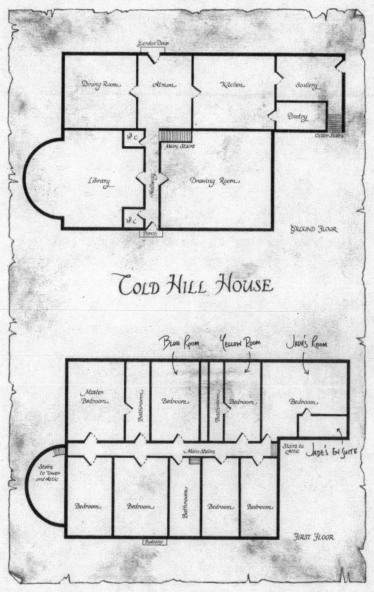

Cold Hill House

1

'Are we nearly there yet?'

Johnny, a smouldering cigar in his mouth, looked in the rear-view mirror. He loved his kids, but Felix, who had just turned eight, could be an irritating little sod sometimes. 'That's the third time you've asked in ten minutes,' he said, loudly, above the sound of the Kinks' 'Sunny Afternoon' blaring from the radio. Then he took the cigar out and sang along to the tune. '*The tax man's taken all my dough and left me in my stately home—*'

'I need to wee,' Daisy said.

'Are we? Are we nearly there?' Felix whined again.

Johnny shot a grin at Rowena, who was luxuriating on the huge front passenger seat of the red and white Cadillac Eldorado. She looked happy, ridiculously happy. Everything was ridiculous right now. This classic 1966 left-hand-drive monster was a ridiculous car for these narrow country lanes but he liked it because it was flash, and in his role as a rock promoter, he was flash all over. And their new home was ridiculous as well. Ridiculously – but very seriously – flash. Rowena loved it, too. She could see herself in a few years' time as the lady of the manor, and she could picture the grand parties they would hold! There was something very special about this place. But first it was badly in need of a makeover and a lot of TLC.

They'd bought the house despite the surveyor's report, which had been twenty-seven pages of doom and gloom. The window frames were badly rotted, the roof needed replacing, there were large patches of damp and the cellar and some of the roof timbers had dangerous infestations of dry rot. But nothing that the shedloads of money he was making right now could not fix.

'Dad, can we have the top down?' Felix said. 'Can we?'

'It's too windy, darling!' Rowena said.

Although the late-October sun was shining brightly, straight in their faces, it was blowing a hooley, and darkening storm clouds were massing on the horizon.

'We'll be there in five minutes,' Johnny announced. 'This is the village now.'

They passed a sign saying COLD HILL – PLEASE DRIVE SLOWLY, with 30 mph warning roundels on either side of the narrow road, then swooped over a humpback bridge, passing a cricket pitch to their left. To their right was a decrepit-looking Norman church. It was set well back and perched dominatingly high above the road. The graveyard, bounded by a low flint wall, was pretty, with rows of weathered headstones, many of them tilting, and some partially concealed beneath the spreading branches of a massive yew tree.

'Are there dead people in there, Mum?' Daisy asked.

'It's a graveyard, darling, yes, there are.' She glanced at the low flint wall.

Daisy pressed her face against the window. 'Is that where we'll go when we're dead?'

Their daughter was obsessed with death. Last year they'd gone on a fishing holiday to Ireland, and the highlight of the trip for Daisy, who was six, had been visiting a graveyard where she discovered she could see into some of the tombs and look down at the bones below.

Rowena turned round. 'Let's talk about something more cheerful, shall we? Are you looking forward to our new home?'

Daisy cuddled her toy monkey to her chest. 'Yes,' she said, a tad reluctantly. 'Maybe.'

'Only *maybe*?' Johnny asked.

They drove past a row of terraced Victorian artisan cottages, a rather drab-looking pub called The Crown, a smithy, a cottage with a 'Bed & Breakfast' sign, and a village store. The road wound steeply uphill, past detached houses and bungalows of various sizes on either side. A white van came tearing down the hill towards them without slowing. Johnny, cursing, pulled the massive car as far over to the left as he could, scraping against bushes, and the van passed with inches to spare.

'I think we're going to need another car for our new country life,' Rowena said. 'Something more sensible.'

'I don't do *sensible*,' Johnny replied.

'Don't I know it! That's why I love you, my darling! But I'm not going to be able to walk the kids round the corner to school any more when the new term starts. And I can hardly do the school run in this.'

Johnny slowed the car and pulled down the right-turn indicator. 'Here we are! The O'Hare family has arrived!'

On their right, opposite a red postbox, were two stone pillars, topped with savage-looking ornamental wyverns, and with open, rusted, wrought-iron gates. Below the large Strutt and Parker 'Sold' board, fixed to the right-hand gate-post, was a smaller, barely legible sign announcing COLD HILL HOUSE.

As he turned in, Johnny stopped the car for a moment,

watching in the rear-view mirror for the removals van; then he saw it as a tiny lumbering speck in the distance. He carried on up the steep, winding, potholed tarmac drive. It was bounded on each side by a railed metal fence, beyond which sheep grazed on the steeply sloping fields. All this land belonged to the house, but was leased to a local tenant farmer.

After a quarter of a mile, the drive curved sharply to the right and they crossed a cattle grid. As they reached a gravel-surfaced plateau at the top of the hill, the house came into view ahead.

'Is that it?' Felix said. 'Wow! Wowwwwww!'

'It's a palace!' Daisy squealed, excitedly. 'We're going to live in a palace!'

The central part of the house was fronted by a classically proportioned Georgian facade clad in weather-stained grey rendering, on three floors, or four if the cellar was included. There was a porch with a columned balcony above it – 'Like a super-grand Juliet balcony!' Rowena had said the first time she had seen it. On either side were tall sash windows and there were two dormer windows in the slate-tiled roof.

On the left side of the building was, incongruously, a crenellated tower with windows at the very top, and on the right was a two-storey extension which, the estate agent had told them, had been added a century after the main house had been built.

'Who's that?' Rowena asked, pointing up at a window.

'What?' Johnny replied.

'There's a woman up in that window – up in that dormer in the attic – looking at us.'

'Maybe it's the cleaners still here.' He peered up through the windscreen. 'I can't see anyone.'

The car rocked in a gust of wind, and an unseasonably cold draught blew through the interior. With a huge grin, Johnny pulled up right in front of the porch, jammed his cigar back in his mouth, took a puff, and through a cloud of smoke said, 'Here we are, guys! Home sweet home!'

The sky darkened, suddenly. There was a rumble above them that sounded, to him, ominously like thunder.

'Oh God,' Rowena said, reaching for the door handle. 'Let's get inside quickly.'

As she spoke, a solitary slate broke free and began sliding down the roof, dislodging and collecting more slates in its path, creating a small avalanche. They smashed through the rusted guttering and fell, gathering speed, sharp as razors, slicing through the fabric roof of the Cadillac, one severing Rowena's right arm, another splitting Johnny's head in two, like a wood axe through a log.

As Rowena and the children screamed, chunks of masonry began raining down on them, ripping through the roof, smashing their skulls and bones. Then an entire slab of stonework fell from near the top of the facade, landing directly on the remains of the roof, flattening the car down on its suspension, buckling its wheels, and crushing its four occupants into a mangled pulp of flesh and bone and blood.

Minutes later, as the removals van crested the hill, all the driver and his crewmates could see was a small mountain of stonework, slates and timber. And above the sound of the howling wind, they could hear the monotone blare of a car horn.

2

Friday, 4 September

Ollie Harcourt was an eternal optimist. A glass half-full guy, who always believed things would work out for the best. Thirty-nine, with rugged good looks, an unruly mop of fair hair, and arty spectacles, he was dressed in a baggy cardigan, equally baggy jeans and Wolverine work boots, and sported an IWC wristwatch.

Caro was the polar opposite. Three years younger, with neat dark hair, wearing a brand-new blue Barbour jacket, tight-fitting trousers and black suede boots. Just as she always dressed appropriately for the office, so today, on this wet and windy September morning, she was dressed appropriately – if a little too perfectly – for the countryside. A born worrier, all the more so in the twelve years since their daughter, Jade, had come along, she fretted increasingly about everything. If Ollie's mantra was, *Hey, everything works out for the best*, hers was, *Shit happens, constantly*.

And she should know. She worked as a solicitor in a law firm in Brighton, doing conveyancing. Not many people went to lawyers because they were happy. She was burdened daily with non-stop meetings, calls and emails from clients fretting over their house purchases or sales, quite often as a result of bitter divorces, or equally bitter disputes with other relatives over inheritances. And because she cared so much, she carried most of their woes home in her heart, and in her briefcase, every weekday night, and often at weekends, too.

Ollie joked that if worrying was an Olympic sport, Caro could represent Great Britain.

She didn't find that funny, particularly as right now, while Ollie worked hard on building his website design business, she was the principal breadwinner. And at this moment, heading towards their new home on the big day of the move, although she was excited, she was also saddled with worries. Had they taken on too much? As a born and bred townie, how would she cope with life in an isolated country house? How would Jade take to it? And she wished Ollie wasn't driving so fast. Especially in this pelting rain, which the wipers were struggling to clear.

'Thirty limit, darling!' she cautioned, as they approached a sign announcing COLD HILL. 'There might be a speed trap. It wouldn't be good to be seen being stopped on our first day here.'

'Tummy tickler!' Ollie said, blithely ignoring her, as the Range Rover became airborne for an instant over a hump-back bridge.

'Fail, Dad!' shouted Jade, bouncing up on the rear seat and struggling to hold on to her iPhone and the carriers containing their two cats on the seat beside her.

They passed a cricket pitch to their left, then a Norman church to their right, its graveyard carpeted with fallen leaves. They carried on up a gradient, passing a row of cottages, one with a handwritten sign offering 'Free-range Eggs For Sale', a drab-looking pub, The Crown, a smithy, a 'Bed & Breakfast' sign and a village store. Finally, as they passed rows of detached houses and bungalows, then a small cottage to their left, Ollie braked hard.

'Dad!' Jade protested again. 'You're upsetting Bombay

7

and Sapphire!' Then she focused back on the photographs of the journey to their new home she was sharing on Instagram.

It was Ollie who had jokingly suggested naming the cats after the gin brand, and both Jade and Caro had instantly liked the names, so they had stuck.

To their right, opposite a red postbox partially engulfed by an unruly hedge, were two stone pillars, topped with sinister-looking wyverns, and with open, rusted, wrought-iron gates. A large sign, in much better condition than the pillars and gates, proudly proclaimed: RICHWARDS ESTATE AGENCY – SOLD!

Ollie stopped, indicating right, as a tractor towing a trailer spewing strands of straw came down the hill towards them at an almost reckless speed, passing them with just inches to spare. Then he swung the car in through the entrance, and sped up the steep, winding, potholed drive, bounded by railed fences in a poor state of repair. On one side of them was a herd of gloomy-looking brown and white cattle; on the other was a field full of alpacas. As the car lurched and bounced, Jade shouted out, again, 'Dad!' Then she saw the animals.

'Oh wow, what are those?'

'Llamas,' her mother said.

'I think they're alpacas!' Ollie said. 'Aren't alpacas smaller?'

'They're so cute!' Jade watched the animals for some moments, then returned her attention to her screen.

A quarter of a mile on they rattled over a cattle grid, and the house came into view. Ollie slowed down, scarcely able to believe this was now their home. It looked almost magical, but with a melancholic air. He felt as if he were a century or more back in time. He could see a horse-drawn carriage pulling up here. It looked like something out of a romantic novel or a movie, perhaps *Rebecca*'s 'Mandalay'.

He pulled the car to a halt on the crunching mossy gravel, behind Caro's Golf, which they had left here earlier in the day when they'd brought their first load of stuff over. The rain rattled down on the roof, as loud as hailstones, and the Range Rover rocked in the howling wind. 'Home sweet home!' he announced.

'Why's it called Cold Hill House?' Jade asked, still focused on her iPhone and tapping away hard.

'Because we're in Cold Hill village, lovely,' he said, unclipping his seat belt.

'Why's it called Cold Hill village?'

'Probably because it's north facing,' Caro replied. 'So it doesn't get as much sun as some places – and it's a bit of a wind trap.' She looked up at the recently restored grey facade, the white-painted sash windows and the metal wall-ties high up – the few parts of the property that had been worked on – filled with worry about the work that would be needed.

She wished she had put her foot down when they had first seen this place. But it had been high summer then. The surrounding fields had been full of yellow wheat and rape. The paddock had been full of wild flowers, the five acres of sweeping lawns had been neatly mown, and the lake was flat as a millpond, filled with lilies, the willow tree on the tiny island shining golden in the brilliant sunlight. There had been dozens of ducks and ducklings and a pair of coots.

Now the fields were a barren wilderness of mud and stubble. The front lawn was overgrown, and the windows of the house, which had seemed then to be filled with light, were now dark and gloomy, like the sunken eyes of a fish that was past its prime.

The porch also looked as if it had aged two decades since they had last been here. The paintwork, which had been new and fresh back then, was already flaking. The brass lion's-head knocker, which she had been certain was shiny and gleaming last time they saw it, was a dull green-hued colour. And the circular driveway was more weed than gravel.

The house had been empty for over thirty years, after part of it had collapsed, the irrepressibly jolly estate agent, Paul Jordan, had told them. A property development company had bought it, intending to restore it and turn it into an old people's home, but they had gone bankrupt in the last property crash after only completing a small part of the renovation work. It had so much scope, Jordan had enthused. It needed an owner with vision. And Ollie, who had great taste – and vision – had convinced her. They'd already moved house three times in the fifteen years since they were married, buying wrecks, doing them up and moving on with a good profit. It was that, and the lump sum Ollie had received from selling his property-search website, which had enabled them to afford this grand old wreck of a place. And, Ollie had persuaded her, they could double their money in five years' time – if they wanted to move again.

'God, I can't believe it's finally ours!' Ollie leaned over and kissed her on the cheek. 'Can you, darling?'

'No,' she said, apprehensively. 'No. It is beautiful. But—'

Close up, and real now, she could see the cracks in the front masonry, the patches of damp on the library wall, the peeling paint on the window frames. The sheer scale of the task ahead of them.

'How'm I going to get to see my friends in Brighton?' Jade interrupted. 'How'm I going to see Phoebe, Olivia, Lara – and Ruari?' Ruari was her boyfriend. She'd told her parents that they'd shared a last, tearful raspberry and mango milkshake yesterday afternoon in Drury's cafe in Richardson Road, round the corner from their old home.

'There's a regular bus service!' Ollie said.

'Yeah, right. Twice a day from the village, which is, like, a mile walk.'

'Your mum and I can drive you in when you want to go.'

'How about now?'

In his rear-view mirror, Ollie saw the small Volvo of his in-laws and, behind them, the removals truck lumbering up the drive. 'I think we ought to get moved into our new home first, darling, don't you think?'

'I want to go home!'

'You are home.'

'This place looks like it's about to fall down.'

Ollie grinned and looked at his wife. 'It's stunning. We are going to be very happy here. It'll just take a bit of getting used to our new lifestyle.'

'I liked our old lifestyle,' Jade retorted. 'I liked Carlisle Road.'

Ollie squeezed Caro's hand. She squeezed back. Then she turned to their daughter. 'We'll make sure you see your friends whenever you want to. And you'll make new friends out here.'

'Yeah? What? Cows? Llamas? Alpacas?'

Caro laughed and tousled Jade's hair. Her daughter pulled her head back, irritated; she never liked her hair being touched. Caro wanted so badly to feel good about being here, to share in Ollie's enthusiasm. She was determined to make an effort. As a city girl, she'd always dreamed of living in the countryside, too. But on this rainy September day, heading towards winter, all the work they had to do on the house seemed daunting. And she'd never in her life lived without neighbours. Noise. Human life. 'You love animals, Jade, darling,' she said. 'You wanted a dog – we could get one.'

'A dog?' Jade said, her face suddenly animated. 'We can really have a dog? A puppy?'

'Yes!' Caro replied.

'When?'

'Well, we could perhaps start looking around the rescue homes as soon as we're straight here.'

Jade brightened considerably. 'What kind of dog?'

'Let's see what's around!' Ollie replied. 'I think a rescue dog would be nice, don't you, lovely?'

'Something fluffy?' Jade asked. 'Big and fluffy?'

'Sure,' he said. 'Big and fluffy.'

'How about a labradoodle?'

'Well, let's see, darling!' Caro laughed. Ollie smiled. Everything was going to be fine. Their dream life in their dream new home. Well, project of a home, anyway.

Caro opened the car door and the howling gale blew it back on its hinges, bending them, the door mirror hitting the front wing of the car so hard the glass shattered.

'That's seven years' bad luck!' Jade said.

'Lucky I'm not superstitious,' Ollie replied.

'Mum is,' Jade said, breezily. 'We're doomed!'

3

'Shit!' Ollie said, standing in the stinging wind and rain, inspecting the damaged door. 'Go in the porch, darling,' he said to Caro. 'And you too, Jade. I'll unlock the front door in a sec and bring the stuff in from the car.'

'In a moment, Dad,' Jade said, looking down at her phone.

'It's OK, I'll help you,' Caro said.

As she jumped down, he put his arm round her. 'The start of our new, beautiful adventure!' he said, and kissed her.

Caro nodded. 'Yes,' she said. She stared up at the vast front of the building, and at the balustrading above the columned porch, which made it look very grand. The house they had just left was a large Victorian semi in Hove, a short distance from the seafront. That had been pretty grand, with six windows on the front and five bedrooms. This place had eight bedrooms – ten, if you included two small box rooms in the attic. It was huge. Gorgeous. But in need of more than just tender love and care. Turning her head away from the wind, she looked back at Ollie, who was trying to shut the car door, aware that both of them probably had very different thoughts going through their minds.

She knew he was thrilled to bits that today had finally come and they were moving in. She'd been driven along by his enthusiasm, but now they were actually here, their bridges burnt, new people already moving into their old house, she was suddenly, unaccountably, nervous. Nervous about a whole bunch of things.

This place was ridiculous. That was one of the few things they'd agreed on. Totally ridiculous. It was far too big. Far too expensive. Far too isolated. Far too dilapidated. And just plain too far. Too far from friends, family, shops. From anywhere. It needed a huge amount of work – starting with rewiring and replumbing. Many of the windows were rotten and their sash cords were broken. There was no loft insulation and there was damp in the cellar, which needed urgent action.

'It's beautiful, but you're bonkers,' her mother had said when she first saw it. Her father had said nothing, he'd just climbed out of the car, stood and stared at it, shaking his head.

Why?

Why?

Why, Caro was wondering, *had she agreed?*

Neither of them had ever lived in the country before. They were townies, through and through.

'You have to have vision,' Ollie had repeatedly told her. His dreary parents, whom he had always rebelled against, were now confined within the walls of their old people's sheltered housing, which they had entered far too young. They'd never had any vision; it was as if their entire lives had been one steady, plodding journey towards their eventual demise. They seemed to embrace all the ailments old age threw at them as if these were some kind of vindication of their planning.

'Sure it's a wreck but, God, it could be so beautiful, in time,' Ollie had enthused.

'It might be haunted,' she'd said.

'I know your mother believes in ghosts, bless her, but I don't. The dead don't frighten me, it's the living I'm scared of.'

Caro had learned, early on in their relationship, way before they were married, that once Ollie had his mind set on something there was no dissuading him. He wasn't an idiot, he had a great commercial brain. And besides, she had secretly liked the whole idea of a grand country life-style. Lady of the Manor of Cold Hill House.

Ollie removed his arm and opened the rear door for Jade, but his daughter, engrossed in her iPhone, carried on Instagramming.

'Out, sweetheart!'

'Give me a minute, this is important!'

'Out!' he said, reaching in and unclipping her seat belt, then lifting out the cat carriers.

She scowled, and pulled her hood up over her head, jammed her phone into her hoodie pocket, jumped down, then made a dash for the porch. Ollie lugged the carriers over and set them down, then ran back to the car, opened the two halves of the tailgate, grabbed a suitcase and hauled it out, followed by another.

Caro tugged out two of her cases, then trailed him into the porch. He put the bags down and fumbled with the vast assortment of keys on the ring that the estate agent had given him, selected what he hoped was the right one, slot-ted it in the lock and turned it. Then he pushed the heavy front door open, into the long, dark hallway.

At the end of the hallway to the right was the staircase up to the first floor. Beyond that, the hall led into a small, oak-panelled anteroom with three doors, which the estate agent said was called the atrium. One door, to the left, went through into the dining room, one on the right was to the kitchen, and the third door opened directly on to the grounds at the back. The estate agent had told them it was rumoured that the oak for the panelling had come from one of Nelson's ships, *Agamemnon*.

Ollie was greeted with a strong smell of floor polish, and a milder, zesty smell of cleaning fluid. A firm of professional house cleaners had spent two days in here, sprucing it up for them. And because of the poor condition of the house, the vendor's solicitors had permitted them to do some essential decorating of their basic living areas before completion.

Jade followed him in, holding the cat carriers and looking around curiously, followed by her mother. Ollie dumped the two suitcases at the foot of the staircase, then hurried back outside to greet his in-laws and the removals men, the first of whom, a shaven-headed man-mountain in a Meatloaf T-shirt and ancient stone-washed jeans, had just jumped down from the cab and was looking up at the house admiringly. He'd admitted, proudly, to Ollie a couple of days ago, while boxing up their possessions in the old house, that he'd only recently come out of jail for an offence he hadn't actually disclosed.

'Bleedin' gorgeous place you've got yourselves, guv!' he conceded. 'Love that tower.' Then, cupping his hand over his roll-up, seemingly oblivious to the elements, he leaned forward conspiratorially and nodded up at the first floor of the tower. 'Planning to put the missus up there when she gets a bit antsy?'

Ollie grinned. 'Actually, it's going to be my office.'

'Good one!'

He saw Caro's mother clambering out of the driving seat of the Volvo, or the *Ovlov* as he jokingly called it. A doughty lady, and a Brighton and Hove magistrate, Pamela Reilly, in a hooded anorak and baggy waterproof trousers, looked at this moment dressed for a polar expedition.

Her husband, Dennis, who, like his daughter, had always been a consummate worrier, was suffering from early-stage dementia and becoming increasingly forgetful and erratic. A retired Lloyds actuary, his profession had suited him perfectly. A career spent in calculating risk, he now applied that same skill set to everything he encountered in his retirement. A diminutive, balding and meek man, he was dressed in one of his habitual three-piece tweed suits and City livery ties, beneath a fur-trimmed coat and a black astrakhan hat that gave him the appearance of a bonsai Russian oligarch.

Twenty minutes later, after the kettle had boiled on the Aga, and tea and coffee had been distributed in mismatched mugs – all they had been able to find so far – and a packet of digestive biscuits torn open, they had an organized team. Caro stood at the bottom of the stairs, just before the atrium, directing the items which the chain of removal men carried in. Dennis stood at the top with a list created by Caro's organized mind of what went where, studying it with a furrowed brow in childlike concentration, occasionally looking around in total, but enthusiastic, bewilderment. Jade let the cats out of their carriers, closed the kitchen doors to keep them contained, then went exploring.

Ollie stood with Pamela in the porch, with a checklist of which of the carefully labelled boxes should go into the house, and which belonged in the outbuildings around the rear, for now, until work inside the house was completed.

The shaven-headed man-mountain lugged a massive box, labelled BEDROOM 1 (MASTER), past them, with a grin.

Ollie ticked it off the list. He watched Caro, inside, look

at the label and direct the removals man up the stairs. Then, as the man disappeared from sight, Ollie glimpsed a shadow crossing the atrium, like the flit of a bird across a fanlight.

His mother-in-law turned to him with a smile, her eyes wide open, almost bulging in excitement. 'Did you see that?' she asked.

Pamela, despite being an extremely well-respected magistrate, had a fey side to her. Early on in his relationship with Caro, Pamela had confided in him that, although she wasn't sure if she was actually *psychic* – whatever that really meant – she would always know when someone was going to die, because she would have a recurring dream. It involved a black raven, a lake and a tombstone with the person's name engraved on it.

What had she seen?

Caro was already uneasy enough about moving here, to this isolated property, without her mother spooking her out. It was the last thing he needed on this first day here, the first day of their new, dream life.

'Did you see it?' she asked again.

Her smile suddenly irritated him. There was a smugness, a *told-you-so* something about it.

'No,' he said, emphatically. 'No, I didn't see anything.'

4

Sunday, 6 September

Jade, her long fair hair clipped back, dressed in jeans, socks and a crop top, with a note to herself written in blue ink on her left hand, was in her bedroom, which had wallpaper that she thought was a bit naff. She had spent much of this first weekend sorting her things out, with the occasional help of her mother. Her favourite song, 'Uptown Funk' by Bruno Mars and Mark Ronson, was blasting out from the Sonos speaker on top of a wooden chest of drawers.

It was Sunday evening and she was bored of unpacking now. Stuff lay ankle-deep on the floor, and Bombay was curled up on the patchwork quilt of her wrought-iron bed. The tortoiseshell moggie, which had adopted Jade within hours of being brought home from the rescue centre three years ago, lay contentedly amid a pile of cushions, her head resting on Blankie, the grey blanket Jade had had with her since she was an infant, and nuzzled up against Jade's yellow, bug-eyed minion. Above the cat, Duckie, her gangly, mangy cream duck, with yellow feet and yellow bill, that she'd had almost as long as Blankie, its feet entwined in the metal latticework of the headboard, hung down gormlessly. Suspended from the other side of the headboard was her purple dream-catcher.

She'd had to admit, reluctantly, that this was a nicer room than her previous one, although it was a yucky pink.

About five times larger, and – big bonus! – it had an en-suite bathroom, with a huge, old-fashioned bathtub with brass taps. She'd already luxuriated in it last night with a Lush bath-bomb, and felt like a queen.

On the curved shelves on the far side of her bedside table, she'd arranged some of her silver trophies, including her *Virgin Active Brighton Tennis Club Championships*, *Mini Green Runner-up 2013* and *Star of the Week Dance Club, 2013*, along with a photograph of the rear of a pink American convertible with a surfboard sticking out of the back seat. Next to it was propped her guitar in a maroon case, alongside a music stand on which lay a curled book titled *Easy Guitar Lessons*. She'd already unpacked most of her books, and put them on the shelves on the opposite wall. All her sets of *The Hunger Games* and *Harry Potter* were in their correct order, as well as her collection of David Walliams, except for one, *Ratburger*, which was on her bedside table. Also next to it on the table were piled several books on training dogs, as well as one she loved, called *Understanding Your Cat*.

In front of the huge sash window was her wooden dressing table, minus its mirror which her father had not yet fixed into place. The surface was littered with cans of her body sprays, bottles of perfumes and Zoella products. Her orange plastic chair sat in front of it.

She was feeling lonely. On weekends in Brighton she would have walked round to Phoebe, Olivia or Lara's house, or they would have come round to her, and made music videos together, or she'd have seen Ruari. Right now her parents, and her gran and gramps, were flat-out downstairs, busy unpacking boxes and getting the house in some kind of order – at least, the rooms they could live in for now, until the builders and decorators had got the house straight. Which was going to take months. Years. Forever.

The large window looked past the row of garages, over the vast rear garden and the lake, a couple of hundred yards in the distance, to the paddock, and the steep rise of the hill beyond. Her mother had told her the paddock would be perfect for the pony she had always hankered after. That brightened her a little, although she was keener at this moment on a labradoodle puppy. She'd spent a lot of time googling dog rescue centres and labradoodle breeders, and looking up all sorts of possible alternatives on Dogs 101. So far she'd found no rescue places or breeders in their area with any puppies, but there was one breeder about an hour away who was expecting a litter soon.

It was coming up to eight o'clock. No doubt one of her parents would be up soon to tell her 'no more screen time' and to get ready for bed. She went over to her dressing table, picked up her phone, and for some moments gazed wistfully at a video clip of Ruari, with his sharp hairstyle, nodding his head and grinning to a piece of music. Then she dialled Phoebe on her FaceTime app.

It was still light outside, despite the dark clouds and the rain, which had not relented throughout the weekend, pattering against the rattling window in front of her. 'Uptown Funk' was playing again at full blast. That was another plus about this new house – her room was at the far end of the first floor, with empty rooms between, so she could play her music as loudly as she liked without her parents coming in to tell her to turn it down. Mostly in their previous home she'd had to resort to wearing her headphones. At this moment she didn't even know where the headphones were. Buried somewhere in one of the four huge boxes of her stuff that she had still not yet unpacked.

Beep, beep, beep.

The phone went dead.

'Come on, come on!' The internet connection here was rubbish. Her dad had promised to get it sorted tomorrow, but he was so useless at dealing with things it would probably take a week, knowing him. They were all going to have to change phone providers. God, it wasn't like they were in the back of beyond or anything – they were only ten miles from Brighton. But at this moment, they might as well have been on the moon!

She tried again. Then, dialling for the third time, she suddenly saw Phoebe's face filling the screen, blonde hair hanging over her forehead, and her own face in a small square in the corner.

Her friend, grinning and chewing gum, said, 'Hey, Jade!'

Then she lost the signal, and Phoebe with it. 'Come on, come on, come on!' she shouted at the screen, and re-dialled. Moments later she was reconnected.

'Sorry about that, Phebes!'

'You OK?'

'I am so not OK! I miss you tons!'

'Me you, Jade! Mum's in a shit mood with Dad, and taking it out on me. And all the gerbils escaped. It's, like, not been a great day. Mungo was running around with my favourite, Julius, in her mouth, with his legs wriggling, then she shot off down the garden.'

'Did she kill him?'

'Dad buried him – what was left of him. I hate that cat!'

'No! Did you get the rest of them back?'

'They were all under the sofa in the sitting room, huddled together, looking terrified. Why would they want to escape? They had everything they needed – food, water, toys.'

'Maybe they don't like the weather and decided to go south for a holiday?'

Phoebe laughed. Then she said, '"Uptown Funk"! Turn it up!'

'OK.'

'What do you think – I've bought the latest *Now* CD for Lara for her birthday?'

'Does she still have a CD player, Phebes?'

There was a long silence. Then a defensive, 'She must have.'

'I don't think we have one any more.'

'Whatever. When are you coming over?'

'I have to negotiate an exit from here with the Cold Hill House Escape Committee. But my parents say I can have a birthday party here. Three weeks' time! I'm going to have a retro photo booth with Polaroid cameras! And we're going to have pizzas – everyone can order them and Dad said he'd collect them.'

'Epic! But that's three weeks, can I come over and see your place before then?'

'Yes. I've got a great room – the biggest bath you've ever seen. You can almost swim in it! Can you come the weekend after next? Sleepover Saturday night? Ruari said his mum's going to drive him over on the Sunday.'

'Maybe we can have a swim in your pool, if it's nice?'

'I'll have to get Dad to remove the dead frogs first. And fill it and heat it. That is so not going to happen.'

'Yech!' Then suddenly Phoebe's voice changed. 'Hey, Jade, who's that?'

'Who's what?'

'That woman!'

'Woman? What woman?'

'Er, the one right behind you? Hello!'

Jade spun round. There was no one. She turned back to the phone. 'What woman?'

Then her phone screen went blank. Annoyed, she re-dialled. She heard the sound of the connection being made, and then Phoebe's face reappeared.

'What did you mean, Phebes? What woman?'

'I can't see her now, she's gone. She was standing behind you, by the door.'

'There wasn't anyone!'

'I saw her!'

Jade crossed over to the door, opened it and looked out onto the landing. She held up her phone, pointing it down the landing so Phoebe could see, then she closed the door behind her, walked back across the room and sat down again. 'There's no one been in, Phoebe, I'd have heard them.'

'There was, I saw her clearly,' her friend insisted. 'I'm not making it up, Jade, honestly!'

Jade shuddered, feeling cold suddenly. She turned round again and stared at the closed door. 'What – what did you see?'

'She was, like, an old lady, in a blue dress. She had a really mean look on her face. Who is she?'

'The only old lady here's my Gran. She's here with Gramps, helping unpack stuff downstairs.' Jade shrugged. 'They're both a bit weird.'

Twenty minutes later, when she had ended the conversation, Jade went downstairs. Her parents were sitting at the refectory table in the kitchen, piles of unopened boxes still on the floor around them, drinking red wine, with the bottle on the table in front of them as they opened all the 'Good Luck In Your New Home' cards sent by friends and relatives. Sapphire was crunching dry food in a bowl close to the Aga.

'Hi, darling,' her mother said. 'Are you ready for tomorrow?'

'Sort of.'

'Time for bed. Big day – your new school!'

Jade stared at her glumly. She was thinking about all her time at school in Brighton. She had loved being in charge of the School Walking Bus. Making the phone calls every morning, starting off with one friend, collecting another, then another, so by the time they arrived at school there were ten of them altogether. Now the rest of them would be doing this tomorrow, without her. She would be going instead to bloody St Paul's Catholic College in Burgess Hill. *Nowheresville.*

And they didn't even go to church regularly!

'Where are Gran and Gramps?' she asked.

'They went home a short while ago, darling,' her mother responded. 'Gramps was very tired. They said to say goodbye and give you their love.'

'Gran came up to my room.'

'Good,' her mother said.

'But she didn't say anything, and went out again. That was strange of her. She always kisses me goodbye.'

'Were you on your computer?'

'I was talking to Phoebe.'

'Maybe she didn't want to disturb you, darling.'

Jade shrugged. 'Maybe.'

Her father looked up and frowned. But he said nothing.

5

Monday, 7 September

Monday morning came as something of a relief to Ollie. The rain had finally stopped and a brilliant, warm, late-summer sun was shining. Caro had gone to work at her office in Brighton shortly after 7.30 a.m. and at 8.00 a.m., listening to the Radio Four news, he got out Jade's Cheerios for her breakfast, while she busied herself, first feeding the cats, then switching on the Nespresso machine, which she loved using, to make her father a coffee. Amazingly, Ollie thought, she had actually got up early this morning! But even so they were running short of time and, anxious not to be late for her first day at her new school, he gulped down his muesli, then hurried her out to the car and checked she had belted up.

As he drove, Jade, in her uniform of black jacket, yellow blouse and black pleated skirt, sat beside him in nervous silence. Neil Pringle was on Radio Sussex, talking to a Lewes artist called Tom Homewood about his latest exhibition.

'Looking forward to your new school?' Ollie asked.

'LOL.'

'What's that meant to mean?'

'Yeah, right. All my friends are still going to King's in Portslade.' She looked down at her phone. '*St Paul's, Burgess Hill.* It sounds like a church, Dad!'

26

'It seems to be a lovely school, and you know the Bartletts? Their triplets went there and loved it.'

Ollie saw her checking her phone; she was back on Instagram. At the top of the display was *Jade_Harcourt_x0x0*. Below she had rows and rows of thumbs-down emoticons alternating with scowly faces.

'Listen, lovely,' he said. 'Give it a chance, OK?'

'I don't have much choice, do I?' she said without raising her head.

He drove on in silence for some moments, then he said, 'So your Gran came up to your room yesterday evening, but didn't say anything?'

'Uh-huh.'

'Are you sure?'

'Phebes saw her – we were FaceTiming.'

'And your Gran didn't say anything?'

'No, she just went out again. Is she angry with me or something?'

'Why should she be angry with you?'

'Phebes said she was looking kind of grumpy.'

Ollie drove the rest of the short journey in silence, thinking, while pinging and clicking noises came from his daughter's phone. Thinking about last night. His parents-in-law had sat with him and Caro in the kitchen. He'd given Dennis a large whisky and Pamela, who was driving as she had to these days, drank one tiny drop of red wine. They'd seen them off, Pamela telling him to say goodbye from them to Jade.

She had very definitely not gone upstairs.

6

Monday, 7 September

Arriving back home thirty minutes later, Ollie parked alongside a battered-looking red van belonging to the builders, who had arrived early and were down in the cellar, starting work on the damp. He sat for some moments, listening to Danny Pike on Radio Sussex taking a Green Party councillor in Brighton to task over a new bus lane proposal that the presenter clearly thought was absurd. He always liked Pike's combative but informed interviewing style.

As he jumped down from the car, he caught a flash of movement to his right. It was a grey squirrel, darting up the trunk of the tall gingko tree in the centre of the circle of lawn in front of the house.

He watched the beautiful animal climb. *Tree rats*, Caro called them. She hated them, telling him they stripped off the bark, and, after seeing another one over the weekend, had told him to go and buy an airgun and shoot it. He watched it sit on a cross-branch and eat a nut that it held in its paws. There was no way he could shoot it. He didn't want to kill anything here. Except maybe the rabbits, which overran the garden.

There was a smell of manure in the air, faint but distinct. Some distance above him he saw a tractor looking the size of a toy crossing the brow of Cold Hill, too far away to hear its engine. He stared around at the fields, then at the front facade of the house, still scarcely able to believe that they now lived here; this was their home, this was where, maybe, hopefully, they could actually settle, and spend the rest of their lives. Their *forever* home.

He pulled out his phone and took a series of photographs in all directions. He looked at the columned, covered porch, with its balustrading above, at the two sets of windows on either side of it, then up at the rows of windows on the two floors above, still struggling to orientate himself.

To the left of the front entrance was a WC, then the door to the library. To the right was the drawing room. Further along to the left there was another toilet, before the long hallway opened out into the atrium. To the left of the atrium was the huge dining room. All these rooms had high, stuccoed ceilings. Through the atrium door to the right was the kitchen and, beyond that, the downstairs part of the extension; a pantry and scullery from which the stairs ran down to the cellar with its vaulted brick ceiling. Part of the cellar housed a long-disused kitchen with a range that had not been lit in decades, once the domain of the live-in household staff. The other end of the cellar contained dusty wine racks. One day, when their finances allowed, they would stock all those racks with wine, another of their shared passions.

He'd checked out all the rooms, briefly and excitedly, on Friday, as they were moving in. God, he loved this place! He'd taken photographs of each room. Many were in a terrible state of repair and they'd have to stay that way for a long while yet. It didn't matter; for now all they needed was to get the kitchen, drawing room and dining room straight, and one of the spare bedrooms. Their own bedroom, which had ancient red flock wallpaper, and Jade's, were in a reasonable condition – some work had been done on them before the developers had gone bust and also before they'd moved in. The priority at the moment was the rot, the electricity and the ropy plumbing.

He stared back at the porch, and the handsome front door with its corroded brass lion's-head knocker, and thought back, as he had several times, to that moment on Friday when he was standing there with his mother-in-law and had seen, fleetingly, that shadow. Trick of the light, or a removals man, or maybe some bird or animal – possibly the squirrel?

He went inside, through the atrium, and turned right into the kitchen. In the scullery beyond was a deep butler's sink, a draining board and a wooden clothes-drying rack on a rope and pulley system to raise and lower it. There was also an ancient metal pump, fixed to the wall, for drawing water from the well that was supposedly under the house, but which no one had yet managed to find.

The cellar door, at the rear of the scullery, had an enormous, rusty lock on it, with a huge key, like a jailer's. It was ajar. He went down the steep brick steps to see if the builders were OK and to tell them to help themselves to tea and coffee up in the kitchen, but they cheerily told him that they had their thermoses and were self-sufficient.

Then he climbed up the three flights of stairs to his chaotic office in the round tower on the west side of the house. It was a great space, about twenty feet in diameter, with a high ceiling, and windows giving fabulous views, one of them onto the steep, grassy slope of the hill rising out of sight. He waded through the unopened boxes and towers of files littering the floor, carefully stepping past a row of framed pictures stacked against a wall, reached his desk, and switched on his radio to Radio Sussex. As he heard the presenter grilling the Chief Executive of the Royal Sussex County Hospital over waiting times in A&E, his phone pinged with an incoming text.

It was from one of his two closest friends, Rob, asking if he fancied a long mountain bike ride round Box Hill next Sunday morning. He replied:

> **Sorry, mate, going to be spending time sorting out the house with Caro. And five acres of lawns to mow. Come over and see the place at the w/e.**

He sent it and moments later the single-word reply pinged back.

> **Tosser.**

He grinned. Rob and he had barely said a polite word to each other throughout their fifteen-year friendship. He sat down, retuned the radio to Radio 4, and logged on to his computer, checking his emails for anything urgent, then had a quick look at Twitter and Facebook, aware that he had not posted anything on either about the move yet. He also wanted to post some pictures of the worst dilapidations in the house on his Instagram page to show before and after. He and Caro had discussed approaching the TV show *Restoration Man*, but decided against because of wanting privacy.

But before any of that he had an urgent job to complete, and although the internet connection wasn't great, it was working, sort of. His Apple Mac geek – as he jokingly referred to his computer engineer – was coming over that afternoon to try to sort it all out, but in the meantime he just had to get on with it, with an urgent deadline for a new client, the grandly titled Charles Cholmondley Classic Motors, *Purveyors of Horseless Carriages to the Nobility and*

Gentry since 1911. They traded top-end classic and vintage sports cars, and had taken several large and very expensive stands at a classic car show that was looming up in Dubai, next month, and for next year's Goodwood Festival of Speed. They needed an urgent revamp of their very dull and old-fashioned website.

If he got it right, it could open the door to the whole world of classic cars which he had always loved. He'd made a serious stash of cash from his previous website business, an innovative search site for people looking for properties. If he could repeat this success in the lucrative world of classic cars, they would be sorted. They'd have the money to do everything they wanted to this house.

He harboured doubts about the provenance of Charles Cholmondley Classic Motors, as the company had only been registered nine years ago. Its proprietor was a diminutive, self-important man in his fifties. On the two occasions when Ollie had met Charles Cholmondley himself, he had been flamboyantly dressed in a cream linen suit, bow tie and tasselled loafers, with silver hair that looked freshly coiffed. It was exactly the image of him that fronted the website, the dealer standing between a gleaming 1950s Bentley Continental and a Ferrari of similar vintage.

Personally, Ollie thought the message this gave off was, 'Come and get royally screwed by me!' He'd tried, subtly, to dissuade him from wearing the bow tie, but Cholmondley would have none of it. *You have to understand, Mr Harcourt, that the people I am dealing with are very rich indeed. They like the feeling of dealing with their own kind. They see this bow tie and they see someone of distinction.*

Something really did not smell right about Charles Cholmondley, and Ollie even wondered if this was his real name. But hey, he was paying good money, which at this moment he needed badly, both for this house and, if there was any surplus, to finish the restoration of his beloved Jaguar E-Type which was languishing in a lock-up in Hove until he could clear out enough space for it in one of the garages behind the house. At the moment, with all the work needed on the house, that Jag was going to be, unfortunately, a low priority.

Moments after he had settled down, Caro phoned to ask if the plumber had arrived to start work on their bathroom, and Ollie told her there'd been no sign of him yet.

'Can you call him?' she asked. 'The bloody people were meant to start work at nine today.'

'I will, darling,' he said, trying not to sound irritated. Caro could never get her head around the fact that, although his office was based at home, he was actually working just as hard as she was. He dialled the plumber, left a message on his voicemail, then focused on his client's website. The radio continued in the background; he listened to it all the time he was working, either Radio Sussex or Radio 4, and on Saturdays, after *Saturday Live*, he loved to listen to the football show, *The Albion Roar*, on Radio Reverb. When there was nothing on the radio he fancied, he tuned his computer to Brighton's dedicated television station, *Latest TV*.

He began surfing the sites of other classic car dealers, and became frustrated, in minutes, with the slow and flaky internet connection. Several times during the next hour he shouted at the computer in anger, and wondered just how much of his life had been wasted waiting for the sodding internet. Then, at 10.30 a.m., he went downstairs to make himself a coffee.

He climbed down the steep, spiral staircase, walked a short distance along the first-floor landing, then went down the stairs to the hall, turned right and entered the oak-panelled atrium that was the anteroom to the kitchen. As he did so he saw Bombay and Sapphire both standing in the middle of the room, their hackles up, watching something.

He stopped, curious, wondering what it was. Their eyes were darting around, right then left, then up, then to the right again, in absolute synch, almost as if they were watching a movie. What were they looking at? He stood with them but could see nothing. 'What is it, chaps?'

The cats continued to stand there, ignoring him, hackles still up, eyes still moving together, utterly absorbed.

'What is it, chaps?' he said again, watching them, watching their eyes. It was giving him the creeps.

Then suddenly they both howled, as if in pain, shot out of the room and disappeared along the hallway.

Deeply puzzled, he walked through into the huge kitchen. It had a low, oak-beamed ceiling, an ancient blue four-oven Aga, a twelve-seater oak refectory table which had come with the property, a pine dresser, rows of pine-fronted fitted shelves and a double sink with a large window above it looking out across the rear lawn and grounds.

He made himself a mug of latte on the Nespresso machine and carried it back into the atrium. And stopped in his tracks.

Dozens of tiny spheres of translucent white light were floating in the air, moving across the room. They ranged in size from little bigger than a pinhead to about a quarter of an inch, and all had a different density of light. They reminded him, for an instant, of living organisms he had observed through a microscope in school biology lessons. They were grouped within a narrow band, no more than a couple of feet across and rising from the floor to head height.

What on earth were they?

Was it his glasses, catching the sunlight at an odd angle? He removed them, and put them on again, and the lights had gone.

Strange, he thought, looking around. He hadn't imagined them, surely? To his left was the long, windowless hallway leading to the front door. To his right was the small door on the far side of the atrium, which had two glass panes, and opened onto the rear terrace.

His glasses must have caught the reflection of some rays of sunlight, he decided, as he climbed back up to his office. He settled back down to work. Just as he did, Caro rang again. 'Hi, Ols, did the new fridge turn up?'

'No, it hasn't turned up yet. Nor has the bloody electrician or the sodding plumber!'

'Will you chase them?'

'Yes, darling,' he said, patiently. 'The plumber called me back and is coming in an hour. I'll chase the others.' Caro had two secretaries at her disposal, plus a legal assistant. Why, he wondered, frustrated, did she never use them to help out?

He dutifully made the calls then returned to his work. Shortly after 1.00 p.m. he went back downstairs to make himself a sandwich. As he entered the atrium again, he felt a stream of cool air on his neck. He turned, sharply. The windows and the door to the rear garden were shut. Then he saw tiny flashes of light around him. They were a familiar precursor to the severe migraines he occasionally suffered from. They were different from the spheres he had seen earlier, but maybe those had been another manifestation of the same symptoms, he realized. He wasn't surprised, with all the stress right now. But he didn't have time to be ill.

He went through the kitchen into the scullery and down the stone cellar stairs. A radio at the bottom was blaring out music, and the two builders were sitting, drinking tea and eating their lunch. One was tall, in his early thirties; the other was shorter and looked close to retirement. 'How's it going?' Ollie asked.

'The damp's pretty bad,' the older one said, unwrapping a Mars bar and giving a sharp intake of breath. 'You're going to need a damp-proof membrane down here, otherwise it's going to recur. Surprised no one ever done it.'

Ollie knew very little about building work. 'Can you do it?'

'We'll get the guv to give you a quote.'

'Good,' he said. 'Thank you. Might as well get it done properly. Right, well, I'll leave you to get on with it. I've got to shoot out later and pick up my daughter from school. What time are you off?'

'About five,' the younger one said.

'Fine – if I'm not around, just let yourselves out and shut the front door. See you tomorrow?'

'I'm not sure,' the older one said. 'We've got an outside job and if the weather holds the guv may want us on that for a couple of days. But we'll be back before the end of the week.'

Ollie looked at them, biting his tongue. He remembered beating their boss, Bryan Barker, down on price on the agreement that his workmen could do outside jobs as and when the weather permitted.

'OK, thanks,' Ollie said, and went back upstairs, swallowed two Migraleve tablets then made himself a tuna sandwich. He sat at the refectory table with a glass of water, and as he ate he flipped through the newspapers he liked to read daily, the *Argus*, *The Times* and *Daily Mail*, that he had picked up on his way home after dropping off Jade at school.

When he had finished his lunch he climbed back up to his office, relieved not to have developed any more migraine symptoms, so far. The tablets were doing their stuff. He stared for some minutes at a photograph of a white 1965 BMW going almost sideways, at high speed, through Graham Hill Bend at Brands Hatch. It was one of a series of images of the car, which had a strong racing pedigree, for sale on the Cholmondley website. Then he heard the front doorbell ringing. It was Chris Webb, his computer engineer, with an armful of kit, who had come to sort his internet out.

He let him in, gratefully.

A few hours later, after collecting Jade from school and returning to work, he heard Caro's Golf scrunch to a halt on the gravel outside. Jade had long been up in her room, closeted with her mountain of homework, and Chris Webb, hunched over the Mac up in his office, was still hard at work sorting out his new connection. Chris looked up, mug of coffee in one hand, cigarette burning in the ashtray Ollie had found for him.

'It's the curvature of the hill that's your problem,' he said.

'Curvature?'

'There are phone masts on the top of the Downs, but the curvature of this slope effectively shields you from them. The best solution,' Webb said, 'would be to demolish this house and rebuild nearer the top of the hill.'

Ollie grinned. 'Yep, well, I think we'll have to go with another option. Plan B?'

'I'm working on it.'

Ollie hurried downstairs to greet his wife, opening the

front door for her and kissing her. Even after fourteen years of marriage, he always felt a beat of excitement when she arrived home. 'How was your day, darling?'

'Awful! I've had one of the worst Mondays of my life. Three clients in a row who've been gazumped on their house purchases, and one nutter.' She was holding two large plastic bags. 'I've bought a load of torches, as you suggested, and candles.'

'Brilliant! We'll put torches around the place. Glass of wine?'

'A large one! How was your day?'

'Not great either. One distraction after another with the builders, the electricians, the plumber. And the architect called to say that our planning application to have a new window in our bedroom has been turned down because the house is a listed building.'

'It's only Grade 2. Why?'

Ollie shrugged. 'Every generation who's owned this place over the past two hundred and fifty years has made changes to it. Why do they sodding think in the twenty-first century that now has to stop?'

'We can appeal it.'

'Yes – at a cost of thousands.'

'I need that drink.'

He led the way along the hall and through the atrium, then into the kitchen. He took a bottle of Provence rosé out of the fridge and opened it. As he poured he said, 'Want to take a walk around the grounds? It's such a beautiful evening.'

Peeling off her jacket and slinging it over the back of a chair, she said, 'I'd like that. How's Jade? How was her first day at school?'

'She's fine. A bit quiet and still sullen, but I get the feeling she secretly quite enjoyed it. Or that it wasn't as bad as she thought. She's doing homework.'

He said nothing about Jade's insistence that her grandmother had come into her room last night.

While Caro went upstairs to see their daughter, Ollie carried their glasses out onto the rear terrace, where their outside dining table and chairs were set up, and onto the lawn. Caro came back down. 'God, it's so glorious – if we could get the pool cleaned up we could have a swim on evenings like this next year!' She smiled. 'You're right – Jade does seem to have got on OK today.'

'Yes, thank heavens! The local pool company's coming on Friday,' Ollie said. 'To give me an estimate on what it will take to replace the damaged tiles and get the heating up and running again.'

'Good! Can't believe how warm it is – half past six in the evening!'

The sun was still high in the sky over the fields to the west. Caro gave him a hug and kissed him. 'I was really worried about moving here,' she said. 'But driving out of Brighton tonight, it was such a joy to leave the city – I think we've made the right decision.'

He smiled, hugged her back and kissed her. 'We have. I just love it. I think we're going to be so happy here.'

'We will be. It's a happy house!'

7

Tuesday, 8 September

The following morning brought the start of an Indian summer heatwave. Ollie, dressed in shorts, T-shirt and trainers, again dropped Jade off at school. She'd found her first day OK, but was still not happy about being separated from all her old friends. He returned home, relieved that the Migraleve tablets he had been taking seemed to have warded off any migraine. He had a lot to do on his client's website this morning.

But no sooner had he sat down in his office, than his distractions continued, starting with a visit from the boss of the building contractors, Bryan Barker, who read out a litany of doom and gloom that further inspection of the house had revealed, in his irrepressibly cheerful way that made everything seem somehow less bad than it really was.

Barker started with the rot in the cellar, then the damp beneath all of the windows on the front facade, which took the brunt of the weather, then the leaking roof. They could do it all in one go, Barker told him, or do it piecemeal, but that would be a false economy. Then, almost by way of reducing the impact, Barker mentioned Ollie's Specialized hybrid bike that he had seen in one of the outbuildings and invited him to join a regular weekly boys' bike ride around the area.

As the builder spoke, pound signs with several rows

of noughts after them flashed, constantly, through Ollie's mind. Then the electrician arrived with a story of equal doom and gloom. The current electrics in the house were, in his view, a serious fire hazard, and if they weren't replaced could invalidate the insurance.

Their plumber, who appeared at the same time, a chatty Irishman called Michael Maguire, told him the results of his inspection yesterday. Much of the piping was lead, which would eventually give them all brain damage from the drinking water if they left it in situ. It would be wise to replace the lot with modern plastic piping. The painter's news was no more encouraging. It seemed that the property development company had employed a total bodger of a builder, who, instead of having walls stripped down, had merely painted over them – possibly just to tart this place up in order to sell it.

The warnings had all been there, in those stark pages of the survey. But they had been panicked into making a decision when the estate agents informed them there was another buyer in the frame. Ollie had convinced Caro there would be no urgency to do the work – they could do it bit by bit over a few years. That no longer seemed to be the case. It had been a financial stretch to buy the house and they thought they had budgeted sufficient for the first year to carry out the renovations. Now, after listening to Barker, Ollie realized they were going to have to add thousands to this figure – and somehow find the money. They were in this financially up to their necks. To make things worse, the market had turned in the time since they had exchanged contracts and if they tried to put it back on the market they would be facing a substantial loss. They had no option but to make it work.

And they damned well would!

In the middle of his discussions with the painter, a neighbour appeared, asking him for a subscription to the local parish magazine – which he agreed to. It was close to midday before, almost brain-dead, he began work again on the Charles Cholmondley Classic Motors, *Purveyors of Horseless Carriages to the Nobility and Gentry since 1911*, website, making sure the pages were clear and readable on tablets and on phone screens. Next, he checked all the links worked – the client's email address, the Twitter, Facebook and Instagram pages.

At 1.30 p.m., finally satisfied, he emailed a link for the test site to his client, then took a break and went back downstairs to make himself some lunch. When he reached the atrium he stopped and looked around for any sign of the lights he had seen here yesterday, but all he could see were a few dust motes in front of the windowpanes in the door. The pills had done the trick, he thought, relieved.

He made himself a Cheddar and Branston pickle sandwich, poured himself a glass of chilled water from the fridge, and carried them, together with the morning's copy of *The Times*, out onto the rear terrace, blinking against the brilliant sunlight. He set everything down and went back inside to find his sunglasses. As he did so, the front doorbell rang. It was a large delivery of flat-pack wardrobes.

Ten minutes later he returned to his lunch. As he read the paper and ate his sandwich, he looked up occasionally, watching a pair of ducks paddling across the lake. Afterwards, he walked round the side of the house, down the drive, and out through the front gates, deciding to stroll down towards the village and look around before returning to work.

As he headed down the narrow lane, which had no pavement and was bounded by trees and hedgerows on both sides, breathing in the country scents, his phone vibrated. It was an email from his new client, Charles Cholmondley, saying he loved the website and would come back to him later in the day, or tomorrow, with his amendments. Ollie felt suddenly incredibly happy. Cold Hill House was going to be a lucky home for them. Sure, there was a massive amount of work to be done, but his new business was on its way. Everything was going to be fine!

As he passed a small, dilapidated Victorian cottage on his right, with an overgrown front garden, he saw an elderly man in a baggy shirt, grey trousers and hiking boots striding up the hill towards him, holding a stout stick, and with an unlit briar pipe in his mouth. He had a wiry figure, white hair styled in an old-fashioned boyish quiff, a goatee beard and leathery, wrinkled skin. As they drew close, Ollie smiled. 'Good afternoon,' he said.

'Good afternoon,' the man replied in a rural Sussex burr, removing his pipe. Then he stopped and pointed the stem in the air. 'Mr Harcourt, would it be?'

'Yes?' Ollie said, still smiling.

'You're the gentleman who just bought the big house?'

'Cold Hill House?'

The old man gripped his walking stick hard, letting it support some of his weight. His rheumy eyes were like molluscs peeping out beneath spiky fringes of white hair. 'Cold Hill House, that would be it. How you getting on with your lady, then?' He stared hard at Ollie.

'*Lady?*' Ollie retorted. 'What *lady*?'

He gave Ollie a strange smile. 'Maybe she's not there no more.'

'Tell me?'

'Oh, I wouldn't want to frighten you, not when you've just moved in.'

'Yeah, well I'm frightened enough already – by the estimates I'm going to be getting from the builders!' He held out his hand. 'Nice to meet you – you're local?'

'You could say that.' He nodded and pursed his lips, but made no attempt to take the proffered hand.

Ollie withdrew his hand, awkwardly. 'It's a delightful contrast to Brighton, I have to say.'

The old man shook his head. 'Not been to Brighton.'

'Never?' Ollie said, surprised.

'I don't like big cities, and I don't like to travel much.'

Ollie smiled. Brighton was less than ten miles away. 'Tell me – you said you don't want to frighten me. Is this *lady* something I should be frightened of?'

The old man gave him a penetrating stare. 'I'm going back some years now – I worked for Sir Henry and Lady Rothberg, when they owned this place, when I was a young man. Bankers they were. I were one of the gardeners. One day they asked me if I could do a bit of caretaking for them while they were abroad. They used to have live-in staff and that, but Sir Henry lost a lot of money and had to let them all go.' He hesitated. 'That room they called the *atrium*, that still there?'

'The oak-panelled room with the two columns? The one you go through before the kitchen?'

'That used to be the chapel when it was a monastery, back in the Middle Ages – before most of the house, as it is today, was built.'

'Really? I didn't know that,' Ollie said. 'I didn't know there was anything remaining of the monastery.'

'Sir Henry and Lady Rothberg used it as a kind of snug – because it was next to the kitchen, it were always cosy in winter from the heat from the oven, and it were cheaper than heating the bigger rooms in the house just for the two of them.'

'They had no children?'

'None that survived childhood, no.'

'How sad.'

The old man did not react. He went on, 'They were going away for a few days and asked me to house-sit for them, to look after the dogs and that. They had a couple of them old-fashioned wing-back chair things in there. On the Sunday night I was sitting listening to the radio, and the two dogs, in the kitchen, began growling. Wasn't a normal sound, it was really eerie, set me off shivering. I can still hear it, that sound, all these years on. They came out into the atrium, their fur standing on end. Then suddenly they both began backing away, and I saw her.'

'Her?'

'The *lady*.' The old man nodded.

'What did she look like? What did she do?'

'She was an old lady, with a horrible expression on her face, all dressed in blue silk crinoline, or something like that, and yellow shoes. She came out of the wall, walked towards me, flicked me in the face so hard with her fan it stung my cheek, and left a mark, and vanished into the wall behind me.'

Ollie shivered, eyeing the man carefully. 'Bloody hell. What happened then?'

'Oh, I didn't hang around. I took off. Just grabbed my things as fast as I could and left. I phoned Mr Rothberg, told him I was sorry, but I couldn't stay there no more.'

'Did he ask you why not?'

'Oh, he did, and I told him.'

'What did he say?'

'He weren't very happy. But he said I wasn't the first to have seen her, the lady. I found that out for myself.'

'What – did you find out?'

'Well . . .' the old man stopped and pursed his lips, then he shook his head. For the first time, Ollie saw fear in his eyes. 'Like I said – it's not my place to frighten you. Not my place.' He began walking on.

Ollie hurried after him for a few paces. 'Please tell me a bit more about her?'

The old man shook his head, continuing to walk. Without turning his head, he added, 'I've said enough. I've said quite enough. Except for one thing. Ask about the digger.'

'Digger?'

'Ask someone about the mechanical digger.'

'What's your name?' Ollie called out.

But, shaking his head, the old man carried on.

8

Ollie stood still and watched the strange character walk on up the lane. He wasn't sure if it was his imagination, but the old man seemed to quicken his pace as he passed the entrance gates to Cold Hill House, slowing down again on the far side.

Digger? What the hell did he mean, *Ask someone about the mechanical digger?*

He felt disturbed by the encounter, and determined to press the old man for more information. There would be other opportunities, he decided. He'd bump into him again, or perhaps he'd find him one evening in the pub and buy him a pint or two, and get him to loosen up.

He walked on, further than he had intended, right down into the village, with the hope he might meet the old man again when he went back up to the house, and entered the small, cluttered shop with faded, old-fashioned sign-writing across the lintel proclaiming COLD HILL VILLAGE STORES. It smelled of freshly baked bread, which masked the dry, slightly musty smell that reminded him of ironmongers' stores. The elderly proprietor and his wife seemed to know all about him already. Clearly the new occupants of Cold Hill House were a major source of village gossip.

He discovered to his delight that they would do a daily newspaper delivery. He gave a list of the papers and magazines he and Caro wanted: *The Times*, *Mail*, the *Argus*, the weekly *Brighton and Hove Independent*, the *Mid-Sussex Times* and the monthly *Motor Sport*, *Classic Cars* and *Sussex Life* magazines. He bought a homemade lemon drizzle cake and a loaf of locally made wholemeal bread, then went back out into the sunshine.

He looked up the hill, trying to spot the old man. A tiny woman in a Nissan Micra was coming down towards him, the top of her head barely visible above the dashboard, with a green van impatiently tailgating her. As he headed back up the hill, he was deep in troubled thought. Was the old man a nutter? He didn't think so. The fear in his eyes had seemed very genuine.

Should he tell Caro?

But what good would that do? Frighten her into imagining something that might not be there? He would wait, he decided. His thoughts returned to the website for Charles Cholmondley Classic Motors. One of the most expensive cars on the list that he'd had to provide copy for was a stunningly fine 1924 Rolls-Royce Silver Ghost Canterbury Landaulette, priced at £198,000, a black sedan with whitewall tyres, and an open roof above the driver's cab, and a complete ownership history. *Ghost*, how very appropriate, he thought with a grin. As he reached the front gates of the house, he stood and waited for some moments, looking up the hill again for any sign of the old man heading back down. But there was none.

He walked up the drive. As he approached the house his spirits lifted once more. The warm sunshine beat down on him, and his T-shirt stuck to his back with perspiration. Then, suddenly, looking up at the sun, high in the sky, he stopped and thought hard.

Thought back to the pinpricks of light he had seen in the atrium.

He had dismissed them as either reflections of the sunlight through the windowpanes in the rear door, or symptoms of an approaching migraine. But the rear of the house faced north and, he now realized, however high the sun was as it traversed from east to west across the sky, it would not shine in through that rear door.

Which made it impossible for those spheres he had seen to have been reflections of sunlight. So it must have been a migraine.

9

On this weekend, every year, Ollie would normally be watching the classic and historic car racing at the Goodwood Revival meeting, his favourite motoring event of the year. But right now, instead of wandering around the famous motor-racing circuit, dressed in vintage clothing, ogling the millions of pounds' worth of fabulous cars, and watching the racing with some of his mates, he stood in the early-morning sunshine in a sodden T-shirt, Lycra shorts and cycling shoes, staring down at a dead frog floating in a puddle at the bottom of the empty swimming pool.

There were already a lot of changes to their lifestyle due to this huge commitment they had taken on with the house, but just over a week after moving here he was loving the challenge and not regretting it for a moment.

'Breakfast, darling!' Caro called out.

'OK – just need to have a quick shower!'

He'd completed a fifteen-mile bike ride, exploring some of the surrounding lanes, and was feeling exhilarated and happy, although a lot more tired by the ride than he would normally have been, he thought. Perhaps because he'd had no rest so far this weekend. Yesterday he'd taken a few hours out from helping Caro to move furniture, unpack and unwrap their best crockery and glasses, hang paintings, and pore over paint charts and wallpaper and fabric swatches, to drive across West Sussex to the Goodwood race meeting.

But it was a short visit, principally to see his client, Charles Cholmondley, and photograph his stand at the Revival meeting to add to the website, but he'd also wanted to visit the other classic car companies which had stands and put his business card around. He was going to need to generate a lot of business to earn enough to get this place into shape. Caro's income would cover the hefty mortgage and additional bank loan interest payment, but he was going to have to start earning serious money again to pay for the renovations. It was only after living here for the past week that he'd started to realize the full enormity of their undertaking. Everything was in even worse condition than they had realized, and the pool was just a tiny part of it. Despite that, he still loved it here.

The pool was surrounded by a collapsing wooden safety fence, and tiles had fallen in big chunks off the sides of it. The large pool house, close by, was so rotten he could push his finger right through parts of its walls.

A man from the pool company had been to survey it, and confirmed just what a poor state of repair it was in. Many of the remaining tiles were loose, and there were deep cracks in the walls. The heating and filtration system were archaic, and had not been used for decades. Just about everything would need replacing. Pool parties looked like a very distant dream. Right now he was even reluctant to pay the cost of having the Range Rover's busted wing mirror repaired.

He turned and gazed at the rear of the house. It was quite different this side from the elegant Georgian facade. It was more stark and institutional-looking, and cluttered on one side with the old stable block, part of which had been converted into the garages, outbuildings and two storage sheds. One housed the lawn tractor, strimmer, hedge-cutter, chainsaw and other garden maintenance equipment they'd had to buy, the other was filled with rolls of rusting chicken wire and a large stack of logs that looked, mostly, infested with woodworm.

He stared at the windows, trying to work out which belonged to which room. The downstairs at least was fairly straightforward with the kitchen and scullery windows, the door leading out from the atrium, then the twin sash windows of the dining room. The upstairs, with its different levels, was harder to figure out.

Twenty minutes later, showered and dressed in jeans and a fresh T-shirt, he had a quick breakfast of cereal and fruit, glanced through the Sunday papers, then helped Caro to lay the table. She had a girlfriend popping over to see the house this morning, then the in-laws were coming to lunch.

'Try and get Jade up,' she asked him. 'I've tried to wake her twice already.'

Despite the fact that he'd driven their daughter into Brighton yesterday morning and let her stay with Phoebe until 10 p.m., she'd thrown a strop in the car on the way home because she was going to have to stay in and have lunch with, as she called them, *the old people*, instead of being able to go back into Brighton and spend Sunday with her boyfriend, Ruari, and her other best friends, Olivia and Lara.

Ollie went into her bedroom, opened the curtains, and pulled back her duvet. Bombay was asleep, curled up beside her.

'Dad!' she protested.

'Your mother needs help. Up!' he said.

The cat eyed him warily.

Jade lay in her pyjamas and looked up at him with her large blue eyes. 'Did you mean what you said about getting a dog? A labradoodle?'

'Yes, darling, I did. I think a labradoodle would be great!'

'Olivia's getting a Schnauzer next week. And guess what, I've found a labradoodle breeder in Cowfold that's expecting a litter next month!' she said.

'OK, we'll go and have a look after they're born.'

Jade suddenly cheered up. 'Great! Promise?'

'I promise! So long as you promise to look after the dog. Deal?'

'Deal! Can we get an alpaca of our own, too?'

'Shall we get a dog first? There are enough alpacas out in the field!'

'OK.'

Ollie then climbed up to his office to work on the final revisions of the classic car website. He had promised Cholmondley yesterday that he would send the amended test site to him by the middle of the week for final approval.

As he sat in front of his computer, tantalizing smells of roasting beef wafted up. Two hours later, at 12.30, he heard the sound of a car, and peered down from the window overlooking the drive. His in-laws' maroon Volvo was pulling up beside his Range Rover and Caro's Golf. Moments later he heard the doorbell.

Normally he would have waited until Caro called him, but today he was on a mission. As the doorbell rang, he logged off, then hurried downstairs, just in time to join Caro in greeting the sweet pair of oddballs and lead them through into the drawing room.

His father-in-law, Dennis, was dressed as usual in a

tweedy three-piece suit. His only concession to the heat-wave was to have the top button of his Viyella shirt open and to sport a paisley cravat instead of a tie. His mother-in-law, Pamela, wore a white lace-trimmed blouse and a floral confection of a skirt, with pink Crocs.

'So, it's still standing, eh!' Dennis said with a smile, looking up and around him. 'And you've made up your mind to buy it, then?'

'They have bought it, Dennis,' his wife reminded him. 'We helped them move in last week.'

Dennis frowned, looking bewildered. 'Ah, right, if you say so, dear.'

'You've done wonders with this room,' Pamela said, enthusiastically. 'What a transformation!'

'It's coming along, isn't it?' Caro said.

'G and T, Pamela?' Ollie asked his mother-in-law.

'I'll pass on the G and just have the T, thank you.'

'A snifter before lunch?' he asked his father-in-law.

'Hmmn,' the old man said, peering at the fireplace. 'Rather fine marble this. Could be an Adam. Hmmn. Make sure the buggers don't try to remove it if you do buy the place. I fancy this would be worth a few bob to some of those dealers down the Lanes.' He then peered up at the ceiling. 'Nasty damp patch up there. I'd get a survey report before you make an offer. Yes, I think an Amontillado sherry, thank you, Ollie.' He pulled a leather cigar case from his inside pocket. 'Want to join me outside in a little smoke before lunch?'

'We thought we'd have lunch outside, actually, Dennis. I'd love a cigar later.'

'Do you have some shade?' Pamela asked, dubiously.

'Yes! Bought some big parasol umbrellas from the local garden centre yesterday.' Ollie led them through the atrium and straight out onto the rear terrace. As his father-in-law lit a cigar he went back indoors to prepare their drinks.

When he returned, Dennis was wandering down the lawn towards the lake, puffing away. Pamela was sitting in the shade of the two huge umbrellas, clearly uncomfortable in the sticky heat. Ollie put her tonic on the table, then sat beside her, cradling a bottle of cold Grolsch, and looked around. Neither Caro nor Dennis was in earshot.

'Pamela, Friday last week, the day we moved in, when you and I were standing in the porch, you saw something, didn't you?'

She raised her glass. 'Cheers!'

He clinked the neck of his bottle against it. 'Cheers.'

She gave him a strange, almost evasive smile, and sipped her drink.

'What was it you saw?' he pressed.

'I thought you'd seen it too,' she said.

Out of the corner of his eye he noticed Dennis walking back towards them.

'Darling,' Caro called out from the doorway. 'Please go and get Jade up!'

'OK, in a moment!'

'Please go now, the beef's going to be ruined! Tell her if she wants us to drive her into Brighton this afternoon, to see Ruari, then she needs to be polite and join us for lunch.' Caro disappeared back inside.

He turned back to his mother-in-law. 'All I saw was a shadow in the atrium.'

'A shadow?'

'I thought I had imagined it. Or that it might have been a bird flitting past or something. What did you see?'

'Do you need to know, Ollie?'

'Yes.'

'Are you sure?'

'Yes, I'm sure. I didn't want to spook Caro out on the day we moved in, which is why I dismissed it. But now I do need to know.'

She nodded, and peered into her tumbler, inspecting the contents with an eagle eye. She poked a flake of lemon suspended among the tiny bubbles like a microorganism. 'I really did think you'd seen it, too,' she said finally.

He shook his head. Dennis was only yards away. 'Please tell me, it's really important.'

'I saw an elderly lady in a blue dress. She appeared out of the wall on the left, glided across the room and disappeared into the wall on the right.' She gave him a quizzical stare.

He looked back at her numbly.

'Are you going to tell Caro?' she asked.

'You've got a lot of damned weed in that lake, Ollie,' Dennis said, bluntly crashing in on the conversation. 'That's another thing you'd have to consider – grass-eating carp.'

'Grass-eating carp?'

'Might be just the ticket.' He took a puff on his cigar then laid it in the ashtray Ollie had provided on the table, and set his empty sherry glass down beside it.

'It's not a high priority – need to get the house done before we start spending money on the grounds,' Ollie replied, and shot a glance at his mother-in-law. She gave him a to-be-continued smile in return.

Dennis looked around suddenly with a bewildered expression, as if he had lost his bearings.

'A top-up, Dennis?' Ollie asked.

'Huh?'

'Some more sherry?'

'Ah, no, right. I'll wait until lunch, I'll have a glass of wine at lunch. Have you booked a table somewhere?'

'We're having lunch here, Dennis,' Pamela said, a tad sharply.

'Really? That's jolly decent of them – they must be keen to sell!' He looked around again then said, 'Are we allowed to use the little boy's room?'

'Straight through the door, it's on the left.'

'Jolly decent of them!' He entered the house.

As soon as the old man was out of earshot, Ollie leaned across to Pamela. 'What do you think? Should I tell Caro?'

'She hasn't seen her?'

'No.' He took a swig of his beer. 'Well, she certainly hasn't said anything if she has.'

'Have you seen anything since?'

Ollie hesitated. 'No.'

'It's possible you might never see her again,' she said. 'I think you might find it helpful to see if you can discover any background, who this woman might be – or rather, might have *been*.'

'I've tried googling already and doing some other internet searches on the house and the village, but so far nothing. I thought of going to the County Records Office to see if I can find anything there about the place.'

'You'd probably do better talking to some of the older locals. There must be a few who've been here for generations.'

He nodded, thinking about the old man he'd seen in the lane. He'd go into the village and track him down tomorrow, he decided.

A couple of minutes later, Dennis came back out. 'She's a bit of a surly one, the housekeeper,' he said.

'Housekeeper?' Ollie said.

'Well, I presume that's who it was. Woman in an old-fashioned dress. I said good afternoon to her and she just blanked me.'

10

'It's your birthday soon,' Caro said, during a commercial break in the TV programme. 'You're going to be an old man!'

'Yep, tell me about it,' Ollie replied.

'Forty! Still, you're wearing pretty well.'

He smiled.

'We haven't discussed how to celebrate.'

'I think we just do something low key until we're sorted here. Then we could think about a big party – if we can afford it. Maybe dinner with a few friends? Martin and Judith? The Hodges? Iain and Georgie?'

They were lying naked in bed, with the Sunday papers spread across the duvet and on the floor either side of them. *Downton Abbey*, which they'd recorded earlier, was playing on the television on the wall. Caro had not missed an episode. Ollie kept an occasional eye on it while he worked his way through the *Sunday Times* sections. The windows were wide open. It was a warm, balmy night. Almost too hot for the duvet.

'You seemed very distracted today,' she said.

'Sorry, darling, a lot on my mind.' He was looking up at the large brown water stain on the ceiling. At the old, faded wallpaper, not yet stripped, at the walls not yet ready for the new paint colours Caro and he had chosen, and the bare floorboards that they had decided to have sanded and varnished, and cover with rugs. At the huge old-fashioned radiators which the plumber reckoned he could get a decent price for at an architectural salvage place. At the cracked marble fireplace. At the rusty old lock on the door. The brand-new cream curtains only accentuated the poor state of decoration of the rest of the room.

The house was warm at the moment, but in another month, with the October gales coming in, all that would change. The temperature could drop within a week or so. The heating barely worked at the moment, but to replace the system, they would have to be without heat totally for a week, the plumber had estimated. They'd given him the go-ahead to get the new boiler and replace all the piping and they'd been assured the work would be completed by the end of September. It had to be or the place would start feeling pretty miserable.

'You mean the website? Charles Cholmondley? How do you pronounce it?'

'Chumley.' Ollie nodded. 'Partly that.'

'I think it looks great.'

'I think the client likes it.'

'Of course he does, you've done a great job – particularly considering everything else you've had to deal with this week! I meant to ask, did you remember to put the sign for a cleaning lady up on the village shop noticeboard?'

'Yes – Ron, who runs the shop with his wife, Madge, said there were a couple of people they thought might be interested.'

'On first-name terms with the locals after just a week?' she said with a grin.

'They're a lovely couple. He's a retired accountant and

she was a teacher. The shop's a labour of love – they do it for pin money.'

'Nice there are people like that in the world,' she said. 'And I like that you're getting to know the place a bit. We ought to go in the pub sometime. Perhaps see if they do Sunday lunch? We need to try to be a bit involved in the community – and there might be some other girls here around Jade's age she could become friends with.'

'Yes, absolutely. Maybe you could join the local jam-making class?' he joked.

'There is one?'

'There was an ad in the store!' He fell silent. He'd still not told Caro about the old lady. Fortunately, it seemed to have slipped from his father-in-law's mind and he had not mentioned her again at lunch. But at some point soon, Ollie knew, he would have to say something to Caro. Hopefully in the coming days he'd find the strange old man again and pump him for more about the background of the apparition. If both his in-laws had seen her, and he'd seen something too, then others must have seen her as well. Presumably it was someone who had lived here in the past. Did the estate agent know about her? Was there any legal obligation for it to have been disclosed?

And if it had been disclosed, would that have made a difference? Would they have still bought the house if they'd known it had a ghost?

Whatever ghosts were . . .

He wasn't so much frightened by the idea of the house having a ghost, as intrigued. But Caro wouldn't have agreed to buying this place in a million years if she'd known.

He stared at the paper, at the headline of the article in the 'News Review' section. As if it had been planted there by an unseen hand.

DO GHOSTS EXIST?

He grinned at the coincidence. Then, before he had a chance to start reading, he felt Caro's fingers trace softly down his navel, then further down still, and she turned and nuzzled his ear. 'We've been here over a week,' she said. 'We haven't had a date night and we haven't done anything naughty in all that time. That's far too long.'

'Far too long,' he echoed, feeling suddenly deeply aroused. They'd promised each other when they had got engaged that they would not become like some couples and let the romance in their relationship ever fade. As part of that resolve they had a date night once a week and had rarely missed one, except in the period around Jade's birth. That had been a terrible time in which Caro had nearly died, and she had been left unable to conceive again.

With her free hand she switched off the television, placed the remote on her bedside table and began lifting sections of the paper and magazines off the bed and chucking them on the floor. Then her left hand moved lower still, and he winced in pleasure, then gasped as she closed her fingers around him.

He leaned away from her, for an instant, to turn off the over-head light, leaving just his bedside table lamp on. Then he turned back to face her. 'I love you,' he said.

She stared at him, as if examining his face, with a quizzical look. As her reply she kissed him.

Minutes later, lying on top of her and deep inside her, Ollie had the sudden sensation of being watched. Distracted, he turned his head, suddenly and sharply, towards the door. But it was closed. There was no one there.

'What is it?' she murmured.

'Sorry – I thought – I thought I heard Jade come in.' He

kissed her and held her tightly, his arms round her, pressing their cheeks tightly together. 'I love you so much,' he said.

'You too.'

Afterwards, Ollie fell asleep within minutes. He awoke a while later from a bad dream, drenched in perspiration, confused, unsure for some moments where he was. A hotel room? Their old house in Brighton? The green glow of his clock radio was the only light in the room. He saw the time flip from 2.47 to 2.48. Outside, an owl hooted. Moments later it hooted again.

Fragments of the dream remained. The old woman in a blue dress chasing him down the corridors of the house, then appearing in front of him, making him turn back. Then running into a tiny room and realizing he was trapped, turning round and seeing the old man with the briar pipe glaring at him, malevolently.

He wriggled up the bed a little to try to shake the dream away, and reached out in the darkness for the tumbler of water he kept by the bed. Caro slept deeply beside him, on her stomach, her arms round her pillow as if it were a life raft. She always slept soundly; she was capable of sleeping through a thunderstorm, and he envied her that. He envied her untroubled sleep right now, as he listened to the sound of her rhythmic breathing and the occasional little *put-put* sound of air bubbles through her lips.

He sipped the water and replaced the glass then, suddenly, a deep, paralysing chill gripped his body. He heard the click of the door opening. Then someone – or something – entered the room. He held his breath. He could just make out the dark shape moving, then stopping and standing right in front of the bed, staring at him. It was motionless. Goose pimples rippled down his skin and the hair rose up on the back of his neck. Was it a burglar? What weapon could he grab? The glass? The bedside lamp? His phone? His phone had a flashlight – he could flip it on.

Slowly, as silently as he could, he moved his hand towards the phone.

Then he heard Jade say urgently, from the foot of the bed, 'There's someone in my room!'

11

The alarm clock radio came on at 6.20 a.m., as it did every weekday morning. Ollie, as usual, rolled over and pressed the ten-minute snooze button.

Caro, who had slept fitfully after getting up in the middle of the night to settle Jade after her nightmare, was instantly awake, and thinking about the full day she had ahead of her at work. She kissed Ollie on the cheek, then climbed out of bed, went into the bathroom and ran the elderly, noisy electric shower.

It took some moments for the water to heat up sufficiently, then she stepped in and ducked her head beneath the shower head, grateful for the stream of hot water that was waking her more every second. She reached for the shampoo, tipped some into her hand, and massaged it into her hair.

Then she smelled the pungent reek of burning plastic.

The water stopped.

She heard the crackle of a fire.

Opening her eyes, stinging from soap, she saw to her horror flames shooting around the blackened shower controls.

'Ollie!' she shrieked, pushing open the shower door and stepping back into the bathroom. She stood transfixed like a rabbit caught in headlights, as flames licked the controls then died down, acrid black smoke rising around them.

'Ollie!' she called out again, running through into the bedroom, dripping wet, shivering, blinking away the soap. He was sound asleep.

'Ollie!'

He did not stir.

She ran back into the bathroom and peered into the shower. The smoke was dying down. 'Fuck!' she said, watching the control unit warily. The last wisps of smoke rose and then there was nothing.

'Fuck,' she said again, touching her soapy hair, and walked over to the washbasin. She turned on the mixer tap and, to her relief, water poured out. She waited until the temperature was OK, then ducked her head under the stream.

As she rinsed off the shampoo she suddenly felt a sharp tug on the left side of her head. Then a harder tug that hurt, making her cry out in pain.

Something was yanking her hair, pulling it down.

She tried to raise her head, but she was being pulled down further. Further. Further.

It felt as though a hand was trying to pull her down into the plughole.

'OLLIE!' she screamed, trying desperately to raise her head, feeling her hair tugging painfully against her scalp. 'OLLIE!'

Then she heard his voice. 'Darling, what is it?'

'HELP ME!'

The water stopped, abruptly. Ollie said, 'It's OK, darling. It's OK.'

She felt his hands on her hair. Then, suddenly, the pain stopped. Gingerly, she stood up. 'Oh my God,' she said.

'You're OK, darling. You're OK. You just got it caught on the plughole.'

'I'm sorry,' she gasped. 'It freaked me out. I really felt like someone was pulling it.'

'Why didn't you use the shower?'

12

Monday, 14 September

It was a warm morning, the heatwave continuing. An hour and a half later, as Ollie drove Jade for the start of her second week at school, she told him about her nightmare last night in which a woman, with an expression of menace, was standing at the end of her bed.

When she had been younger, Jade had suffered from night terrors. Terrible dreams that had made her sleepwalk around the house in her onesie, totally unaware. They had found the solution, which was to talk jokingly to her and make her laugh. Saying, repeatedly, 'Hi, darling, stick your tongue out,' was something that normally worked. Her face would turn from an expression of fear into a big smile. Then they could put her back to bed.

But last night she had been too afraid to leave her parents' room, until he and Caro had finally coaxed her back to her own bed, and then let her sleep with the lights on. It had taken Ollie a long time to get back to sleep. He had lain until dawn, his mind whirring, thinking. Thinking. Thinking.

Deeply disturbed.

After dropping a yawning Jade off at school and returning to the house, Ollie had an immediate word with the plumber about the shower. Maguire told him it was over thirty years old and it looked as if, at some time, the wiring had been gnawed by rodents. He told Ollie that, like so much in this house, it should have been scrapped a long time ago.

After instructing Maguire to replace it as quickly as possible, he briefly discussed various issues and queries the workmen had raised. Then he climbed up to his office and immediately settled down to work, checking carefully through the amendments he had carried out to the Chol-mondley Classics website. There were so many cars on it that he coveted. He paused for some moments to admire an immaculate blue and cream 1967 Mercedes 280SL Pagoda before, with some trepidation, emailing his client the link to the finished site.

He frittered away the next fifteen minutes replying to emails, Tweets and Facebook posts which had been coming in daily, wishing him and his family luck in their new home. There were dozens of comments in response to his Insta-gram posts too, as well as a ton of spam from various trade companies. Then he turned his attention to a less urgent, but equally challenging commission from another client, a revamp of the very basic website of an Indian restaurant in the centre of Brighton, The Chattri House.

This was a complete back-to-the-drawing-board job, to which the client, Anup Bhattacharya, whom he had met with last week, enthusiastically agreed. The man owned a chain of twelve themed Indian restaurants around the country – so a lot was riding on getting this right. He looked through the notes he had made on his iPad at their meeting: the look and the feel of the site that Bhattacharya wanted; the road map of contents; the number of pages; the social media interaction and links. There was an e-commerce side as well, with branded food products to go on sale in the entrepreneur's online deli.

At 11.00 when he went down for his mid-morning coffee, he hesitated before entering the atrium, as he now did each time, looking around carefully. As he stepped into the room the only thing he noticed, and perhaps it was his imagination, was that the temperature seemed to have dropped a fraction. He stopped and looked around. It wasn't a big room – it was square, about fifteen feet by fifteen. To the left, the panelling was shaped into three arches, which fitted with this once having been the altar of the chapel of the monastery. Ahead was the window and door out onto the rear garden and grounds. To the right, past two wooden Doric-style columns, was the doorway into the kitchen.

This was the area where his mother-in-law had very clearly seen what he could only presume was a ghost. The same one described by the old man in the lane. And from the sound of it, the one seen by his father-in-law, Dennis, yesterday. Gliding out of the altar wall to the left, moving across the tiled floor and disappearing into the wall to the right of the kitchen door.

He suddenly felt uncomfortable standing here, feeling again as he had last night that someone was watching him. He walked through to the kitchen, selected a strong capsule for the Nespresso machine, switched it on, then checked the water level at the rear, waiting for its its twin green lights to stop blinking. The feeling that someone was watching him persisted. Someone standing behind him.

He turned round, sharply. There was no one.

This is not going to get to me, he thought. I'm not going to let it.

Below in the cellar he could hear the whine of a drill. Somewhere above him was the sound of hammering on metal. One of the painters outside, working on the worst of the window frames, had a radio blaring out music. A clean protective runner had been laid along the hallway by the builders. He could smell fresh paint.

He carried his coffee up to the bedroom, where there was still a smell of burnt plastic from the shower, retrieved the section of the *Sunday Times* where he had seen the article on ghosts last night, and carried it on up to his office. Then he sat at his desk, in the upright orthopaedic chair Caro had insisted he buy, to improve his posture and stop him getting stooped from so many hours crouched over his computer. He opened the paper out and began to read.

Fifteen minutes later, he tore the page containing the article out, folded it and placed it in a drawer. There were a couple of names in there that might be useful, he decided. Then, fighting the distraction, he focused on The Chattri House website for the next two hours.

Shortly after 1.30 p.m. he decided to take a break and walk down into the village to see if he could find the old man. He planned to grab a bite of lunch in The Crown pub and see what kind of food it served – and perhaps book for Sunday lunch for Caro, himself, Jade and her friend Phoebe, who was coming over for a sleepover on Saturday night, and Ruari, who was joining them on Sunday. Then, on second thoughts, he decided it would be nicer to have the lunch at home – and a lot cheaper.

As he reached the front gate he heard the roar and clatter of a tractor towing a large piece of agricultural machinery on a trailer up the lane at speed. A grizzled man in a tweed cap, sitting in the cab, stared rigidly ahead. As he waited for it to pass, Ollie gave him a wave, but got no acknowledgement.

He watched it for some moments rattling on up the

road, almost expecting to suddenly see the old man walking down the hill. But there was no sign of him in either direction. He noticed to his irritation an empty Coke can and discarded food wrapper lying close to the front gates. Litter louts made him furious – what the hell gave people the right to just throw things out of their cars at random because they were too lazy to find a bin? He made a mental note to pick them up on his return.

He headed down the hill. As he reached the dilapidated-looking cottage on his right, with the very faded sign, GARDEN COTTAGE, he saw the front door was a few inches ajar, and decided to go and introduce himself, as this was his nearest neighbour. The gate was sagging so much on its hinges that the latch no longer closed properly. He pushed it open, feeling it scrape along the bricks of the garden path, then pushed it shut behind him and went up to the front door.

'Hello!' he called out. There had been a knocker once but all that remained were the two corroded brass clasps that had held it. There was no sign of a bell. He rapped with his bare knuckles and called out, again, 'Hello!'

'Yes, who is it?' asked a friendly, female voice, with a booming, county accent that seemed very grand for this little abode.

He heard a loud meow, then the woman saying, 'There's someone at the door, Horatio!'

A moment later Ollie was facing a tall, elderly woman, with flowing white hair, fine features and clear blue eyes, who stood there with an inquisitive smile. She was dressed in flip-flops, dungarees covered in flecks of what looked like dried clay, and a frayed cream blouse, with more flecks of the stuff on her face.

'Oh – I'm sorry to bother you,' he said, politely, removing his sunglasses for a moment. 'I'm Oliver Harcourt – my wife and I have recently moved into Cold Hill House. I thought I would just pop round and say hello as we're neighbours.'

'Well, how jolly nice of you! And welcome to Cold Hill – hope you'll be jolly happy here. Excuse my appearance, I've been throwing pots.'

Ollie wondered for a moment if she was bonkers, then he realized what she meant. 'Clay? You're a potter?'

'Yes, I've got my wheel and kiln out in the back. Tell you what, I'll make you and your wife—?'

'Caro.'

'Caro! I'll make you and Caro a vase, as a moving-in present. My name's Annie Porter.'

'Are you a famous potter?'

She laughed. 'Good God, no. Most of my stuff explodes in the damned kiln anyway – but every now and then something survives! Do you like elderflower cordial?'

'Not sure I've ever tried it.'

'Got some of my own homemade in the fridge. Jolly good it is, too. Come in and have a glass and tell me a bit about yourselves. I hear you've a little girl. Nice to have a young couple come to the village – too many old fogeys like myself here!'

What little he saw of the interior house as he followed her through into the rear garden was as dilapidated as the exterior, although evidently good quality. There was a threadbare Persian hall carpet and a handsome grandfather clock. On one wall was a photograph of a man in naval uniform next to a frame containing a row of medals, and on the opposite wall, a couple of fine seascapes in ornate frames, and a black-and-white photograph of a modern warship. Several gaily painted vases and mugs were arranged on shelves in the kitchen, which they passed through on their way out to the unkempt rear garden. It was filled mostly with vegetables, Ollie noticed, rather than flowers, and there was a row of cloches. At the far end was a shed that looked in imminent danger of collapse, which presumably housed her pottery studio.

They sat at a small round metal table on hard chairs, under the glare of the sun, and he gratefully sipped the sweet but refreshingly cold cordial. It was several minutes of being pumped with questions by Annie about himself, Caro and Jade, before he had the opportunity to ask her anything back.

'So how long have you lived here, Annie?' he said, finally.

'In Cold Hill? Gosh, let me think. About thirty-five years. We bought this place as a bit of a retirement dream – my late husband and I. But you know how things work out.' She shrugged.

'I'm sorry – did you split up?'

'Oh no, nothing like that.' She looked sad, suddenly, for the first time. 'No, Angus died in the Falklands War – his ship was hit by one of those Exocet missiles.'

'I'm really sorry.'

She shrugged. 'That's how life goes sometimes, isn't it?' She pointed at a small bed planted with tall sunflowers. 'They always make me smile, sunflowers!'

'They make everyone smile,' Ollie said.

'Daft-looking things. Daft but happy. We all need a few daft things in our lives, don't you think?'

'I guess!' He smiled and sipped some more of his drink, wondering whether it would be polite or rude to ask any more about her life. 'This is delicious.'

She beamed. 'Good, I'll give you a couple of bottles to

put in your fridge. I always make far too much of the bloody stuff! I give it out to several people in the village. The shop want me to go into mass production so they can stock it, but I can't be bothered with all that!'

'You must know most of the people here, I imagine?' Ollie said.

'Oh, everybody, dear. Everybody. Well, nearly everybody. Most people who come here stay – for a good long while, at any rate. So, are you all happy in the house?'

After a moment Ollie said, 'Yes, yes, we are. Very. Well, my daughter, Jade, is a bit miffed about being separated from all her friends. We lived in the centre of Brighton previously – well, Hove, actually. Are there any young girls, around twelve, here in the village? I'd like to try and find her some friends.'

'There's one other family with young children, in the Old Rectory – that Victorian house at the far end. You might not have noticed it, because it's behind gates, set back quite a long way, like your house. The Donaldsons. He's some bigwig corporate lawyer who commutes to London, a bit aloof, but his wife is very friendly. She comes along to the informal pottery classes I hold every now and then. I'll introduce you. I know most people around here.'

'Thank you, I'd appreciate that. There's a chap just thundered past in a tractor a few minutes ago, going up the hill. Who's he?'

She grinned. 'That'll be Arthur Fears. His family have farmed around here for generations. They own quite a bit of grazing land on the hill. He's a miserable bugger, and he always drives too fast. I think he reckons he owns the road.'

'I waved at him and he just blanked me.'

'I wouldn't worry about that – he ignores me, too. He only speaks to locals, and in his view you're not a local unless you were born here!' She smiled. 'Some of the older country people have strange views. But, anyhow, you're settling in?'

'Yes. Sort of.' He shrugged.

She saw his hesitation. 'Oh?'

'Actually,' he went on, 'there's one person I'd like to ask you about. An old boy I met in the lane. He had a pipe and walking stick. He was very odd.'

She frowned. 'A pipe and a walking stick? Doesn't ring a bell.'

'He's a local, he told me.'

She shook her head. 'I can't think who you mean. Can you describe him a bit more?'

Ollie sipped some more cordial then put the glass down, thinking hard. 'Yes, I would guess in his late seventies, quite wiry, with a beard and very white hair. Oh yes, he had a briar pipe in his mouth and a very gnarled stick. We had a conversation – he asked me where I was from and when I told him Brighton, he shook his head and said something that made me smile. He said he'd never been there – he didn't like big cities!'

'He sounds like a rambler. A bit nutty?'

'He was definitely odd.'

She shook her head. 'There's really no one around here I can think of who fits that description.'

'He's very definitely a local. He said he used to work at our house years back.'

'I honestly can't think who you mean. There's definitely no one in the village of that description. I know everyone, trust me.'

13

'I'm being shown a house,' Kingsley Parkin said, totally out of the blue.

'I beg your pardon?' Caro said to her client.

'A house! I'm being shown a very big country house – not far from Brighton!'

Caro's modern office, in the centre of Brighton, had a window that looked directly down on the courtyard in front of the city's Jubilee Library. Not that she ever had time to take in the view. From the moment she arrived in her office, in the small law firm in which she was a junior partner, before 8.00 a.m. every morning, she was full-on, reading documents, drafting and redrafting transfers and leases. At 9.00 a.m. the phone would begin to ring, incessantly, until the switchboard closed at 5.00 p.m. Some clients would email or phone her – or both – several times a day, anxious about properties they were buying or selling.

Additionally, she had meetings throughout the day both with existing clients and to take new instructions. Mostly she enjoyed face-to-face meetings, they were her favourite part of her work. She had a natural instinct to help people, and she enjoyed the challenge of pointing out pitfalls in property transactions. But with the way her days stacked up, she needed to keep her client meetings as brief as possible and to the point; there was little time to spare for small talk.

Which was why this new client, seated in front of her, a pleasant, but very, very long-winded man, vacillating over whether to bid for a potential student housing property which was shortly coming up at auction, was beginning to irk her.

He was an elfin creature, of indeterminate age somewhere north of sixty, in a high-collared emerald shirt beneath a shiny black jacket on which the tailor's white stitching was part of the design, silver trousers, and patent-leather Cuban-heeled boots. His fingers were adorned with large jewelled rings. His hair was jet black, his skin was pockmarked and sallow, as if rarely exposed to daylight, and he reeked of tobacco. He'd once been the lead singer of a 60s rock band that was something of a one-hit wonder, and had scraped a living doing pub gigs and cruise ships on the back of it ever since, he had told her. Now he was looking to shore up his finances for his old age with some property investments.

'There are a couple of things I need to make you aware of,' Caro said, reading through a long email from the vendor's solicitor, a particularly sharp character called Simon Alldis.

Mr Parkin picked up his cup of coffee and held it daintily in the air. 'Listen, my love,' he said in his coarse, gravelly voice. 'I'm being told something.'

'Told something?'

'Happens to me all the time. The spirits won't leave me alone – know what I mean?' He flapped his hands in the air, as if they were a pair of butterflies he was trying to shake free from his bangled wrists.

'Ah.' She frowned, not knowing what he meant at all. 'Spirits?'

'I'm a conduit, my love, from the spirit world. I just can't help it. They give me messages to pass on.'

'Right,' she said, focusing back on the document in the hope it would concentrate his mind on the business in hand.

'You've just moved into a new house, Mrs Harcourt?'

'How do you know that?' she asked sharply, uncomfortably surprised. She did not like her clients knowing about her private life, which was why she kept her office bland, with just one photograph facing her on her desk, of Ollie and Jade holding paddleball bats on the beach in Rock, Cornwall.

The two butterflies flitted around above his head again. 'I have an elderly lady with me, who passed last year!' he said. 'You see, the spirits tell me things, I can't switch them on and off. I hear a *click* and then someone is there. They can be very irritating sometimes, you know? They can piss me off.'

'Who tells you?'

'Well, it varies, you see!'

'Shall we concentrate, Mr Parkin?' She looked back down at the document on her desk.

'I have a message for you,' he said.

'That's very nice,' she said, sarcastically, glancing at her watch, the Cartier Tank that Ollie had bought her for their tenth wedding anniversary. 'The document I have here—'

He cut her off in mid-stream. 'Can I ask you something very personal, Mrs Harcourt?'

'I have another client immediately after you, Mr Parkin. I really think we should concentrate.'

'Please hear me out for a moment, OK?'

'OK,' she said, reluctantly.

'I don't go looking for spirits, right? They find me. I'm just passing on what I get told. Does that make any sense?'

'Honestly? Not much, no.'

'I'm being shown a house. A very big place, Georgian-looking, with a tower at one end. Does that mean anything?'

Now he had her attention. 'You saw the estate agent's particulars?'

'I'm just passing on what the spirits are telling me.' He shrugged. 'I'm just a conduit.'

'So what are these *spirits* telling you?'

'This is just one particular spirit. She wants me to tell you there are problems with your new home.'

'Thank you, but we already know that.'

'No, I don't think you do.'

'We're well aware of them, Mr Parkin,' she replied, coldly. 'We had a survey done and we know what we're in for.'

'I don't think what I'm being told would have shown up on a survey, my love.'

His familiarity annoyed her.

'There are a lot of things you don't know about this house,' he went on. 'You're in danger. There are very big problems. I'm being told you really ought to think about moving out, while you still can. Your husband, Ollie, your daughter, Jade, and yourself.'

'How the hell do you know all this about us?' she rounded on him.

'I told you already about the spirits. They tell me everything. But many people don't like to believe them. Maybe you are one of those?'

'I'm a solicitor,' she said. 'A lawyer. I'm very down to

earth. I deal with human beings. I don't believe in – what do you call them – spirits? Ghosts? I'm afraid I don't believe in any of that.' She refrained from adding *all that rubbish*.

Kingsley Parkin rocked his head, defensively, from side to side, the butterflies soaring once more, light glinting off the rubies, emeralds and sapphires. 'Admirable sentiments, of course!' he said. 'But have you considered this? Ghosts might not care that you don't believe in them? If they believe in you?'

He grinned, showing a row of teeth that looked un-naturally white. 'You're going to need help very soon,' he said. 'Trust me. This is what I'm being told.'

She was beginning to feel very unsettled by the man. 'Told by whom?'

'I have this elderly lady with me who passed in spring last year. She had a grey cat who passed the year before, who is in spirit with her. She's telling me her name was – hmmm, it's not clear. Marcie? Maddie. Marjie?'

Caro fell silent. Her mother's sister, her aunt Marjory, had died in April last year. Everyone called her Aunt Marjie. She'd had a grey cat which had died a few months before she did.

14

Ollie left the old lady, Annie Porter, his head spinning. She was wrong. She *must* be. Maybe her memory wasn't too great.

He walked on down into the village, deep in thought, as the tractor driven by grim, surly Arthur Fears, local farmer and frustrated Formula One driver, rocketed by, blasting him with its slipstream. He passed the village store, then hesitated when he reached the pub. Much in character with the village, The Crown was a Georgian building, but with a rather shabby extension to the left covered with a corrugated iron roof. It was set well back from the road, with a scrubby, uneven lawn in front of it, on which were dotted around several wooden tables and benches – a couple of them occupied.

He walked up the path. In small gold letters above the saloon bar door, were the words: LICENSED PROPRIETOR, LESTER BEESON.

If he ever had to create the interior of an iconic English country pub for a website, Ollie thought, as the ingrained sour reek of beer struck his nostrils, this place would be it. Booths recessed into the walls, wooden tables and chairs, window seats, and a warren of doorways leading to other rooms. The ochre walls were hung with ancient agricultural artefacts, and there was a row of horseshoes along one side, along with a dartboard.

Presiding over the L-shaped bar was a massively tall man in his late fifties, with a mane of hair, a cream shirt with the top two buttons undone and a gut the size of a rugby ball bulging his midriff. Behind his head were rows of optics, a photograph of a cricket team, and several pewter tankards.

'Good afternoon,' the landlord greeted him warmly, lifting a pint glass up and drying it with a cloth.

'Good afternoon!'

'Mr Harcourt would it be, by any chance?' He set the glass down.

Ollie grinned, surprised. 'Yes.' He held out his hand. 'Ollie Harcourt.'

The landlord shook it firmly. 'Les,' he said. 'All of us in Cold Hill are very happy to have you and your family with us. We need a little rejuvenation. What can I offer you as a drink on the house?'

Normally, Ollie avoided drinking alcohol at lunchtime, but didn't want to look a prig. 'Well, that's very kind of you, thank you. I'd like a draught Guinness – and also a lunch menu, please.'

The plastic-coated menu appeared in front of him instantly, as if conjured from out of the ether by the land-lord. The Guinness took some minutes longer. As Lester Beeson stood over the glass, which was steadily filling with black liquid and cream foam, Ollie ventured, 'Do you by chance know an old guy in the village, with a briar pipe and walking stick?'

'Pipe and walking stick?' He thought for a moment. 'Doesn't ring a bell. Local, is he?'

Ollie nodded. 'A wiry little fellow with a goatee beard and very white hair. In his seventies or even eighties?'

'No, doesn't ring any bells.'

'I understand he lives here, in the village. I met him last week – I wanted to have another chat with him.'

'I thought I knew everyone.' The landlord looked puzzled. He turned towards an elderly, morose couple seated in a window booth, eating in silence as if they had run out of conversation with each other years earlier. 'Morris!' he called out. 'You know an old fellow who smokes a pipe and has a walking stick?'

After some moments the man, who had lank white hair hanging down either side of his face, as if a damp mop had been plonked on his head, set down his knife and fork, picked up his pint of beer and sipped it.

Ollie thought at first he couldn't have heard the landlord. But then he said, suddenly, in a northern accent, 'Pipe and a walking stick.' He licked froth from his lips, revealing just two teeth, like a pair of tilting tombstones, at the front of his otherwise barren mouth.

The landlord looked at Ollie for confirmation. He nodded.

'That's right, Morris. A beard and white hair,' Beeson added.

The old couple looked at each other for a moment and both shrugged.

'He's as old as God, Morris is!' Beeson said to Ollie with a grin, and loudly enough for the old man to hear, then turned towards him. 'You've been here in the village – what – forty years, Morris?'

'Forty-two it is, this Christmas,' the old woman said.

Her husband nodded. 'Aye, forty-two. We came down here because our son and his family moved here.'

'Morris were engineer on the railways,' she said, inconsequentially.

'Ah,' said Ollie, as if that explained everything. 'Right.'

'Don't know of anyone like that,' she said.

'I'll ask around for you,' Beeson said to Ollie, helpfully.

'Thank you. I'll give you my home and mobile phone numbers – if you hear anything.'

'If he lives anywhere around here, someone will know him.'

'Old as God, did you say?' the old man suddenly called out to Beeson. 'I'll have you know, young man . . . !' Then he began chuckling.

Later that day, when Caro came home from work, Ollie again said nothing to her about the strange old man with the pipe.

Caro said nothing to Ollie about her encounter with Kingsley Parkin.

15

Monday, 14 September

With Katy Perry belting out through the Sonos speaker, Jade sat at her dressing table, which doubled as her desk, doing her maths homework, and allowing herself – *willing herself* – to be distracted by just about anything. She hated maths, although at least her new teacher at St Paul's made it more interesting than the dull one at her old school.

That, she had gleefully Instagrammed to all her old friends, was one very big plus of St Paul's. No more annoying Mr G! God, he was so dreary. So – well – just so *annoying*.

Annnnnooooooyyyyyyyyyinggggg! she typed out and posted beneath a photograph she had taken, surreptitiously, of Mr G in class some months ago, then pinged it to all her old schoolmates.

She put her iPhone back down on the table, then watched several ducks in the distance swimming in convoy across the lake, heading to their island sanctuary in the middle. Good, she thought. Smart ducks! Keep safe from the foxes overnight! As if reading her mind, Bombay suddenly arched her back, jumped down from the bed, walked over to the water bowl Jade kept up here for her, and began lapping at it.

'I bet you'd like a duck if you weren't so lazy, wouldn't you, Bombers?' She slipped off her chair, knelt beside the cat and began stroking her. Bombay nuzzled her head against Jade's hand and started purring. 'But I would not be happy about that, OK? No ducks!'

Her room was a lot straighter now, at least, with all of her things out of the boxes and on shelves or in cupboards. But she wasn't entirely happy. She still felt too isolated from her friends. And Ruari wasn't messaging her as often as he usually did. What was that about, she wondered, suspiciously? And although there seemed to be some nice people at St Paul's, she'd not yet made any new friends. In fact, there were a couple of girls in her class who seemed quite bossy and rude.

She sat back at her desk and, instead of returning to her maths, opened up the Videostar app on her iPad and went to the current pop video she was making with Phoebe, which she hoped to complete at the weekend.

In the video, set to 'Uptown Funk', she and Phoebe, in matching zebra-striped onesies, were dancing, alternately in colour, then in black and white, then just in silhouette. She'd got the idea from some of the silhouette shows she had watched on YouTube. As the video progressed, they were to fade more and more into silhouette, but the idea was not yet coming across as she wanted.

Her phone rang. She froze the video, picked the phone up and saw it was Phoebe on FaceTime, her blonde hair hanging untidily over her face as normal in a ragged fringe.

'Hey.'

'Hey.'

'Missing you, Jade!'

'Me too. I wish I was back with you guys.' Then she paused for a moment. 'You know what – I was just watching the shadows. I think I've had an idea! We can do this over the weekend – I've—'

Phoebe frowned. 'You've got a visitor,' she said, suddenly.

'That's Bombay! She's with me all the time, just like in Carlisle Road.'

'Not the cat, your gran.'

'Gran?'

'Behind you!'

Jade felt a sudden icy chill and spun round. There was no one there. The door was closed. She shivered and turned back to her phone. Then she shot another wary glance over her shoulder.

'Phebes, my gran's not here today.' She was conscious that her voice was shaking.

'I saw her, honestly, Jade. The same lady that came in last week – last Sunday?'

'Describe her?'

'I could see her more clearly this time, she was closer, only a few feet behind you. All in blue, with a creepy old-woman face.'

'Yeah, yeah, yeah!'

'No, no, *for real*, Jade!'

Taking the phone with her, Jade walked over to the door, waited a moment, then pulled it open sharply. There was nothing there. Just the long, empty landing, with closed doors to the spare rooms, the door to her parents' room some distance along, the stairs up to her father's office in the tower at the far end, and the staircase down to the hall. 'There's no one here. Are you joking, Phebes? You're trying to spook me out, aren't you?'

'Honest, I'm not!'

'Whose idea is it? Yours? Liv's? Lara's? Ruari's? Trying to freak me out for a prank?'

'No, I promise you, Jade!'

'Yeah, right.'

16

'Hey!' Ollie called out, immensely relieved to see the old man again. He was standing at the bottom of the drive between the entrance pillars, pipe clenched in his mouth, staring up at him, squinting against the intensely bright sunlight. Ollie ran the last few yards as if terrified the old man would walk off. 'I've been trying to find you, but it's not easy!'

'No, well, it wouldn't be,' he said. 'That's for sure.'

He looked exactly as he had last week, with his rheumy eyes, his pipe and his gnarled walking stick.

'I never got your name?' Ollie quizzed him.

'Oh, I like to keep meself to meself.' He nodded with an almost sage-like expression on his face.

Ollie proffered his hand. This time the old man took it and shook it, weakly, with bony, clammy fingers. 'I needed to come and find you again, Mr Harcourt, you see. There's things you need to know about your house.'

'That's why I was trying to find you. I wanted to ask you more about what you told me last week. Would you like to come up and have a cuppa, or a cold drink?'

The man looked afraid suddenly and shook his head vigorously, almost in a panic. 'Oh no, thank you, I don't drink nothing.'

'Nothing?'

'I'm not coming up to the house. Not going near that place, thank you very much.' He stared at Ollie levelly, his eyes filled with an almost immeasurable sadness. 'I don't know what to tell you, that's the truth. I don't know. Have you seen her yet?'

'The *lady*?'

'Have you seen her?'

Ollie suddenly had the idea of taking a photograph of the man. If he showed a photograph, then someone would identify him.

He didn't think the old man would give permission if he asked him straight out, so while they talked he sneaked a glance at his iPhone, which he was holding in his right hand, and swiped the camera symbol up with his thumb. Just as the old man appeared, blurrily, within the camera viewing screen, the phone rang. It was Caro.

Ollie couldn't believe his luck!

Seizing the chance, he raised the phone and pressed the red button to kill the call, but pretended to answer it. 'Hi, darling!' he said. 'I'm just chatting to a lovely gentleman in the lane. Call you back!' While he was speaking, the camera viewfinder returned, and still holding the phone up, he took a clear photograph of the man, before pocketing the phone. Then he said to the old man, 'Apologies, my beloved.'

'So,' the old man said again, more insistently. 'Have you seen her? Have you?'

'I think both my in-laws may have done.'

Suddenly, gripping his stick with a clenched fist, he looked around, wildly, with fear in his eyes. 'I have to be on my way now, I have to be off.'

'Wait, please, can't you tell me more about this – this thing you saw here? The lady? Is it something we need to be worried about, do you think? There was a big piece on ghosts in the *Sunday Times* I've been reading. It talks about imprints in the atmosphere, energy they've left behind, that sort of thing, trapped in a space–time continuum. There's tons of stuff on the web, all kinds of theories. One is they're the spirits of people who don't realize their bodies are dead and haven't found their way to the next plane. *Earthbound souls*, I think is the expression. Or that they have unfinished business. They're spooky, but does anyone actually need to be afraid of them? I mean – can ghosts ever actually do anything?'

'What about that Hamlet's father?' the old man replied.

'That was a play, it was fiction, just a story,' Ollie said, surprised to have Shakespeare thrown at him by this man.

Abruptly, the old man turned away, just as he had done the previous time they'd met. 'I have to go now,' he said, and started walking off.

Ollie hurried after him and drew level. 'Please – please just tell me a bit more about her, this lady.'

'Ask someone to tell you about the digger.'

'You mentioned it last time – tell me what about the digger?'

'The mechanical digger.'

'What digger do you mean?'

'No one leaves your house. They all stay.'

'All stay? What do you mean?'

'Ask about the digger.'

'What about the digger?'

But the stranger quickened his pace, striking the ground with his stick, staring fixedly ahead in silence, his face livid with anger, as if he resented Ollie's presence.

Ollie stopped and watched him walk on, feeling confused by the encounter. He turned to go back up to the house, but instead of the long driveway, he was suddenly staring at the front of their old home, their Victorian terrace in Carlisle Road in Hove. He walked slowly towards the front door, feeling as if it were the natural thing to do. As he reached the porch, the door opened, and there was Caro, smiling happily.

'Darling,' she said. 'We have a visitor!'

It was the old man. He appeared in the doorway, looking very comfortable, as if he had come to stay and was settling in nicely, and raised his pipe in the air. 'Mr Harcourt, nice to see you, welcome home!'

Then a steady *peep . . . peep . . . peep . . . peep* intruded. His alarm clock.

He had been dreaming. A weird dream – or a nightmare.

Caro leaped out of bed instantly. 'Got to get in really early today,' she said. 'I've got a completion going on this morning and I have to go and see a client who's in the Martlets Hospice.'

As he heard the sound of Caro in the bathroom, Ollie sat up, remnants of the strange dream still going around his head, and silenced the alarm repeat. 6.30 a.m. God, it had seemed so real, so vivid.

He reached out for his phone to check Sky News, as was his ritual, and saw to his surprise the red low-battery warning. He was sure it had been fully charged last night. Then he realized that the camera app was running.

He wondered if he was still dreaming. Out of curiosity, he clicked on Photos. There was a new image in the bottom left of the screen.

And now for sure he knew he was dreaming.

He jumped out of bed and ran over to the bathroom, his heart pounding. Caro was stepping out of the shower, one towel wrapped round her body, another, like a turban, round her head.

'Take a look at this!' he said, urgently, and held up the screen. 'Tell me I'm not dreaming, please?'

She peered at it for a moment then said, in the acidly pleasant-but-dismissive tone she sometimes adopted when she was required to be polite about something she really did not care for, 'What a *sweet* little old man. Why did you photograph him?'

17

The heatwave was over and the morning sky was grey and laden with rain. A light drizzle was falling and the wipers, on intermittent, swept it away every thirty seconds or so. He glanced at his daughter, proudly and with deep affection. In her smart uniform, with her hair neatly pulled back into a ponytail, he could see that in a few years' time she would blossom into a beautiful young woman. And he wondered what kind of boyfriend trouble would then lie in store for him. Her relationship with Ruari amused him; it seemed a kind of innocent puppy-love. But this wasn't a world where innocence lasted long. He hoped he and Caro could get her childhood to last as long as possible. And she was, at least, a very sensible girl. They'd always talked openly with her, and encouraged her to be open back to them. He tried never to shirk from any question she lobbed at them.

'Do you believe in ghosts, Dad?' Jade said suddenly, shaking Ollie out of his troubled thoughts, as they waited in a long line of traffic at roadworks for a temporary traffic light to change. He looked at the car clock, anxious that she would be late.

'Why?'

She shrugged.

'Something on your mind?' He reached out and stroked her hair.

Almost instantly she shook her head, brushing his hand away. 'Daaaaddd!'

The light changed to green and the traffic began to move. Ollie put the Range Rover into 'drive' and they inched forward. 'Why did you ask about ghosts? Do you believe in them?'

She looked down at her phone for some moments, then stared ahead, through the windscreen, playing with the strap on her bag. 'Phoebe was pranking with me last night, she really freaked me out.'

'How come?'

'I was on FaceTime chatting to her, she was just being silly.'

'What was she doing?'

'She told me she could see Gran standing behind me, in my room.'

'Gran?'

'She wasn't here last night, was she?'

He thought for some moments before replying. Wondering, remembering the first Sunday night when Jade had asked if her grandmother had come up to her room. 'No, she wasn't.'

'She said she saw this creepy-looking old lady in blue.'

'I don't think your gran wears blue much, does she?'

Jade shook her head. Then she said, 'Have you ever seen a ghost?'

'No.'

'Would you be scared if you saw one?'

'I'm not sure how I'd feel,' he replied, openly.

'Can ghosts hurt people?'

'I think it's the living who hurt people, lovely. Not ghosts. If ghosts exist.'

'I think Phoebe was just being mean.'

'It sounds like it. She's coming on Saturday for a sleepover, right?'

Jade nodded.

'We could play a trick on her, if you like? Scare her? I could put a sheet over my head and appear out of a cupboard – what do you think?'

A huge smile appeared on her face. 'Yes! Will you, Dad? Will you? Then I could put it in our video!'

'Great! Are you looking forward to your birthday party – it's not long now. Will you invite anyone from St Paul's?'

'There were so many annoying people yesterday. They all kept coming up to me wanting to be friends with me. Except one gang of four boys, I don't think they're very nice.'

'There's nothing wrong with people wanting to be friends with you, lovely. That's a nice thing, isn't it?'

'Just so embarrassing. I want *my* friends.'

'You still have your friends. But it would be nice to make some new ones at the school. Was there anyone you particularly liked?'

She thought for a moment. 'Well, there's a possible one called Niamh. I don't know yet.' She was silent again for some moments, then suddenly, looking worried, she asked, 'I know I'm going to have to wait till the Saturday for my party, but I will still get my presents on the Thursday, won't I?'

'Of course! From all the family, anyway. You might get some more from your friends on Saturday – so that'll be like having two birthdays.'

'Brilliant! Hey, maybe next year we could have a pool party for my birthday? That would be epic!'

He smiled. 'Maybe!'

Then his thoughts returned to his strange and disturbing dream last night.

Ask someone to tell you about the digger.

No one leaves your house. They all stay.

Cholmondley rang Ollie as he drove back from the school to say he was happy with everything, and could he now get the website live as soon as possible. Ollie told him he would upload the site to his server and it would be live within the next hour.

Then his thoughts returned yet again to the weird dream, and the words of the old man, and the photograph that had appeared on his phone overnight. Then his daughter's question in the car a short while ago. Coincidence?

He wished it was as simple as dismissing it that way. But he couldn't. There was one burning question in his mind right now: was he going crazy?

People said that moving house was the most stressful thing a human being could do. Was the stress of this, the stress of his financial worries and the stress of trying to build his new business getting to him? Had he forgotten he'd taken a photograph of the strange old man when he'd met him last week? Or was it some weird thing that had happened through the Cloud? Ever since synching his iPhone, iPad and laptop to the Cloud there had been the occasional oddity. Was this just one of them?

It had to be.

There was one possible way, he realized, of finding out.

18

Arriving back home shortly after 9.00 a.m., Ollie was disappointed by the absence of any vans outside the house. Not one of the small army of workmen had turned up so far. Ollie hurried up to his office and spent the next hour getting the Cholmondley website up and running. He checked it carefully and by 11.00 a.m., after a few emails back and forth with his client, he had sorted a couple of minor glitches and Cholmondley was a happy bunny.

Then he phoned his computer engineer, Chris Webb, who knew everything there was to know about Apple Macs, and more, to discuss the photograph of the old man that had appeared on his iPhone overnight. While they were talking, he emailed it to Webb.

'Maybe you went sleepwalking?' Webb said.

'But this photo was taken in daylight!'

'It's odd,' he said after a while. 'I'm looking at your albums stored on the Cloud – everything's dated, except for this one photograph. There's no date and no geo tag. It's sort of appeared out of nowhere, mate!'

'Yep, it has.'

'You know what I think may have happened?' Webb said.

'What?'

'One possibility is you took a phone call while you were talking to this old boy, and you accidently took a photo?'

'Possible – but I'm sure I didn't take my phone out while I was talking to him,' Ollie said. *Except in my dream*, he thought.

'I find Photo does odd things sometimes. I've not heard of it happening – but I suppose it could.' Ollie heard a slurp – it sounded as though Webb was having a drink of something. Then he continued. 'Remember in the old days when you took actual film into a shop to get it developed?'

'That does seem a long while back!'

'Yeah. Well, in those days – it happened to me a couple of times – when I got my photos back sometimes there'd be a rogue one slipped in among them somehow – totally random – another couple's baby, or holiday snap.'

'And that might have happened here? Chris, the coincidence would be – insane! I saw this old boy last week, chatted to him, then I wake up this morning and there's his photograph on the phone. Come on, what are the chances of that happening – that somehow the Cloud has delivered someone else's photograph of him to me? How many gazillion to one?'

'Coincidences happen.'

'I know, but this. I just . . .' He fell silent.

After some moments Webb said, sounding bemused, 'I'm sorry, Ollie, it's the best explanation I can give you. Otherwise I'm stumped. I'll have a word with someone I know at Apple and see if I can find out how often something like this does happen.'

'I'd be very grateful, Chris.'

Ollie ended the call and stayed at his desk, staring down at the old man. He couldn't place the background, which was indistinct. He enlarged his face, as he had done several times earlier, to make absolutely sure he wasn't mistaken. But it wasn't just the face, it was his briar pipe, that gnarled walking stick, that strange quiff-like hairstyle, the rheumy eyes. Chris Webb was usually right, and what he had said, however far-fetched, was the only possible explanation.

He went downstairs, dressed in jeans and a sweatshirt, and pulled on the new wellington boots Caro had given him as an early birthday present last month. He had already told Caro his birthday was to be a quiet affair – just dinner with a few friends. The wild party would have to wait until their finances had recovered from buying and renovating this place. Just then, the builders arrived full of excuses – they'd been held up at a supplier waiting for some damp-proofing material they'd been promised. But, frustratingly, there was still no sign of the electrician or plumber.

He tugged on a baseball cap then set off in the drizzle down the drive, walking at a faster stride than normal, on a mission. He was deep in thought and ignored the comic-looking alpacas in the field to his right, trotting inquisitively over towards him.

He looked up at the sinister wyverns on the gate pillars, as he walked through into the lane, then stopped as the red post van roared up the hill, its right-turn indicator winking. It pulled up beside him and the driver greeted him.

'Mr Harcourt?' He held up several envelopes, held together with a rubber band. 'Want these or shall I pop them through the letter box?'

'If you wouldn't mind taking them up to the house?'

'Not at all! Moved in all right?'

'Just about! Tell me – what time do you collect the post from there?' Ollie pointed at the small red Royal Mail post-box, half-hidden by the hedgerow on the other side of the lane.

'One collection a day – around half past four weekday afternoons, about midday on Saturdays. If you need later your best bet would be the post office in Hassocks.'

Ollie thanked him, and the mail van roared off up the drive. Then he glanced up and down the lane, and was disappointed to see it was deserted. The wet weather had intensified the smells of the leaves and grasses and he breathed the air in, savouring it as he set off down the hill.

A few minutes later he pushed open the gate of Garden Cottage and walked up the path. The decrepit front door was, as before, ajar. He called out, 'Hello!'

Annie Porter appeared in grubby dungarees, her hands caked with clay. She seemed delighted to see him. 'Ollie! Do come in! You've come for some more of my elderflower cordial, have you? Pretty addictive stuff – some of the locals here call my cordial the crack cocaine of Cold Hill!'

Ollie laughed.

He was soon seated at the small pine table in her kitchen. Annie Porter rinsed her hands, brewed coffee, then opened a tin and arranged homemade shortbread on a plate while he waited patiently.

Finally, the coffee made, she sat down opposite him. 'It's good you're here, you've saved me a trip – I've actually got the bottled cordial I was going to bring up to you, and some ginger marmalade.'

'Thank you!'

'As I said, it's a delight to have new faces here in the village.' She waited for Ollie to pour some milk in his coffee then helped herself to some. 'So, you know, I've really been puzzling about this fellow you asked me about. I just can't think who it could be.'

Taking his cue, Ollie removed his phone from his pocket, clicked on the photograph of the old man to enlarge it, and then showed the image to her. 'This is him.'

She looked at it and frowned. 'This?'

'Yes.'

'This is the man you saw in the lane last week?'

'Yes. Do you recognize him now?'

She gave Ollie a very strange look, then she took the iPhone from him and peered closely at the photograph for several seconds. 'You saw him in the lane last week? This man?'

'Yes – er –' he thought for a moment – 'last Tuesday.'

She shook her head. 'Last Tuesday? You couldn't have done.'

'I had a conversation with him. I think I told you yesterday, he said he used to work at our house.'

She studied the picture again then asked, 'Where did you take this, Ollie?'

'Do you recognize him?' He ignored her question, deliberately.

'Yes,' she replied. 'Absolutely.'

'Who is he? What's his name?'

'I'm sorry,' she said. 'I'm really finding this very strange. You say you saw him last week?'

He nodded.

'You couldn't have done – he must have a double.'

'Why's that, Annie?' he asked, feeling a sudden cold void in the pit of his stomach. Was he still dreaming?

'Well, this is Harry Walters, I'm sure of it. But there's no way you could have seen him last week.' She gave him a very frosty stare. 'You know,' she said, 'you're really making me feel very uncomfortable.'

Ollie raised his arms. 'I'm sorry. I—'

'What exactly is your angle here?' Her voice had become cold.

'Angle?'

'Game? Are you playing a game?' She stared again at the image. Ollie sipped his coffee. It was good but, perturbed by her sudden change of demeanour, he barely noticed the taste.

'I don't quite get what you're trying to do,' she said, eventually.

'All I'm trying to do is to find out who this chap is, so I can find him and talk to him again.'

She gave him a bemused look, across the table. 'You don't strike me as a loony, Ollie.'

He grinned. 'Well, that's good to know.'

'But you want me to believe you had a chat with Harry Walters last week and took his photograph?'

Ollie shrugged his shoulders. 'Yup – well—'

'And you want me to tell you where to find him?'

'Please, I really do need to speak to him.'

She looked straight at him. Her eyes were a clear grey-blue. Very beautiful and honest eyes. 'This conversation you had with Harry Walters – last week?'

He nodded.

'He told you he used to work at Cold Hill House?'

'Yes.'

'What did he say?'

'He told me that he'd been asked to house-sit for the owners – Sir Henry and Lady Rothberg. I googled them but couldn't find much. He was a banker, and they both died in 1980.'

'Yes, that was only a few months after we came here.' She studied the photograph intently. 'This is just uncanny,' she said without lifting her eyes. 'You haven't told me where you took this.'

He hesitated, not wanting to tell a lie that could compound itself. 'Well . . .'

'This is definitely Harry. But he's dead.'

'Dead?'

'He died – oh – quite a few years ago. I remember the date roughly because a property company bought your house and there was a lot of gossip in the village about what they were going to do with it. Some silly old fool put a rumour around that they were going to tear it down and build a tower-block of flats. Anyhow, they were doing a lot of work on renovating the place, and Harry went back to work as a gardener there – his wife had died and he was happy to have something to do. He was a jolly good gardener – helped us a bit when we first moved in. I learned quite a bit about growing vegetables from him.' Her expression became wistful. 'Poor old Harry.'

The cat wandered in and meowed.

'What do you want, Horatio?' she asked.

The cat meowed again and wandered disdainfully back out.

'He actually died on your property,' she said. 'There've been a few tragedies there over the years, unfortunately.'

His unease deepened. 'What happened to Harry Walters?'

'Well, what I heard was that he was working around the edge of the lake, using one of those backhoes to pull reeds out. There'd been heavy rain in the previous weeks, and the bank just gave way under the weight of the machine. It toppled sideways, then rolled on to him and pinned him down just below the surface. He drowned in only about a foot of water.'

'Backhoe? A digger?'

'Yes, that's right, a mechanical digger.'

19

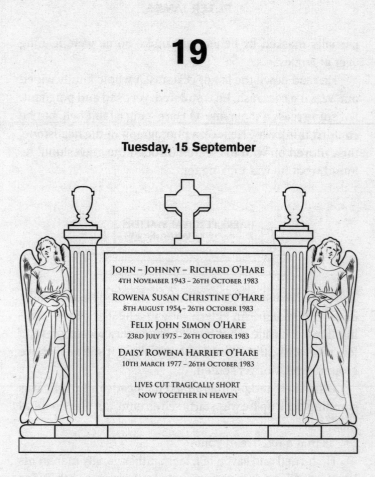

JOHN – JOHNNY – RICHARD O'HARE
4TH NOVEMBER 1943 – 26TH OCTOBER 1983

ROWENA SUSAN CHRISTINE O'HARE
8TH AUGUST 1954 – 26TH OCTOBER 1983

FELIX JOHN SIMON O'HARE
23RD JULY 1975 – 26TH OCTOBER 1983

DAISY ROWENA HARRIET O'HARE
10TH MARCH 1977 – 26TH OCTOBER 1983

LIVES CUT TRAGICALLY SHORT
NOW TOGETHER IN HEAVEN

Ollie stood in the steeply banked graveyard at the rear of the Norman church. Beyond the far wall, sheep grazed on the hillside. He stopped at this large marble headstone, with carved angels on either side. It had the air of a family mausoleum, and was much grander than the rest of the headstones here, many of which were so weather-beaten their engravings had almost faded completely, or were partially masked by lichen and moss. Some were leaning over at angles.

He read down the list of O'Hares. A whole family wiped out. Was it a car crash, he wondered. Very sad and poignant. For some reason the name 'O'Hare' rang a faint bell, but he couldn't think why. He took a photograph of the headstone, then moved on with his search through the graves until he found what he was looking for.

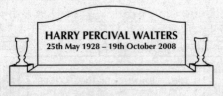

The plain headstone looked much more modern than most of the others here. An elderly lady in a headscarf was placing flowers beside what looked like a very recent grave, a few rows away, the mound of earth along it still well above ground level, not yet settled.

Ollie knelt and photographed the headstone. As he was standing back up he was startled by a cultured voice behind him.

'Is that a relative of yours?'

He turned and saw a tall, lean, rather gangly man in his late forties, wearing a crew-neck Aran jumper with a dog collar just visible, blue jeans and black boots. He had thinning fair hair and a handsome face with an insouciant, rather world-weary expression that reminded Ollie of a younger version of the actor Alan Rickman.

'No, just someone I'm rather interested in!' He held out his hand. 'Oliver Harcourt – we've just moved into the village.'

'Yes, indeed, Cold Hill House? I'm Roland Fortinbrass, the vicar here.' He shook Ollie's hand firmly.

'A very Shakespearean name,' Ollie replied, thinking of the odd coincidence of Harry Walters mentioning Shakespeare in his dream.

'Ah yes, a very minor character, I'm afraid. And he only had one "s" – I have two. Still, it has its advantages.' He smiled. 'People tend to remember my name! So, are you all settling in? I was planning to pay you a visit soon to introduce myself, and see if I can encourage you into joining a few of our activities.'

The drizzle was coming down more heavily now, but the vicar did not seem bothered by it.

'Actually, my wife, Caro, and I were saying that we should try to get involved in village life a bit.'

'Excellent! You have a little girl, I believe?'

'Jade. She's just turning thirteen.'

'Perhaps she'd like to join in some of our youth activities? Does she sing?'

Privately, Ollie thought Jade would rather take poison than join in any local church activities. 'Well . . . I'll have a word with her.'

'We could do with a few more in our choir. What about you and your wife?'

'I'm afraid neither of us would be much of an asset.'

'Pity. But if you're keen to join activities, we've plenty on offer. When would be a good time for me to pop up?'

'Caro's at work all week – she's a solicitor. Perhaps Saturday sometime?' He looked back at the grave for a moment. 'Actually, there is something I'd—' He stopped.

'Yes?'

'No, it's OK.' He looked back at the tombstone. 'Did you know this man – Harry Walters?'

'Before my time, I'm afraid. My predecessor would have – Bob Manthorpe. He's retired now, but I have his contact details. May I ask what your interest is?' The vicar shot a glance at his watch. 'Look, tell you what, I'm free for half an hour or so – I've got a couple coming to talk about their wedding plans at one o'clock. Fancy coming out of the rain and having a cuppa?'

'Well – OK – if it's no trouble?'

Roland Fortinbrass smiled. 'I'm here for the community. It would be a pleasure. My wife's out but she might be back in time to meet you.'

The vicarage was a small modern box of a house, spartanly furnished. Ollie sat on a sofa, cradling a mug of scalding coffee, while the vicar sat, legs crossed, in an armchair opposite him. Copies of the parish magazine lay on a simple wooden table between them, next to a plate of gingerbread biscuits. A crucifix hung as the central decoration on one wall and, rather incongruously, a framed colour photograph of a 1930s British Racing Green Bentley three-and-a-half on another. A row of birthday cards was on the mantelpiece, above an empty grate.

Fortinbrass noticed Ollie looking at the car. 'My grandfather's,' he said. 'He was a bit of a motor-racing man. Shame we no longer have it.'

'I have a client who has one up for sale at £160,000,' Ollie said. 'With a decent racing pedigree it could be double that.'

'He raced it at Le Mans, but didn't finish! What line of business are you in – something to do with the web, I believe?'

Ollie grinned. 'Caro and I have always been townies.

When we made the decision to move, someone told me that in a village everyone knows everything about you within minutes!'

'Oh, we're townies, too! My first church was in Brixton. Then Croydon. This is my first foray into the countryside. And I must say, I love it – but you are right, it can be very parochial. I fear I've upset some of the older folk here already by introducing guitar music into some of my services. But we have to do something. When I took over in 2010 we had just seven people coming to Communion, and twenty-three at Matins. I'm happy to say we've increased that now. Anyhow, tell me a bit more about your interest in that grave? Harry Walters?'

'How much do you know about our house, Vicar?'

'Please call me Roland. I always think *vicar* sounds dreadfully old-fashioned and rather stuffy!'

'OK, and I'm Ollie.'

'It's very good to meet you, Ollie.'

'Likewise.'

'So, Cold Hill House. I don't know a great deal, really. I gather it's been in need of some TLC for rather a long time. A big restoration project that needs someone with passion – and quite deep pockets.'

'I was talking to a local, Annie Porter?'

'Good, you've met her. Now she is a really delightful lady! And quite a character. Her late husband was a hero in the Falklands War.'

'So I understand. I really like her.'

'She's most charming!'

'She said there had been a number of tragedies at the house – I think I'm going back a few years here. That's part of my reason for my interest in Harry Walters. He was killed in an accident at the house – or rather, in the grounds.'

'Oh?'

'He drowned in the lake – a mechanical digger he was driving toppled over.'

The vicar looked genuinely shocked. 'That's simply *dreadful.* I hope it hasn't put you off in any way?'

Ollie thought for some moments. This was an opportunity to quiz the vicar on his views on ghosts, and yet he didn't want to come across as a flake on their first meeting. 'Absolutely not. The past is . . .' He fell silent.

'Another country?' Fortinbrass prompted.

Ollie sipped some coffee and smiled. 'That's what I'm hoping.'

20

Tuesday, 15 September

'So did you find that fellow you were looking for?' Lester Beeson asked, placing a Diet Coke on the counter. 'You wanted ice and lemon you said?'

The landlord was distracted today, as there were a dozen elderly, noisy ramblers in the bar, all in soaking wet cagoules, brightly coloured anoraks and muddy boots, a couple of them poring over a soggy map at a table.

'Yes, thanks, ice and lemon is fine. Yes, I've found him.'

'Good.'

'Where are the toilets, please?' a woman called to the landlord.

Beeson jerked a finger over to the far wall.

Ollie ordered a prawn salad, carried his drink over to an alcove, as far away from the ramblers as he could get, and sat down. Then he pulled his phone out of his pocket, opened his photos and looked at the two he had taken an hour earlier in the graveyard, of Harry Percival Walters's headstone. Born May 1928, died October 2008. That made him eighty when he died, he calculated. Then he swiped across to have another look at the photograph of Harry Walters himself.

It was no longer there.

Puzzled, he checked through his albums. All the most recent photographs he had taken, over the weekend and yesterday, chronicling every step of the restoration work on the house, were still there. Even though he backed up all his photographs to his laptop and iPad and to the Cloud, he usually kept them on his phone too, for quick reference.

It definitely wasn't there.

While he waited for his food to come, he phoned his computer man. From the crackling noise on the phone, it sounded as if Chris Webb was either driving or in a poor reception area.

'I'm just on my way home from a client,' Webb said. 'Can I call you back when I get home?'

'No probs.'

Half an hour later, Ollie strode up the drive towards the house, his head bowed against the rain which was now pelting down. He was pleased to see a row of workmen's vans outside the house, and that a skip had been delivered.

He hurried inside, where there was a hive of activity in several of the downstairs rooms and the cellar. As he climbed back up into the kitchen, his phone pinged with a text. It was from Cholmondley, requesting an addition to the website. While he stood reading it, the plumber, Michael Maguire, wriggled out backwards from under the sink and looked round at him. 'Ah, Lord Harcourt! How are you, sir?'

'I'm OK – how's it going?' Ollie raised his phone and took a photograph of the pipework beneath the sink, to add to his photo record of the restoration work.

'I don't know who did this work before, but they were real bodgers!' the Irishman said.

Before he could reply, Ollie's phone rang. It was Chris Webb.

'I'm back now, how can I help?'

Ollie waved for the plumber to carry on, and as he spoke to the computer man he walked back out of the kitchen and headed upstairs, needing to change out of his wet clothes, looking around warily. 'It's OK, Chris, it's just that the photograph I emailed you earlier has gone from my iPhone and I needed you to send it to me. But it's OK, I'm home now, it'll be on my computer. Thanks.'

'No problem!'

Ollie changed in their bedroom, taking a pair of jeans out of the huge Victorian mahogany wardrobe they'd brought from Carlisle Road, a fresh T-shirt and a light sweater, then climbed up the tower to his office, thinking again about the newspaper article about ghosts. Energy seemed a key factor. One of the theories it posited was that energy from dead people could still remain in the place where they had died. Could the energy of some elderly lady who had died here still be around? Was that what his mother-in-law had seen on the day they were moving in? Did that explain the spheres of light he had seen in the atrium?

Why had Jade asked him about ghosts this morning? Had it really been a bad dream that had spooked her on Sunday night – or something more?

What the hell was in this house? Something, for sure. He needed to find out – and find an explanation – before Caro saw something, too, and really freaked out.

Buying this place had been a stretch beyond what they could really afford. They were hocked up to the eyeballs. Moving out and selling right now was not an option. Whatever was going on, he needed to get to the bottom of it and sort it. There were always solutions to every problem. That had always been his philosophy. It was going to be fine.

He sat down at his desk and realized his hands were shaking. They were shaking so much it took him three goes to tap in the correct code to wake up his computer.

He went straight to Photos and checked through it carefully.

All the photos he had taken of the work in the house were there, and the photographs of Harry Walters's headstone, as well as the one he'd just taken of the pipework. But there was no photograph of Harry Walters.

He turned to his iPad, and opened Photos again. It was the same. Everything else he had taken was there. But no photograph of the old man.

Was he going mad?

But Caro had remarked on the photo this morning, and Chris Webb had received it and talked about it. He dialled his number.

'Chris,' he said, when he answered. 'I'm sorry, I do need you to send that photograph. I can't find it.'

'I've got a bit of a problem with that,' Webb replied. 'Must be a bloody iCloud issue, like I said. I'm sorry, mate, it's vanished.'

21

Wednesday, 16 September

Sometimes Caro nudged him gently, or touched his face, to let him know he was snoring. But tonight Ollie was wide awake, unable to sleep. He had watched the dial of his clock radio go from midnight to 00.30 a.m., 00.50 a.m., 1.24 a.m., 2.05 a.m. Now it was her who was snoring, as she lay face down, her arms wrapped round her pillow.

He was thinking about the photograph of Harry Walters. And the name O'Hare that he had seen in the graveyard. Why did that name seem familiar? He heard the hoot of an owl somewhere out in the darkness. Then the terrible squeal of something dying. A rabbit caught by a fox? The food chain. Nature.

Then another sound.

Running water.

He frowned. Where was it coming from? Had he left a tap running in the bathroom?

He slipped out of bed, naked, as quietly as he could, not wanting to wake Caro, and crossed the bare floorboards to the en-suite bathroom, the sound of running water getting louder. He slipped in past the door which was ajar, pulled it shut behind him and switched on the light. And then saw the water gushing from both the hot and cold taps into both of the twin basins.

He strode over to them and turned the taps off. Still the

sound of running water continued, loudly. He turned and looked at the bathtub. Both taps there were gushing out water. He turned them off too. Still he heard the sound, and realized the shower was running as well.

He turned that off. Then stood still. There was no way – no way at all they could have left all these on.

'Dad! Mum!'

It was Jade crying out.

He grabbed his dressing gown off the bathroom door, hurried back in the darkness across the bedroom and heard Caro stir.

'Wasser?' she murmured.

'S'OK, darling.'

He slipped out into the corridor, closed the bedroom door, fumbled for the landing light and switched it on.

'Dad! Mum!'

He ran down the landing and into Jade's room. Her bedside light was on and she was standing, in her T-shirt and shorts, in the doorway of her en-suite bathroom. He could hear the sound of gushing water.

She turned to him with terror in her eyes. 'Dad, look!'

He pushed past her and stopped. Water was brimming over the top of the huge bathtub and the floor was awash. Both taps were spewing water.

He went over to them, sloshing through the puddles on the floor, and turned them off. But he could still hear water.

It was coming from the shower.

He yanked open the door and turned the tap off.

'I turned them off, Dad, I did, before I went to bed! I had a bath and then brushed my teeth.'

He stroked her head. 'I know you did, my lovely.' He grabbed the towels off the rail and dumped them on the floor to mop up the water. 'I'll get you some fresh ones.'

'I did turn them off.'

Down on his knees, trying to mop it up before it went through the ceiling below, he nodded. 'The plumber was here earlier. He must have left a valve open or something.'

His words were enough to calm Jade. But not himself.

And he could still, faintly, hear running water.

His heart pounding, he kissed his daughter goodnight, switched off her light, then rushed downstairs and into the kitchen. Both taps there were going full blast. He turned them off and went through into the scullery where the taps on the butler's sink were gushing water. He turned those off. And could now hear running water outside.

His brain was a maelstrom of confusion. He turned the ancient key in the huge lock on the door to the rear garden, pushed it open and stepped outside into the cool, damp air. The sky was clear and cloudless. A quarter moon was shining above the top of Cold Hill, and the sky was like a black velvet cloth sprinkled with sparkling gemstones.

Something felt totally surreal.

He heard running water even louder now.

He grabbed the torch on the edge of the draining board, switched it on and shone the powerful beam out into the garden. Something in the distance – too far away to tell whether a fox or a badger, perhaps – hurried away. Then he saw the source of the water. It was an outside tap, pelting out water.

He turned it off and yet, as he went back into the house, he could again hear running water.

He locked the door, hurried through the kitchen and atrium and into the downstairs toilet, where both taps were gushing.

I'll kill that sodding plumber! he thought, turning them off. But he could still hear water coming from somewhere.

He ran back upstairs and into one of the spare rooms, which had a washbasin. Again, the taps were running full blast. He turned them off then went into the yellow room, and through into the bathroom. Again, the taps were spewing water.

As he screwed them tight shut he was trying to think rationally through his tiredness. The idiot plumber must have turned on every tap in the house to test the water system, then left without turning them off.

It was the only explanation he could come up with.

He went around the entire house again, to check that every tap was tightly off. Then, before returning to bed, he remembered there was one more bathroom, up in the attic, next to a tiny spare room with an old, very ornate wrought-iron bedstead in it, which was in much better condition than the rest of the house. It looked as if the property development company, which had started renovating the house before going bust, had begun at the top. There was a modern bathroom up here, an electric shower and a marine electric flush toilet.

The sink was bone dry, as was the shower tray, which relieved him. Because of the height of these attic rooms, they were on a different water system to the rest of the house, he seemed to remember being told.

He went back downstairs and crept into bed. This time, Caro did not even stir; she seemed to have slept through the whole thing. He switched off the torch and laid it gently on the floor beside him.

As he did so he heard the sound of running water again. Then it stopped.

22

Wednesday, 16 September

Plock.

A droplet of water landed on Ollie's forehead. He woke up with a start and looked at the clock.

3.03 a.m.

Plock.

Another droplet struck him in the same place.

He raised his hand and touched his forehead. It was wet.

Plock.

'Shit!' he said. 'Fuck!' As another droplet struck his cheek, he reached down beside the bed, fumbling for the torch.

'What is it?' Caro murmured.

'I think we've got a leak.'

He grabbed the torch, but before he could switch it on, there was a crack as loud as a gunshot above them, then a deluge of cold water, plaster and choking dust descended on them.

'Jesus!' Ollie shouted, leaping out of bed. 'Shit, shit, shit!' He switched on the torch.

'What the hell's—?' Caro sat up, sharply. In the beam of his torch, covered in white dust, she looked like a ghost.

'What the – what the—?' Caro said, scrambling out of bed.

Ollie swung the beam upwards. A large chunk of the centre of the ceiling had caved in, leaving a hole several feet in diameter, through which water was cascading.

He grabbed his phone from the bedside table, found the plumber's number and dialled it. After several rings, when he thought it was going to go to voicemail, he suddenly heard a click, followed by a surprisingly breezy Irish voice.

'Squire Harcourt, good morning, sir! Is everything all right?'

23

By midday, it seemed almost every room in the house had workmen in it, plumbers, builders and electricians. The water had seeped through their bedroom floor, which was directly above the kitchen, and shorted out the lights there and in the atrium. Caro had had to go into work for a meeting she couldn't cancel, but said she would try to come home as soon as she could, to help out.

Meanwhile Ollie had done his best in the bedroom, with a mop and bucket, then helped the workmen cover everything there with dust sheets. Bryan Barker explained it would be difficult to repair one individual section of the very old ceiling, which was lath and plaster – a lime mortar mixed with horsehair – without risking more damage. It would be better and faster to take the lot down and then plasterboard it. Ollie made the decision and told him to go ahead. With luck the work could be completed by the end of the week, but until then the bedroom would not be habitable.

The only spare room that was in a fit state to sleep in was the tiny room up in the attic, with the wrought-iron bedstead; he and Caro could camp there, he decided. His tiredness was starting to make him feel irritable. The house was a cacophony of radios blaring out pop music, hammering, the whine of power tools and the rasp of sawing. He needed, badly, to lock himself away in his office and focus on work for a few hours. Cholmondley had already left two messages for him this morning, sounding increasingly impatient, wanting to know when the latest amendment he had texted him about yesterday would be up on the website, and Anup Bhattacharya of The Chattri House had sent him an idea for his website that he wanted, urgently, to discuss today.

Bleary-eyed from lack of sleep, he was desperate for more coffee, but the two strong ones he'd made himself earlier this morning had drained the small water reservoir of the Nespresso machine, and at present the water supply to the house had been isolated and capped off by the plumber. There was some mineral water in the fridge, he remembered, going downstairs and entering the kitchen. An extravagance, he thought wryly, removing the bottle of Evian and filling enough for a large espresso. As he did so a shadow fell across him.

He spun round.

'Sorry, didn't mean to startle you, squire!' It was Michael Maguire, in his boiler suit, looking grimy and exhausted. He'd been here since 4 a.m.

Ollie smiled at him, a quotation he'd come across suddenly echoing in his mind. *To the man who is afraid, everything rustles.* That was how he was feeling right now. 'Want a coffee? I can make it from this,' he said, holding up the bottle.

'We're just rigging up a standpipe now – we'll have your mains water back on by late afternoon. Thanks, I'd appreciate one. So, do you want the good news or the bad news first?'

'I think coffee first,' Ollie said.

A few minutes later they sat down at the kitchen table,

and while Maguire was finishing a phone call to a supplier, ordering materials, Ollie took the opportunity to quickly check his emails on his own phone. When the plumber finished his call, he looked back at Ollie.

'There is *good* news?' Ollie quizzed. 'In all of this? Want to tell me?'

Maguire sat hunched over the table and eyed Ollie warily for a moment. 'Well, the good news is I can get hold of all the materials I'm going to need right away. I'll have some here this afternoon and the rest tomorrow morning.' Then he stared gloomily down at his coffee.

'And the bad?'

'I'll try and work out the cost, but it's going to be expensive. You might be able to get some of it back on insurance, but I don't know how much.'

'The bedroom ceiling, with luck,' Ollie said. 'And the wiring damage in here.' He shrugged. 'So tell me your findings – what caused all the taps to start running?'

'Well, I haven't got to the bottom of it yet, but you know from the survey what a poor condition the plumbing is in. Every single washer in every tap is ancient rubber and has perished. From all the droppings I can see in the loft spaces and wall cavities, you've an infestation of vermin – particularly mice. Those little buggers have eaten through the only modern pipework you have – the plastic ones put in by the developers before they went under. There are air-locks all over the system, causing a lot of hammering and juddering of pipes – and that leads to the degradation of washers, too, causing them to fail.'

Maguire paused to sip his coffee then went on. 'Your plumbing here is a complete mishmash of mainly lead, with some copper and really ancient barrel pipe. Copper piping can, when it gets too old, just pop apart; lead starts to get fine, pinhole perforations, and begins spraying water as if it's sweating. Barrel pipe's made from low carbon steel and the oxygen in the water makes it rust from the inside. The pipe corrodes to a point where water won't move through it any more, like a clogged artery. Then, of course, you get a build-up of pressure from the backed-up water in the system. Something starts making the pipes vibrate, you get the effect of expansion and contraction from the pipes not having seen any hot water through them in years. All that blocked water, with pressure building up, is going to have to go somewhere.'

He looked balefully at Ollie and shrugged. 'The action of the expansion and contraction tends to have one of two effects – either it causes a catastrophic failure of piping joints, or it loosens the blockages in the pipes and you get a surge of water. Get that surge and the taps, with their disintegrated washers, can't hold it back. The problem is compounded by the whole antiquated water system in this house being interlinked. You've got a galvanized service tank in the loft space between the attics, directly above your bedroom. When tanks like that age, they start getting blisters, and there's a danger if pressure builds up too much that the sides can just blow – collapse.'

'That's what happened, you think, Mike?' Ollie sipped his coffee; it tasted good. The aroma gave a momentary respite from the smell of damp that had been pervading the house during the past few hours.

'I can't tell you for certain, Ollie.' The plumber pursed his lips and shook his head from side to side. 'But if you add everything up – the ancient pipework, no lagging anywhere against the ravages of past winters, the vermin infestation, the complete absence of any plumbing maintenance, a service tank fifty years past its sell-by date – you've got all the ingredients for a perfect storm.' He shook his head. 'I think it's criminal anyone allowed such a beautiful house to get into this condition. I'll tell you one thing, you're lucky all the washers are corroded – if the taps had held, then several of the piping joints might have failed and you'd have had flooding in rooms all over the house.'

Ollie listened carefully, drank some more coffee, then thought for some moments. 'OK, what you're saying does make sense, but if all the tap washers were useless, how come I was able to turn the taps off and stop the water? The taps were all opened – surely they couldn't have opened by themselves?'

'Well, they could, Ollie, if there was enough vibration in the pipes. Like the nuts on the wheel of a car can work loose if there's enough vibration for long enough.'

Ollie's phone pinged with an incoming text. He saw it was from Cholmondley but didn't read it. He looked back at the plumber. 'Nearly every tap in the house – and the outside one as well?'

'As I said, Ollie, I can't tell you categorically that this is what happened. There is, of course, another possibility.'

'Which is?'

'Someone causing mischief. Some intruder, vandal?'

'Mike, I can't see anyone breaking into a house at three in the morning and then running around turning all the taps on. That doesn't make any sense.'

'I'm just speculating – couldn't have been your daughter and some of her friends having a bit of a laugh?'

'A bit of a laugh?'

He raised his hands. 'Kids today. Mine are constant mischief.'

'We're lucky with Jade, she's pretty sensible – she—' He stopped and frowned, as a thought occurred to him.

When Jade was younger she had sleepwalked regularly. Could it have been her who had done this? Could she have gone around the entire house, in her sleep, turning on taps? Why? And yet, he did remember one incident, some years back when she was about seven, when she'd gone out into the garden shed, lifted several items out and put them on the lawn. In the morning she'd had absolutely no recollection of doing it. And another occasion, around that same time, when she had gone into the kitchen and emptied everything out of the fridge and freezer and stacked it all neatly on the floor, again with no recollection in the morning.

'My daughter had a sleepwalking problem when she was younger. I wonder – I – I'm just – could she have done this?' Ollie said. 'Just—' He fell silent for some moments, then turned his palms upwards in despair. 'I'm just speculating.'

'That's all I'm doing, too,' Michael Maguire said. 'I'm just speculating.'

24

Ollie went back up to his office. The plumber's explanation for the running taps might account for some of them. But surely not for every damned tap in the entire bloody house? He just couldn't buy that. Although he wished he could.

He'd not yet told Caro about the running taps; until the ceiling had caved in she'd only stirred and not really been aware of the drama around the house. How many taps were there? He started to count in his head. The bathroom in the attic – two in the sink there and a mixer shower – three. But they hadn't been running. On the first floor there were the en-suite ones in their bedroom, Jade's and the yellow room, plus the family bathroom for the other four spare rooms – and the washbasin in the blue room. Downstairs there were two toilets with basins off the hall, and then the kitchen, the scullery and the outside tap.

He noted them down, trying hard to think with his tired brain if he'd missed any out. The sink in the disused kitchen in the cellar, he suddenly remembered, and noted that down also. The more he thought about it, the less convincing the plumber's explanation seemed. Not every tap on the main system, every single one. No way.

Jade?

The possibility that it was Jade doing it in her sleep did make uncomfortable sense.

He thought back again to some of those previous episodes, then he sat at his desk, logged on and googled *sleepwalking*. As he had imagined, there were hundreds and hundreds of sites. He went back and entered some key words to narrow the search parameters. Then he scanned through the shorter list of sites, selected and began to read. The third site he came to interested him the most. He bookmarked it and read through it several times, taking particular note of the list of possible symptoms.

Little or no memory of the event – that had been true. She always had no memory.

Difficulty arousing the sleepwalker during an episode – also true of Jade.

Screaming when sleepwalking occurs in conjunction with sleep terrors.

Jade had screamed last night. He'd run into her room, turned off the taps on the overflowing bathtub and pulled the plug out. She had terror in her eyes, and now, thinking about that more clearly, he could remember that look of frozen fear on her face from years back. It was the same way she used to look straight after waking from a sleepwalking episode when she was seven.

She'd been quiet in the car on the school run this morning, Instagramming all her friends with a dramatic picture of the hole in her parents' bedroom ceiling. He had no idea what she was saying but could see several rows of smiley, scowly, frowny and other emoticons.

Then a thought struck him hard. They'd taken Jade to a child psychologist back then. The woman had put her night terrors and sleepwalking down to her fears at starting at her new school, and predicted they would stop when she settled in and started making friends. The psychologist had been right, that was exactly what happened.

Now Jade was in her early days at another school.

Was the pattern repeating itself?

It made sense.

A flash alert for an incoming email from Chris Webb caught his eye, distracting him, and he opened it.

No luck with that old boy with the pipe, I'm afraid. I went on a Photos forum to see what I could find there – it seems that what usually happens is that photographs get misfiled – but they don't disappear completely. Not like your chap has. Don't know what to suggest. You sure he wasn't a ghost? ☺

25

'Dad, can I invite Charlie as well as Niamh to my birthday party? We will still have it, won't we?'

Pulling the Range Rover away from traffic lights, after he had collected her from school, Ollie reached out and squeezed Jade's arm, lightly. 'Of course we'll still have the party, my lovely.' Then he shot her a glance. 'Charlie – who's that?'

'My friend,' she said, very matter-of-factly. 'She's nice.'

'A new friend?'

She nodded and looked down at her phone, her fingers moving rapidly on the keys.

He was pleased that she looked a lot happier this afternoon. In fact it was the first time in the ten days since she had started at St Paul's that she seemed like her old self. 'Is she at school with you?'

'Yes.'

'OK, that's great. Of course she can come to your party. You can invite anyone else you like from the school, too.'

'There might be two other girls,' she said, then looked solemn. 'But I'm not sure if I really like them, yet.'

'Well, you've got time, over a week still.'

She was focused again on her phone and barely nodded acknowledgement. Then after a few moments she said, 'Charlie's mum works for a vet.'

'OK.'

'Her mum knows a labradoodle breeder – and can you believe it, Dad? They're expecting a litter next week. Can we go and see them, can we? A puppy could be my birthday present, couldn't it?'

'I thought you wanted a new iPad?'

'Well, I do, but I'd rather have a puppy, and you said we could have one.'

'How do you think Bombay and Sapphire would get on with a puppy?'

'I've been reading about it, Dad. I know exactly what to do.'

Ollie smiled. He believed her. When she was eight, Jade had had two gerbils and she had doted on them, keeping their cage immaculate. She had even trained them to go through a mini gymnastics course she had set up on her bedroom floor, and she and her closest friend, Phoebe, had invented gymnastic awards which they'd presented so seriously to them.

Jade had also trained them, much to his and Caro's amusement, to come downstairs on their own. She explained, in the very serious manner she sometimes adopted, that this was in case the house ever caught fire when everyone was out, so they would be able to escape. Neither he nor Caro had wanted to disillusion her by pointing out the one flaw she hadn't spotted, which was that the gerbils would still have been trapped in their cage.

'OK,' he said. 'Your mother and I will need to work out some time when we can go to see them – isn't there another breeder having a litter also?'

'Yes, but that's not for *ages*.'

'I thought you said it would be in about a month?'

'I did, Dad. That's what I mean, *ages*.'

*

Ollie was kept hanging on by Cholmondley. He half wondered if it was deliberate, and the pompous little man was paying him back for not returning his calls this morning.

After several minutes he laid the receiver on the desk, leaving it on loudspeaker, and began to check his emails. The first was from his regular tennis opponent, Bruce Kaplan, an American-born computing science professor at Brighton University. They'd met and become friends whilst studying IT at Reading University. Kaplan had subsequently taken an academic path whilst Ollie had gone down a commercial one. They were closely matched at tennis, and he enjoyed Kaplan's company – he had a massive intellect and frequently an unusual take on the world.

> So did you unpack your tennis racquet yet? Back to usual this week? Friday at Falmer?

He'd had a weekly game with Kaplan at the Falmer Sports Centre, on the University of Sussex campus, for the past ten years or so.

> Prepare for a thrashing.

Ollie typed back.

> In your dreams!

came the reply. It was followed immediately by another email from him.

> Btw, check out a guy called Dr Nick Vaughan in Queensland, Oz, doing interesting research work in macular degeneration. Might be interesting for your mother. B.

Ollie replied, thanking him. His mother had recently been diagnosed with early-stage macular degeneration, but whether she – or his father – would take any notice of anything he sent them, he doubted. They were far too conservative in their views. Their doctor was always right, so far as they were concerned; they weren't interested in anyone else's opinion.

They weren't interested in the new house, either, and that made him sad. He would love them to come down and see the house, and see how well he had done in life, but he doubted they ever would. Before moving in he'd suggested his parents should come for a visit. 'Too long a journey,' his father had replied, bluntly. 'And your mother can't really travel now, not with her eyesight.'

She had never travelled when her eyesight had been perfect, either. Neither of them had, although they could have afforded to. His father had earned a decent living as the works manager of an engineering plant and his mother had been a primary school teacher. Instead, every summer throughout his childhood, for their annual family holiday, Ollie, his brother, Bill, and his sister, Janis, had been driven by their parents thirty miles to Scarborough on the Yorkshire coast, where they'd stayed in a self-catering cottage. It was a lot cheaper than many places in the town, his father boasted every year without fail, because, he would say proudly, 'It doesn't have a sea view. Who the hell needs that when you've got legs to walk to the bloody sea, eh?'

Their parents might not have travelled but their children had. Janis was in Christchurch, New Zealand, married with four children, and Bill was in Los Angeles, living with his boyfriend, and working as a set designer. It had been a couple of years since he had seen either of his siblings, there was quite an age difference between each of them; none of them had been close. That cold and distant relationship he'd always had with his parents was a big part of the reason he tried to keep a closeness with Jade.

Despite his misgivings, he typed out an email to them both with a link to Dr Nick Vaughan's website, and sent it. They wouldn't take any notice, but it was duty done.

Then the penny dropped.

O'Hare.

'Hello? Hello? HELLO?' A disembodied voice snapped him out of his thoughts. Then he realized with a start it was coming from the phone receiver.

He snatched it up. 'Charles?'

'Listen, Mr Harcourt, I'm not very happy about being buggered around all day.'

'I apologize, our bedroom was flooded out in the middle of the night and we've been in chaos.'

'With all due respect, that's not my problem. You could have had one of your staff call me.'

Yes, Ollie nearly said, *who would you have preferred to talk to – Bombay or Sapphire?* Instead he replied, as politely as he could, 'You're such a very important client, Mr Cholmondley, I wouldn't dream of fobbing you off with a junior member of my team.'

A few minutes later, with Cholmondley back in his box, Ollie hung up, then went over to a stack of packing cases he had not yet opened, containing box files of documents. He checked the labels, found the one he wanted and ripped the sealing tape with a paper knife. After a couple of minutes rummaging through it, he lifted out the file he was looking for and carried it back over to his desk.

Through the window, he saw Caro's Golf coming down the drive. Normally he would have run downstairs to greet her, but he was anxious to look at this document, to check. Hopefully he was wrong, mistaken.

Hopefully.

The box was marked, in Caro's handwriting, *COLD HILL HOUSE HISTORIC DOCS.*

He opened it and a musty smell rose up. A few documents down he found the deeds, with old-fashioned script on the front, a red wax seal in the bottom right corner, and green string holding the pages together. He flicked through quickly and saw that Cold Hill House had passed through the hands of several companies until Bardlington Property Developments had purchased it in 2006. There were several accompanying documents in a folder with various architectural drawings on plans they had submitted for the redevelopment of the property; one was for demolishing the house and building a country house hotel; another was for keeping the existing house but building a further ten houses in the grounds; a third was for turning it into sheltered housing accommodation.

He turned back several pages then stopped and stared down in dismay.

Stared at the names.

John Richard O'Hare.

Rowena Susan Christine O'Hare.

On this document they were joint signatories on the purchase of Cold Hill House on 25 October 1983.

He picked up his phone, opened Photos and flicked across to the ones he had taken in the graveyard. He found the one of the headstone of the O'Hare family, and expanded it with his finger and thumb to read the dates that all four of them had died.

26 October 1983.

One day after they had bought the house.

As he went downstairs to greet Caro, he felt a deeply uncomfortable sensation.

26

Ten minutes later, Ollie helped Caro, still in her office clothes, to lug sheets, duvets, pillows and towels up the two flights of stairs to the tiny spare room in the attic. They were going to sleep here for the next couple of nights until their bedroom was habitable again.

'Well, it's going to be cosy, my love!' Caro said as they went in.

'That's for sure!'

Right under the eaves, the room had a sloping roof and a small window looking out on to the rear garden. The ancient wrought-iron double bed took up almost all of the space. It fitted snugly against the right-hand wall, leaving just enough room to open the door and enter. There was a gap of about three feet between the left of the bed and the built-in cupboards that ran the full length of the left wall.

'It reminds me of the bed in that little French hotel we stayed in once on our way down to the south – remember?' she said, staring dubiously at the horribly stained old mattress, before dumping her armful of bedding on it.

'Near Limoges, wasn't it? Which creaked liked crazy when we made love in it!'

She laughed. 'God, yes, and it rocked so much – we thought it was going to collapse!'

136

'And that tight little French woman who ran it and charged us extra for having a bath!' he said.

'And I went out into the corridor in the night to have a pee and walked into someone's bedroom!' She shook her head, grinning at the memory. 'God, this mattress needs airing. I'll bring a fan heater up here and leave it on for a couple of hours.' She wrinkled her nose. 'Let's turn it over and see if it's any better on the other side.'

Ollie dumped the bedding on the floor. Then they lifted the mattress; the ceiling was so low they bashed the bare light bulb, hanging from an ancient cord, in the process.

There was a large brown stain in the centre on the reverse side. 'Yech!' Caro said.

They turned it back again. 'It'll be fine when we've got a clean undersheet and bedding on it, darling,' Ollie said.

'I hope no one died in this.'

Nope, the last owners died before they even got a chance to sleep here, he nearly answered. But instead he said, 'It was probably some servant who was put up here.'

'The mystery is, how on earth did they ever get a bed this size in this room?' she said.

'I would imagine in bits and they assembled it up here. Unless they built the house around it!'

Later, with the clean bedclothes on it, and the pillows freshly plumped, it was looking more inviting. Ollie slipped his arms round Caro's waist. 'Want to try it out?'

'I need to get Jade her supper. What do you fancy tonight?'

He kissed her neck. 'You.'

She turned to face him. 'That was the right answer!'

As they went back downstairs, Caro said, 'It's such a beautiful evening, let's take a walk down to the lake and see the ducks. I was talking to one of the partners who lives out in the country and has ducks on his lake. He said the way to encourage them to stay is to feed them – at least once every day. He keeps an old metal milk churn at the edge with duck food pellets that float. He's given me the name of the stuff to get and a place you can order from online. He said if we throw them a few scoops of food every day we'll soon have a large colony in residence.'

'Milk churn?'

'It stops rats getting the food. You can find them on the internet, apparently.'

'Great, I'll have a look tomorrow.'

'I'll go and put some jeans on.'

Whilst she did so, Ollie unplugged his clock radio alarm, took it up to the attic room, and reset it.

Ten minutes later, holding hands and wearing wellies, Ollie and Caro walked up to the edge of the lake. A solitary coot paddled coyly away from them, its head nodding like a clockwork toy, towards the little island in the middle. A pair of mallards eyed them warily and also moved away, to the far side of the lake.

They walked around, behind tall reeds, then stopped and stared over the wooden rail and post fence at the overgrown paddock, and at the hill rising steeply beyond.

'This would be ideal for Jade's pony,' Caro said. 'But if we got one, we'd need to put up a stable.'

'She seems more into dogs at the moment – a labradoodle,' Ollie said. 'She's not mentioned a pony since we came here.'

'She asked me to book her a lesson for this Saturday. There's a good riding school, apparently, at Clayton – I'm going to see if they can fit her in. I hope she takes to it again

– she's not ridden in a while.' She shrugged. 'I was madly into ponies – until I started dating, then I lost all interest. Do you think that's what's happened with her?'

'I don't think her seeing Ruari is exactly dating,' Ollie said. 'Going for milkshakes in the afternoon is more a kind of play dating.'

'I hope so. I don't want her to lose her innocence too soon. She's a happy soul.'

'And boyfriends make you unhappy?' he said with a quizzical smile.

'God, I remember teenage angst over boys.'

Ollie nodded. 'Yep, same over girls.'

Above them a flock of migrating swallows were heading south, passing high over the roof of the house. Heading to the sun. How nice that would be right now, Ollie thought, envying them the simplicity of their lives.

Caro stared at the house. 'Strange just how different the front and rear look.'

He nodded. Compared to the handsome front, with its finely proportioned windows, the back of the house really was a mishmash. It seemed even more so than when he had last looked at it: partly red brick and partly grey rendering, with windows of different sizes seemingly placed here and there at random, and with an ugly single-storey garage block and assortment of dilapidated outbuildings, some brick, some breeze block and some wooden.

Caro pointed with her finger. 'I still haven't got the hang of the geography. Over to the left, those two windows are the scullery and that's the scullery door. Then the two kitchen windows and the door into the atrium, and the dining room windows to the right.'

'Yes.'

'Going left to right on the first floor is Jade's bedroom.

Then the two back spare bedrooms, then our room at the right?'

Ollie nodded.

Then she pointed up at the row of dormers. 'That one – that's where we're sleeping tonight, right?'

Ollie did a calculation. 'It is.'

'Then the three to the left?'

'They're the other side of the loft space. You get to them via the staircase next to Jade's room. I think they're all part of the old servants' quarters. I'll check.'

'Incredible to be living in a house where we can't even remember all the rooms!'

He grinned. 'Just think how beautiful this place is going to look in a few years' time when we've finished all the restoration!'

She smiled, then said a hesitant, 'Yes.'

'You sound dubious?'

She shrugged. 'No – it's just – it – it's all still so daunting. I hope we haven't taken on too much.'

'We haven't! In a couple of years we'll be laughing that we even worried about it.'

'I hope you're right, darling.'

'I'm right, trust me.'

She gave him a strange look and grimaced.

'What?'

'Nothing.'

'Tell me?'

'Nothing. You're right. And we don't have much option, do we?'

'We could move.'

'With our mortgage? The vendors had dropped the price three times because no one was mad enough to take it on. I don't think we'd find a buyer very easily at all. Not until we have improved it one hell of a lot. So we don't have an option. We're here and we've just got to get on with it.' Again she gave him a strange look and shrugged.

'Don't you love it, though, darling?'

'Ask me in five years' time,' she replied.

27

Caro prepared a simple supper for the three of them, of baked potato with tuna. She made her own version of a tuna salad filling with chopped spring onions and capers, which Ollie particularly loved – and always felt to be a healthy meal.

Ollie's rule – that Caro totally agreed with – was that they turned the television off for meals and talked. They both made a particular effort to instil that in Jade.

'So,' Ollie said, 'tell your mum and me a bit about your new friend, Charlie?'

'New friend, darling?' Caro said.

Jade nodded thoughtfully, as she mixed some tuna into her potato. 'I don't know if she'll be a best friend yet, but she's nice.'

'Did she just join the school, too?'

'Yes. Quite a lot of them have been there since they were eleven, so they can be a little bit cliquey.'

'Do you want to invite her to your party?'

'Well, I think so. There's another girl I might ask also, called Holly.'

Ollie and Caro caught each other's eye and smiled. This was a good sign that she was making new friends.

Afterwards, Jade went up to her room, and Ollie and Caro sat in front of the television, with a glass of white wine, watching an episode of *Breaking Bad* from the box set he had given her last Christmas – they were still less than half-way through the second season. Caro joked that they'd still be watching it well into their old age.

After the episode had finished, Caro stood up, yawning, then walked round the house on her obsessive tour of inspection, exactly as she had done when they lived in the city. She couldn't sleep until she had checked that every door and downstairs window was secure. Then she went round for a second time, double-checking. Ollie let her get on with it. He knew from past experience that otherwise she would wake in the middle of the night in a panic and go downstairs to start checking.

Tonight he joined her, wanting to make sure none of the workmen had left any dangerous electrics on that might cause a fire. There was no sign of improvement in any room so far – wherever the workmen were at the moment looked in a considerably worse state than when they had moved in. They were still at the ripping out and stripping down stage.

'I bloody love you!' Ollie said, as they reached the top of the stairs to the attic bedroom, sliding his hands round Caro's waist.

She turned towards him. 'And I bloody love you, too!'

They kissed. Then kissed again, charged with sudden deep passion. He pushed her T-shirt up her back, then slid his fingers down inside the rear of her jeans.

'Did I ever tell you that you have the most beautiful bum in the world?' he whispered.

'No, Mr Harcourt,' she said, busily unzipping him. 'No, Mr Harcourt, I don't believe you did.'

He worked his hands around her front, then slowly down inside her thighs. As he did so she unbuckled his belt, popped the stud fastener of his trousers and pulled them down, sharply. Then his boxer shorts. She knelt in front of him and cupped him in her cool hands.

He gasped, delicious sensations rippling through him. Then he helped her back to her feet, tugged at the zip of her jeans, pulled them down, too, then her lacy underwear. They staggered through the bedroom door, in a clumsy manoeuvre that was part embrace, part dance, tripping over their trousers, then he eased her backwards on to the bed.

Afterwards, lying on top of her in the dark of the room, lit only by the weak yellow glow from the bare bulb hanging over the staircase, he grinned. 'Hmmmn, I quite like this bed.'

'It's not shit, is it?' she grinned back.

Ten minutes later, their teeth brushed and clothes discarded, they fell asleep, comfortably and happily spooned. 'I love you, babes,' Ollie whispered.

She murmured back, contentedly.

He woke from a nightmare some while later, his entire body pounding, disorientated. Where the hell was he? Something dark, undefined, a terrible dark dread, engulfed him. Then he had the sensation that the bed was moving. Jigging, very slightly. An intense pressure was pinning him to the mattress. It was as if the air had suddenly become leadenly heavy and was pressing down on him, crushing him, smothering him.

He tossed his head wildly from left to right in panic, unable to breathe. Terror spiralled through him. He fought to breathe. Sucking through his mouth, his nostrils. It was as if he was breathing in cloying soot.

Then everything was fine. He could breathe normally again. Beside him he heard the steady rhythm of Caro breathing. His heart hammering, he rolled over and looked down at the clock radio he had placed on the floor last night.

00.00.

He stared at the flashing green digits. That happened when there was a power cut. Were they having one now – or had there been one earlier?

Then something moved.

There was someone in the room.

Jade?

A shadow moved beside him. Shit. Oh shit. Someone was standing over the bed, looking down.

He began to shiver. Was it an intruder? A burglar?

The shadow moved a fraction.

Caro, beside him, did not stir.

He clenched his fists, thinking, his heart hammering even more now, as if it was trying to break out of his chest.

Then a small boy's voice rang out, shrill and crystal clear and excited. 'Are we nearly there yet?'

The voice sounded like it was coming from the end of the bed.

Then a small girl's voice, equally shrill. 'Are there dead people in there, Mum?'

Ollie listened, paralysed by fear. He was dreaming, he had to be.

Then he heard a blood-curdling cry of shock and pain, then screams.

Moments later a man with stark raw terror in his voice howled, 'Oh Jesus!'

Suddenly, Ollie could smell cigar smoke. Not a faint whiff carried on the night breeze from a distant dwelling, but the thick pungent smell of someone smoking a cigar inside this house. Inside this room.

The figure still stood beside the bed, moving a fraction, just enough for Ollie to be certain it was a person and not the shadow of a piece of furniture.

Then he saw a small ring of glowing red, right above him.

It was this man by the bed who was smoking a cigar.

Who are you? Who are you? WHO ARE YOU? WHAT DO YOU WANT? Ollie tried to scream, but the words were trapped in his gullet.

An Arctic gust of fear ripped through him. Christ. Oh Christ.

Then the bed began to rock.

'Ols? Ols? *Ollie?*'

Caro's voice, gentle, anxious.

'Ols? Ols, darling? You're having a nightmare. You're screaming. Ssshhh, darling, you'll wake Jade.'

He opened his eyes, bewildered, feeling Caro's warm breath on his face. His whole body was pounding, and he was shaking. The bedclothes felt sodden with perspiration. 'I'm sorry,' he gasped. 'I'm sorry, darling. I had a – horrible – horrible—'

'Go back to sleep.' She stroked his face tenderly.

He lay for some moments breathing deeply, too scared to close his eyes in case he returned to the dream. His whole body felt heavy, as if gravity was pulling him down deep into the mattress.

Slowly he felt himself drifting away. Lying on a raft on an ocean with Caro beside him, beneath clear blue sky and the yellow disc of the sun. 'So many windows, so many.'

'Lots.'

She was pointing up at the sky. 'So many to count.'

The raft began to rock in the gentle swell. Then the sky darkened and the swell deepened, pitching them up and down, rocking the raft so much they were struggling to cling to it.

Peep . . . peep . . . peep . . .

The alarm was sounding. He opened his eyes, sleepily, blinking. The room was filled with early-morning light. But something was wrong. Where was he? Of course, it was coming back to him now. Of course, in the attic bedroom. But even so, something else was wrong.

Peep . . . peep . . . peep . . .

He suddenly remembered that there had been a power cut in the night, hadn't there? Zeroing the dials on the clock? Shit, what was the time? He reached a hand down to the clock to hit the snooze button, to give him another ten minutes of sleep, but all it hit was the wall. Frowning, he realized he was lying right beside the wall. The concentric circle pattern of the stained Anaglypta wallpaper was inches in front of his eyes.

Where the hell was his clock radio?

Still befuddled by sleep, he remembered the figure standing by the bed, in his dream. Smoking a cigar.

Had they been burgled in their sleep?

Then he heard Caro's voice, sounding very disturbed.

'Ollie?'

'Yurrr.'

'Ollie. What – what – what the hell's happened?'

'Wasshappened?' he said.

'Shit!' she said. 'Shit, shit, shit!' She dug a finger hard into his back.

'What?'

'Look!' There was real terror in her voice.

'Look at what?'

'Look out of the sodding window!'

He stared at the end of the bed, where the window was. Except there was no window.

Slowly, dimly, his memory put things into order. They were up in the attic because their bedroom ceiling had collapsed from the flooding. The window, which had no curtains, had been just beyond the foot of the bed when they had gone to sleep.

Now all he could see instead was the wall to the landing, and the closed door beside it.

He frowned.

The memory was returning. They'd made love with a crazy, urgent passion, last night. Had they slept at the wrong end of the bed?

He sat up with a start and cracked his head against two upright bars of the iron bedstead.

'Ollie,' Caro said, her voice trembling. 'Ollie, what the hell's happened?'

Clarity was returning. A terrible clarity. And with it the realization.

The bed.

The bed had moved during the night.

It had rotated one hundred and eighty degrees.

28

Shaking, Ollie and Caro stood, naked, beside the bed.

'Are we going mad?' she said.

He lifted each corner of the mattress in turn and stared down at the corroded nuts securing the frame to the legs. He tried to turn each one with his fingers but none of the four of them would budge.

'It's just not possible, Ollie,' she said. 'It's not possible.'

He could hear the tremor of terror in her voice. He looked up at the ceiling, around at the walls, then up again, his brain a vortex of confused thoughts. 'Are we sodding dreaming?'

'No, no, we are very definitely not dreaming.'

The clock radio was on the floor, where he had left it last night. The dial said 6.42 a.m. Somehow it had reset itself. The room seemed to tilt sideways, suddenly, and he had to steady himself against the side of the bed to prevent himself from falling over. He looked at his wife, her eyes wide, her face pale with confusion and fear, then he pulled on his jeans and T-shirt.

'I'll be back in a sec.'

He opened the door.

'I'm not staying in this room alone, wait for me.' She tugged on her jeans and sweatshirt, and followed him as he padded, barefoot, down the narrow wooden treads of the steep staircase.

'Go and make sure Jade's awake, darling,' he said, as they reached the first-floor landing.

She nodded and headed, as if in a trance, along towards Jade's room.

Ollie went down into the atrium and hurried through the kitchen to the scullery, where he kept his toolbox. Then he lugged it back up to the attic, took out an adjustable spanner, lifted up a corner of the mattress, and tried to move the corroded nut with the tool. It would not budge.

He put all his strength into it and levered the spanner again. With a protesting groan, the nut moved a fraction of an inch.

'Is this some kind of a joke?' Caro asked, suddenly by his side again. 'Is it?'

Ollie tried again. He tried with each of the four nuts in turn. 'No. No, it's not.'

'A bed can't rotate, Ollie. What's going on, tell me? Is this some kind of a fucking joke? Tell me if it is because I'm really not finding it funny. Is this your idea of some stupid game to try to spook me out?'

He looked up at her. 'Why the hell would I want to do that? Oh sure, I got up in the middle of the night, unscrewed our bed without waking you up and reassembled it in the opposite direction. You really think that, Caro?'

'Do you have a better explanation?'

'There has to be one.' He looked up at the ceiling. Then at the walls, then down at the bed, trying to do the maths. The geometry.

Tears began trickling down Caro's cheeks. He stood up and held her tightly in his arms. 'Look, let's think about this rationally.'

'That's what I'm doing, Ollie, I'm thinking about this rationally.' She was breathing in deep, sobbing gulps. 'I'm thinking fucking rationally. I'm thinking this whole fucking house is cursed.'

'I don't believe in curses.'

'No? Well maybe you'd better start.'

He held her tightly again. 'Come on, let's get showered and have breakfast and we'll try to think this through.'

'It's that bloody woman!' she blurted.

'What woman?'

She calmed down a little, and was silent for some moments. Then she said, 'I think we have a ghost.'

'A ghost?'

'I didn't want to say anything, in case you thought I was going nuts. But I've seen something.'

'What have you seen?'

'The morning after we moved in, you'd gone downstairs and I was sitting at my dressing table putting on my make-up. I saw a woman – a sort of old woman with a pinched face – standing right behind me. I turned round and there was nothing there. I thought it was my imagination. Then I saw her again a few days later. Then on Sunday I saw her in the atrium, sort of gliding across it.'

'Can you describe her?'

Caro described the woman. Ollie realized it was exactly the same description her mother had given him.

'I've seen her too, darling,' he said. 'I didn't want to say anything to you, because I didn't want to spook you out.'

'How fucking great is this? We've moved into our dream home and it has a sodding ghost.'

'There was an article I read in the paper about ghosts, which said that sometimes, when people move into an old

151

house, it activates something there. Some memory of a past resident. But it all settles down after a while.'

'I don't call turning our bed round in the middle of the night settling down, do you?'

'There has to be a rational explanation for what happened last night,' he said. 'There *has* to be.'

'Sure, so tell me. I'm all ears.'

Twenty minutes later, showered and shaved, Ollie went downstairs and collected the papers from the letter box in the front door, then he went into the kitchen. He turned on the radio, out of habit, and began to lay out breakfast on the table, trying to think clearly and rationally. There bloody well *had* to be an explanation for what had happened last night. Could they have imagined it all? Could the bed always have been that way round?

But he remembered the conversation they'd had in bed last night, how they were looking forward to waking in the morning and staring out through the window at the lake.

Was he going insane? Were they both?

He thought about the strange voices he'd heard in the night. Had he imagined them?

Bombay walked into the room and meowed at him. Moments later, Sapphire appeared, too.

'Hungry? Want your breakfast?'

Bombay meowed again.

He poured dried food out for them, filled their water bowl, then went over to a cupboard, took out Jade's Cheerios pack and put it on the table, along with a bowl and milk. He was craving a coffee, and as Jade hadn't yet appeared, he switched on the Nespresso machine, popped a Ristretto capsule in it, placed a cup underneath it, waited for the green lights to stop winking and pressed the one for a long espresso. While it was hissing, he began preparing some fruit for himself and Caro.

'Dad!'

He turned, hearing Jade's reproachful voice.

'Morning, lovely!'

She stood at the entrance to the kitchen in her school uniform, her face looking pale. 'I wanted to make it, that's my job – why didn't you wait?'

'I'm going to need at least two coffees this morning – you can make the second one.'

'Whatever.' She sat down sulkily at the refectory table and reached for the cereal pack.

Peeling a tangerine, Ollie asked, 'How did you sleep?'

'Actually, not very well.'

'Oh?'

'Look, don't tell Mum, right?' She raised a finger to her lips. 'Special secret?'

Ollie raised his own index finger to his lips. 'Special secret! OK! Don't tell your mum what?'

'Well, I think I saw a ghost.'

29

Jade sat in the Range Rover beside Ollie in silence for much of the way to school. She had been silent at breakfast after dropping her little bombshell, and she seemed determined to remain silent now.

He was silent too, deep in his own troubled thoughts. But then, finally, he said, 'OK, enough screen time for one car journey!'

She looked at him with a miffed expression.

'So come on, darling, tell me more. You said you saw a ghost. What did you see?'

'It was a little girl standing at the end of my bed.'

'OK. Did she frighten you?'

'Well, sort of.'

'What did she look like?'

'The same as last time.'

Surprised, Ollie said, 'You've seen her before?'

She nodded.

'How many times?'

'I don't know. Several times.'

'Why didn't you tell me before, or your mum?'

She shrugged. 'I thought Mum would be spooked. You know how nervy she is.'

He smiled. 'OK, so why didn't you tell me?'

154

'I tried to the other day. You were like – sort of a bit dismissive.'

'OK, I'm not being dismissive now. Tell me more about her.'

'There's another thing, Dad. Remember I told you, when I FaceTime with Phoebe, she keeps seeing this old woman behind me.'

He halted the car at traffic lights, frowning. 'Do you remember on our first Sunday in the house – you asked if Gran had come up to your room?'

She nodded.

'But your gran had gone home quite a bit earlier. Did Phoebe see something then, in your room?'

'Yes.'

'So how does all this make you feel?'

'I think it's pretty cool!'

Ollie smiled. 'You do?'

She nodded again, vigorously, her eyes bright with excitement. 'I think it's so cool that we've got a ghost!' Then her demeanour darkened. 'Well, except I'm not sure I like this girl who comes into my room. I don't think she's very nice.'

'Why's that?'

'Well, she doesn't say very nice things.'

'What does she say?' Suddenly the woman in the car in front of him, a small Toyota hatchback, threw a cardboard cup out of the window. He felt a flash of rage. Why? Why did people do shit like that? He looked at his daughter with deep affection. She was a decent human being. She'd never throw litter out of a car window. Or harm an animal. She didn't have a malicious bone in her body. Although some-times he worried she was too trusting.

After some moments, Jade said, 'Each time I see her she

tells me not to worry and that I'll be joining her soon. That we all will be – you, Mum and I.'

'Joining her where?'

'On the other side.'

'That's what she says to you?'

Jade nodded. 'She says we're already dead.'

'What do you say to her?'

'I just tell her she's silly! She is.'

Her attitude cheered him up a fraction and he smiled. 'Yes, she's very silly.'

'Dead people can't hurt you, can they, Dad? You said that to me, didn't you?'

'No, darling, they can't,' he said, trying to sound convincing.

A few minutes later he watched her head off towards the school, with her little multi-coloured rucksack on her back, and her guitar in its maroon case in her hand, hurrying to catch up with a group of girls – her new friends, he wondered?

He sat there for several minutes, long after she had safely disappeared, chatting away happily to a couple of girls in the group. No doubt full of street cred because she had talked to a ghost last night and none of the others had.

Then he drove off, heading home.

Hoping some of the workmen would be there today.

Just what the hell had really happened during the night?

He was nervous, he realized. Nervous right now about being in the house alone.

30

The events of the morning made Caro late arriving in the office. One client was already waiting in reception, and a problem had presented itself for another, the Benson family, a couple with two young children, who were meant to be moving house today. The solicitor for the other side – the purchaser of their bungalow in Peacehaven – had just left a message that his client was having issues with his bank and the money wouldn't come through today. Which meant no completion.

Shit, she thought. That meant she was going to have to call the Bensons, who were in a property chain, and break the bad news. Mrs Benson was placid but her husband, Ron, was a thoroughly neurotic and bad-tempered man and she was certain to get grief from him.

She went up to her office and told her secretary to give her five minutes before sending up the client who was downstairs, and to hold all calls. Then she sat at her desk, looked up the phone number of her strange new client, the medium Kingsley Parkin, and dialled it. To her dismay, after six rings it went to voicemail and she heard his precious-sounding voice.

'You've reached Kingsley Parkin. I'm sorry I can't come to the phone at the moment, due to unforeseen circum-stances. Ha, just my little joke! Please leave a message, and your number if I don't know you, and my people will call your people back!'

Caro looked at her diary and saw that the morning was rammed with clients. There were over a hundred emails in her inbox, and she knew on top of this she had the day's physical mountain of post yet to arrive. She called through to her secretary and instructed her that if Kingsley Parkin returned her call while she was tied up with a client, to tell him she needed to see him extremely urgently, and to ask him if by any chance he'd have time for a quick bite of lunch, locally, today. Otherwise, was there a time she could call him? She also told her secretary that if Parkin could make lunch, to cancel the one she had booked in with her best friend, Helen Hodge.

Her luck was in. Shortly after 10.30 a.m., as her third client of the morning – a sweet elderly widow in the process of buying a bungalow – was settling into the chair opposite her, her secretary buzzed her to say that Kingsley Parkin was suggesting meeting in LoveFit cafe, where it was quiet enough to talk.

Perfect, Caro told her. She knew where LoveFit was, although she'd not been there – it was just a five-minute walk away.

Caro arrived, full of apologies, at almost a quarter past one.

Kingsley Parkin, in bright red trousers, a cerise shirt with a collar so high it enveloped his ears, a white jacket and Cuban-heeled Chelsea boots, jumped to his feet from a brown leather sofa, close to the entrance. He was even shorter than she remembered.

'Never worry about punctuality, love. As an Irish mate

of mine says, when God made time he made plenty of the stuff.'

She grinned then rather awkwardly accepted his embrace and his kiss on both cheeks. She tried to keep relations with clients strictly formal, but this was a different circumstance. He reeked, as before, of tobacco.

'Nice place,' she said approvingly, looking at a wall of surfing pictures and another plain orange wall on which four stripy surfboards hung on display like a piece of modern art, with a palm tree in the middle. 'Do you surf?'

'Only the internet, love! Not much of a one for all that exercise stuff.'

'I really appreciate you seeing me at such short notice,' she said.

'I'm glad you called. I've been really worried about you.'

'You have?'

'I've got us that far table,' he said. And then added, lowering his voice, 'I've asked them to make sure they don't put no one next to us so we can't be overheard – as I think I know what this is about!'

They sat down, tucked away in the far corner, and ordered. While they waited for their food Caro kept to business, updating him on the searches on the property he was considering bidding for. Then they made small talk for a few minutes.

Her chicken salad and coffee arrived. A protein shake, a glass of iced water and a large plate of pitta bread stuffed with falafel were placed in front of the old rocker.

When their bearded waiter had retreated, Parkin said, 'I did try to warn you on Monday, love.' He picked up the pitta with his hands but chunks of falafel tumbled out. So he put it back on the plate and attacked it instead with his knife and fork.

Caro stared down at her mountainous salad. She had no appetite. 'I've not – I – I've never believed in the occult – paranormal – spirits. My mother always has, but she's a little bit – sort of – eccentric.'

'And now something's happened to change your mind, hasn't it, which is why you wanted to see me so urgently?' As he chewed, a tiny sprig of salad bobbed between his gleaming teeth. Just like his jet-black hair, the whiteness of his teeth only served to accentuate the tired, aged skin of his face.

For an instant, Kingsley Parkin reminded her of one of the Mexican Day of the Dead skulls she'd seen on sale at Cancún airport, a few years ago when they'd holidayed there. Some of those skulls wore wigs and had great teeth, too.

She hesitated, as if still reluctant to open up to this man. Then she said, 'We've only just moved into this house – less than two weeks ago. But there's a lot of strange things been happening.'

He watched her face and nodded. 'I know.'

'How?'

'Like I said – your aunt Marjie told me. You've smelled her perfume in your bedroom, haven't you?'

Caro felt her face redden. 'Yes – how . . . ?' Her voice tailed away.

'And you found a silk scarf she'd given you, years ago, on your bed, didn't you?'

She stared at him, wide-eyed.

'She's trying to let you know that she's around and wants to help you.' He closed his eyes. 'She says you, your husband and your daughter are in terrible danger. Your aunt is really very agitated. She wants you to leave. All of you. She's telling me you must leave the house. You must. Just as soon as you can.'

He closed his eyes and balled his knuckles against his forehead in concentration. After some moments he murmured, 'What is it, dear? What is it? I can't hear you very clearly, there's a lot of interference, what is it, what is it?'

Caro stared at him. He nodded several times, then opened his eyes, looked warily at her and placed his bony hands on the table. 'She says that if you don't want to stay there for ever, now is your only chance to leave.'

'We can't just leave,' Caro said, then shrugged. 'We've sunk everything we have into that house. It's – it's our future.'

Closing his eyes again, he began to pound his ears with his knuckles. 'There's something in the house, someone, something, it's very indistinct, there's someone, she's saying, someone who doesn't like to let people leave.'

There was a sharp crack that made them both jump. Caro froze for an instant, in shock and confusion. Then she heard gurgling water.

Parkin leaped to his feet, yelping, looking highly agitated and flapping his napkin. Other diners were looking at them. The bearded waiter was hurrying over with a cloth in his hand.

The medium's glass had shattered. Water, ice cubes and jagged shards of glass poured over the edge of the shiny wooden tabletop.

A couple of minutes later, with order restored, and a fresh glass of water placed in front of Parkin, which Caro eyed nervously, the medium continued.

'See?' he said, staring at her knowingly with gleaming eyes.

'See what?'

'Come on, Mrs Harcourt – Caro – may I call you Caro?'

'Of course,' she said flatly.

'That was a sign from your aunt. She's not happy with your attitude.'

'Oh, come on, it was just a faulty glass. Probably got cracked in the dishwasher and the ice caused it to contract.' She said it without conviction.

'Is that how you want to explain away everything else that's happened in the house? Do you want to be in denial?'

'What else has happened that you know?'

He stared at her again, hard. 'You've seen her, haven't you?'

'I've seen a woman standing behind me in my mirror, yes. Ollie – my husband – has seen her too.'

'Can you describe her?'

'She's not that distinct – an old woman – in her seventies or eighties. Sort of like a translucent shadow.'

He shook his head. 'That's got to be the woman your aunt is telling me about. If you've seen her then you really do have to leave.'

Caro shivered. The events of the night, the presence of this woman in her mirror, and now this medium all went against the grain of what she believed – and what she wanted to believe. And yet he was right, she couldn't be in denial. 'I told you – on Monday – I just don't believe in – I've never believed in, you know – in spirits. Not in the past. I always thought it was rubbish.'

'And now?'

'Now I'm not so sure. Something's happening, isn't it?'

'There's a really bad energy in your house.'

'There must be ways of dealing with bad energy. Shit, you are really spooking me!'

He closed his eyes, and again pressed his knuckles to

his forehead. 'She's showing me a bed. She's showing me something very wrong with a bed. Does that mean anything to you?'

Caro stared back at him. 'Yes, yes it does. Can you help us?'

'I am trying to help you. I'm telling you that you have to leave this house.'

'And I'm telling you that we've sunk every penny we have into it. Surely there has to be a way of making it OK? Aren't there people who can deal with – whatever you want to call it – hauntings – ghosts – poltergeists? Aren't there specialists who know how to clear a house of these things?'

'You mean exorcists?'

'Yes. Do you know any?'

'That doesn't always work. Did you see that old film *The Exorcist*?'

'Yes, a long time ago. I thought it was scary, but stupid.'

He looked down at his plate then up at her again. 'In my view, Caro, the only thing that would be stupid would be to ignore what's happening.'

Caro felt the vibration of her phone, which was on silent, signalling an incoming text. She pulled it out of her handbag and glanced at it.

The message said:

YOU'LL NEVER LEAVE MY HOUSE.

Then, moments later, it vanished.

31

Thursday, 17 September

Ollie had a hectic morning, dealing first with amendments to the Cholmondley website, followed by a lengthy Skype conversation with his new client, Anup Bhattacharya, on the content of his website. He was also pleased to see three new enquiries come in, following his visit to all the stands at the Goodwood Revival last weekend. In some ways he was glad of the distractions of work, but he badly needed time to think.

At least with a blue sky and sunshine outside, the house felt more welcoming and normal than it had during the early hours of this morning. He'd called Caro a couple of times to see how she was, but only got her voicemail. He'd also called the previous vicar of Cold Hill, the Reverend Bob Manthorpe, and had left a message on his voicemail. Now, at 1.45 p.m., having just got off the incredibly long-winded conference call, he was hungry and went downstairs to grab himself some lunch.

The house was a hive of activity, which he was glad about. As he entered the kitchen he saw the head of the building firm, Bryan Barker, in discussion with his foreman, Chris.

Barker, in a lumberjack shirt, jeans and heavy-duty boots, was an affable, energetic man with a dense crop of silver hair and youthful good looks that belied his sixty-seven years.

'Ah, Ollie,' he said. 'I was about to come up and see you. Chris is very worried about the cellar. There are two structural walls down there in extremely bad shape.' He gestured to his foreman, a lean, pensive and pleasant-natured man in his thirties, to continue.

'We're going to have to hire a structural engineer, Mr Harcourt,' the foreman said. 'I think we need some Acrow props urgently. I'll show you where I mean.'

Ollie followed them both down the brick steps into the cellar. Bryan Barker pointed to a large space which led through to the disused kitchen. There had clearly been a wall here at some point. 'This is what we're worried about.'

The foreman pointed up. 'It looks to me as if the developers who were working here before they went bust, as I understand, had taken down a wall to open this space up. But the problem is, this is a main load-bearing wall.' He then pointed at several large cracks in the ceiling. 'I'm not at all happy about these,' he said. 'We've only discovered them since removing the plaster here. I don't want to alarm you, and I can't be certain, but I'm pretty sure these have widened in the last few days.'

'If any of them went,' Barker chipped in, 'it could have a domino effect on all the floors above. It could literally bring down the entire house – this part of it, anyway. I think we should get an engineer out here quickly.'

'How much would he cost?' Ollie asked, gloomily, knowing that underpinning was unlikely to come cheap.

'I think he'd come out for a site visit without charge. Then it would depend on how much work he has to do. I really don't think you have any option.'

'Why the hell didn't the surveyor mention this in his report?'

'He did.'

The foreman nodded, adding his confirmation too.

'Shit, did I miss it?' Yet another thing Ollie realized he had missed – or at least had misinterpreted. There was so much wrong that after a while his eyes had glazed over each time he'd reread the report. He and Caro, who had red-penned a copy of it, realized in the end they were going to have to take a view. Buying the house was a gamble – a massive gamble. They both knew it and they took the risk, thinking they could just do a small bit at a time, room by room. But it hadn't occurred to him – and he was certain not to Caro either – that the place could actually be in real danger of falling down.

'I don't suppose we've any chance of getting any of this on insurance?' Ollie asked.

'Not a hope in hell, I shouldn't think,' Barker said.

The foreman shook his head.

'OK,' Ollie said. 'You'd better do it.' Then he hesitated. 'Bryan, when you have a moment, could you come upstairs and take a look at something for me?'

'Of course. Want to do it now?'

As Ollie led the way up to the attic bedroom, Barker suddenly asked him, 'Were they relatives of yours or Caro's who were here earlier?'

Ollie stopped and turned. 'Relatives? Here earlier? Who do you mean?'

'The couple with two small children.'

Ollie frowned. 'Couple with two small children? I didn't have any – visitors.'

'About an hour ago. He had a big cigar. I thought he must know you pretty well to be smoking in your house!'

Cigar. Ollie was thinking back to last night. The middle of the night. The smell of cigar smoke in the room before the bed had rotated. Barker had seen something, he realized. But he didn't want him getting spooked, and perhaps telling his workmen, and risk some of them leaving. Equally, he knew that Bryan Barker was no fool.

'Oh, right, yes, Caro's brother and his family popped in briefly to see her – so I gave them a quick tour,' he lied. Then he carried on up the stairs to the attic and went in first. The clock radio still lay on the floor. Caro had stripped the bed – there was no way they were going to sleep in this room again, although he hadn't yet figured out where they would sleep tonight. The spare beds they'd brought from Carlisle Road were all dismantled and stacked, at the moment, in the library. They would probably have to make do on the sofas. Barker had a full team working on the ceiling repair and was confident they'd be able to move back into their bedroom by tomorrow afternoon.

'I've not been up here before,' the builder said. 'What a very pretty room. Reminds me of a little hotel in France where Jasmin and I stayed some years ago!'

'That's funny,' Ollie said, grinning, but feeling very uncomfortable being back here, despite the bright daylight streaming through the window. 'Caro and I said the same thing – it's just like a place we stayed in a few years ago, near Limoges.'

'Beautiful old bed – a real antique. Worth a few bob.' Then Bryan Barker frowned. 'A bit odd, though. I would have put it the other way, facing the window rather than the door.'

'Actually,' Ollie said, guardedly, 'that's what I wanted to discuss with you. How easy would it be to rotate it – a hundred and eighty degrees – without dismantling it?'

'Rotate it a hundred and eighty degrees?'

'Yes.'

Barker looked at the bed, around at the walls and up at the ceiling. Then he pulled an industrial-looking tape measure from his back pocket and measured the length, width and height of the bed. Next, he did the same for the room dimensions. When he had finished he did some mental calculations. After some moments he shook his head. 'Wouldn't be possible, Ollie, not without taking it apart.'

'Are you sure?'

'Absolutely sure.'

'How easy would it be to take it apart?'

Barker lifted one corner of the mattress and looked at the nut. 'Doesn't look like this has been touched in years.' Then he checked around the entire bed, lifting each corner of the mattress in turn. When he had finished he said, 'Well, it all comes apart. The easiest way would be to unscrew and reverse the headboard and the footer as they're not welded to the frame.'

'And if we actually wanted to rotate the entire bed?'

The builder gave him a puzzled look. 'The legs would come off all right, with a bit of effort, but that still leaves the frame.' He thought for some moments, looking even more puzzled. 'If we took all four legs off, then we could rotate the frame – but –' he shook his head – 'it's just over two metres long. The room is just under two metres wide.' He opened one of the cupboard doors and peered inside. Then he stepped back. 'We'd have to chop out the cupboard doors and then remove all the shelves. The only way would be to remove the legs, then take the frame out of the room, down the stairs, turn it and bring it back up again. But why do you want to make it so complicated?'

'There's no way two people could rotate this bed, in this room, on their own and without tools?'

'Not in a million years,' Bryan Barker said. 'If it's not a personal question, why are you asking?'

Ollie smiled. 'I'm not very good at spatial stuff. Caro and I had a bet about it last night.'

'And you reckoned it could be done?'

He nodded.

'Hope you didn't put too much money on it. I need you to pay my bills!'

Ollie stared warily around the room, wondering silently, as he had been all morning. What had happened in here last night? What the hell had happened in here?

Then he patted the builder reassuringly on the shoulder. 'Relax, I didn't bet the ranch.'

'I'm glad to hear it.'

32

Twenty minutes later, after wolfing down a ham sandwich, and then a chocolate bar that he found in the fridge, Ollie walked back upstairs and along to the tower, momentarily preoccupied with thoughts about where he and Caro would sleep tonight.

The other spare rooms were in very poor condition, with rotten floorboards, peeling wallpaper, damp and black patches of mould. The big, extra-wide red sofas in the drawing room, which they'd bought some years ago and were great for lounging back in and watching television, seemed a lot more appealing.

That settled, his thoughts returned again to last night. He was still trying to find an explanation for what had happened. The only one so far, and it was a weak one, was that the bed had always been that way round and somehow they were mistaken in thinking otherwise. But he wasn't convincing himself.

And just what the hell had Bryan Barker seen today? The O'Hare family? There had been four of them, according to the headstone in the graveyard. Two adults and two young children.

As he entered his office, his mobile phone rang. He didn't recognize the number on the display.

'Oliver Harcourt,' he answered, warily.

The voice sounded elderly but richly sonorous, as if from someone long used to public speaking. 'It's Bob Manthorpe, you rang me earlier?'

The previous vicar of Cold Hill, Ollie realized. 'Reverend Manthorpe, yes, thank you so much for calling back.'

'Not at all, what can I do for you?'

'Well, the thing is –' Ollie stepped through the maze of packing cases and stacked files to his desk, and sat down – 'my wife and I – we've just moved into a house called Cold Hill. I understand you were the vicar in the village some years ago?'

There was an extremely prolonged silence. Ollie wondered if they had been disconnected – or if the old man had hung up. Then he heard his voice. '*Cold Hill House?*'

'Yes.'

'It was being restored, I recall, a long time back. A very beautiful place indeed. Jolly good. Hope you'll be very happy there.'

Ollie could detect the unease in his voice. 'Thank you, we hope so too. I wanted to ask you a few things about your time here.'

'Well, you know, I've been retired for some years. And these days my memory's not what it was.'

'Is there any chance we could meet? Just for a quick chat? It's really quite important.'

'Well, I suppose so.' He sounded hesitant. 'I'm free all afternoon today if you're able to pop over?'

'Where are you?'

'Do you know Beddingham?'

'Yes – just outside Lewes.'

'I'm in a little cottage just off the roundabout at the bottom of Ranscombe Hill – the junction of the A26 and A27.'

Ollie did a quick calculation. It was about twenty to thirty minutes' drive from here. He looked at his watch. It was 2.20 p.m. Normally he had to pick Jade up from school at 3.30, but she was staying on late today for a school orchestra practice and he'd agreed to collect her at 5.30. 'I could be with you by three,' he said.

'I'll put the kettle on,' Manthorpe said, then gave him a few more details on how to find the house.

Ollie went down to look for Bryan and Chris, and told them he was going out for a bit. Then he climbed into his car and headed out. Driving down the hill and into the village, although he knew it was ridiculous, he still found himself keeping an eye out for Harry Walters.

A short while later he headed down the A23 towards Brighton, then turned left at the roundabout at the bottom of Mill Hill, and up onto the A27, driving fast, thinking about all the questions he wanted to ask the retired vicar.

He passed the sprawling, tree-lined campus of Sussex University to his left, and glanced ruefully at the stunning superstructure of the Amex football stadium to his right. He'd been a season-ticket holder since it opened, but because of buying the house, and having to cut down on all expenses, he'd had to let that go for this new season. Hopefully, he'd be back before too long. He was already missing the Saturday afternoon gatherings there with his mates.

At the next roundabout he carried on along the Lewes bypass. A few minutes later he drove, on the dual carriageway, down a long hill, with sweeping views of Sussex farmland to the right and the gentle slopes of the South Downs and Firle Beacon in the far distance. Many of the fields, harvested now, were just yellow stubble, with rows of round bales. This was normally one of his favourite Sussex views, but today he was too distracted by his troubled thoughts to appreciate it.

At the roundabout at the bottom of the hill he followed the Reverend Manthorpe's instructions, turning right almost immediately onto a slip road. He then made a left and pulled up behind an elderly people carrier parked outside a semi-detached Victorian cottage. A small rusted caravan that the retired vicar had told him to look for was propped up on bricks in the driveway.

He rang the doorbell, feeling nervous suddenly, wondering what reaction he was going to get. The old man had invited him over with considerable reluctance in his voice. A dog yapped inside. Moments later the door was opened by a tall man in jeans, battered slippers and a grey cardigan, holding a smouldering pipe in one hand. He had a mane of white hair that flopped over his face, which, although aged, showed that he must have once been strikingly handsome. He was stooped over, holding the collar of an excited Jack Russell in his free hand. 'Shssshhhh, Jasper!' he said commandingly to the dog. Then he smiled up at Ollie.

'Mr Harcourt? Come on in!'

He stepped back, sideways, in the tiny hallway that reeked of tobacco smoke, and the dog jumped up against Ollie's trouser leg, excitedly wagging its tail.

'Down, Jasper!'

'It's OK, I like dogs,' Ollie said. 'He can probably smell our cats.'

'He's a little bugger, still trying to train him!' Manthorpe said, closing the front door. 'Come on through. Down! Down, Jasper!'

He led Ollie into a cramped, shabby but cosy sitting room, with several logs piled up in an unlit fireplace, a leather couch and two leather armchairs arranged around a wooden chest serving as a coffee table. A large glass ashtray, with a pile of ash, sat on it, and there was a copy of the *Daily Telegraph* and a local parish magazine beside it.

'Hope you don't mind this?' Manthorpe held up his pipe.

'Not at all, I love the smell, it reminds me of my grandfather!'

'Cup of tea? Coffee?'

'Tea would be great. Builder's, please, just a touch of milk and no sugar.'

'Plonk yourself down.' Manthorpe indicated the sofa.

Ollie settled into it and the dog jumped up beside him and pushed his nose against him. He stroked the animal's wiry coat while the vicar went out of the room, and looked around. He glanced at a photograph on the mantelpiece of a much younger Manthorpe, in a grey suit and dog collar, arm-in-arm with a pretty, serious-looking, dark-haired woman. On the wall were several framed watercolours of Sussex rural scenes, one very recognizable as the Seven Sisters.

'My late wife,' Manthorpe said, coming back into the room some minutes later with a tray on which were two steaming mugs and a plate of digestive biscuits. He set it down on top of the papers. 'She was a jolly talented painter. Please help yourself.'

Then he sat in an armchair, lounged back, dug a box of matches out of his pocket and relit his pipe. Ollie found the smell of the curling blue smoke took him back to his childhood.

'It's very good of you to see me,' he said.

'Not at all. To tell you the truth, it's nice to have company. I've been jolly lonely since my wife died.' He looked at the dog. 'He seems to have found a friend!'

'He's gorgeous,' Ollie replied, continuing to stroke the animal and struggling to hold him back from his attempts to sniff his crutch.

'So.' Manthorpe laid his substantial frame right back in the chair, tilting his head at the ceiling, and drew hard on his pipe. 'Cold Hill House?'

'Yes.'

'Quite an undertaking, I would imagine.'

'You could say that.'

'You must have deep pockets.'

'We've only been there a couple of weeks – I'm not sure my pockets are ever going to be deep enough. It's a serious money pit.'

Manthorpe smiled. 'Did you ever see that film?'

'Which film?'

'*The Money Pit.* Tom Hanks. It's very funny.' He hesitated. 'But perhaps not to you. Might be a bit off-putting.' He grinned. 'So anyway, I don't imagine you've come to touch me for a loan – what can I do for you? You said it was urgent.' He sucked hard on his pipe again, then blew a perfect smoke ring which rose almost all the way to the ceiling before starting to lose its halo shape.

'You were in Cold Hill for how long?'

'Yes – gosh – I spent almost thirty years there. Loved it. Never wanted to be anywhere else.'

'You'd have known Annie Porter?'

Manthorpe beamed. 'Annie Porter? What a lovely character!' He pointed at a tall, very slightly uneven vase, painted with a floral design, on a shelf alongside a row of photographs of three children, and a separate photograph of a golden retriever. 'My late wife fired that in her kiln. She used to attend Annie's pottery classes regularly. Annie's still around is she? Must be knocking on a bit.'

'She's in rude health, I'd say.'

'Remember me to her.'

'I will indeed.' Ollie reached for his mug. 'Do you remember someone else who I think was there during your time: Harry Walters?'

Manthorpe eyed him, wary all of a sudden. 'Harry Walters? Silver-haired old boy who also smoked a pipe?'

'That's him.'

'I remember him a little. Bit of an oddball – kept himself to himself. He worked up at your place. Poor bugger died in an accident there.'

'Yes, that's right, apparently a mechanical digger toppled onto him. What about the O'Hare family? Four of them. They were buried in the churchyard in 1983. Do you remember them?'

'Yes,' Manthorpe answered after a short silence. 'Yes, that was terrible. One of the saddest things I ever had to deal with. Happened not long after I arrived there as the vicar.'

'What can you tell me about them?'

'Well, not a lot really, never had time to get to know them.' He leaned back and drew on his pipe, but it had gone out. He struck another match, sucked hard and blew out another perfect smoke ring. Ollie felt his phone vibrate in his pocket, but ignored it. 'Johnny O'Hare – if I remember right – was a big shot in the music business. We had the funeral in the church, and requests for songs from artistes he had worked with. Glen Campbell. Diana Ross. Billy J. Kramer. The Dave Clark Five. The Kinks. He was into some area of management – composers or lyricists, something like that.' The retired vicar's voice changed, and Ollie could detect something wistful in it. 'I can tell you, we had a real *Who's Who* of rock greats in the church that day. I doubt there's ever been anything like it before or after. We had Paul McCartney, Ray Davies, Mick Jagger, Lulu – there were police cordons in the village to keep the crowds back.'

'Amazing!' Ollie said.

'Hmmmn, you could say that. I'll tell you another thing I've just remembered. The deceased's brother – Charlie O'Hare – came to see me a few days before the funeral. He was a little – *eccentric* might be a polite word for him. He told me his brother had never been much for religion, but he thought it would be nice to have a communion service for the funeral. He said Johnny had always been a bit of a bon viveur and rather than have the traditional communion wine and wafer host, asked me whether we could have champagne and caviar blinis instead – oh, and cigars instead of candles. He wondered if everyone in the church could light up a cigar in his brother's memory. Apparently he was very fond of cigars.'

Ollie smiled, pensively. Cigars. Did that explain the smell in the attic room? Barker's sighting?

'I gave him short shrift, I can tell you!'

'I'm not surprised.'

'Do this job for long enough and nothing will surprise you, I can tell you that! Although I've forgotten a lot. I told you on the phone that my memory's not so good these days.'

'It seems pretty sharp to me,' Ollie said. 'So what happened to the O'Hare family? How did they die? It looks as if they all died at the same time – was it a car accident?'

'Well, of sorts, but not in the conventional sense.' Manthorpe relit his pipe yet again, from a fresh match. 'They'd just arrived at the house, pulled up at the front door, when part of the roof and front collapsed on them, crushing them – killing them all instantly.'

Ollie listened in shocked silence. 'On the day they moved in? They all died?'

'Yes. I'm afraid the house has had a few tragedies.' Then he smiled. 'But don't be put off. Some of the older folk in the village used to talk a lot of rubbish about the place being cursed or damned. But the reality is any house of that historic age is more than likely to have had its fair share of deaths. The history of the human race doesn't make happy reading, does it? I've seen a lot of sadness during my time, but I've seen a lot of things that have kept my faith in God and in humanity alive, too. If there were no bad things in the world, we'd have nothing to measure the good against, would we?'

'I guess not.' Ollie sipped his tea.

'The light can only shine in darkness,' Manthorpe said. He gave Ollie a quizzical look. 'Perhaps you and your family will be the light the house needs.'

'It's not looking that way at the moment.'

'Why is that?'

'I feel we've moved into a nightmare.'

Ollie told him everything. From the first day and what he and his mother-in-law had seen in the atrium. Then the spheres he had seen. The young girl and the old woman that Jade had told him about. The episodes with the water. The voices he had heard last night and the bed rotating. And Caro's confession to him about the woman she had seen several times.

When he had finished, Manthorpe nodded silently, and tapped the embers out of his pipe bowl into the growing pile of grey ash in the ashtray. 'Oh dear,' he said finally. 'Oh dear.' He looked at Ollie with a dubious expression. 'Cold Hill House was empty during most of my time there. As I said, there were a lot of rumours about the place – you know, village gossip.'

'What rumours?'

'About it being cursed, if you believe in that sort of thing. And there was one particular rumour.' He shrugged dismissively, produced a tobacco pouch from his pocket and began to refill his pipe. 'The problem is, Mr Harcourt—'

'Please call me Ollie.'

He nodded. 'OK, Ollie, the problem is that in country villages people have time on their hands. Too much of it. They gossip, speculate.'

'What did they speculate about Cold Hill House?'

'How much of its history do you know?'

'So far not much – other than what was in the estate agent's particulars. Before the O'Hares bought it, the house was owned by a Lord and Lady Rothberg – he was heir to a banking dynasty, apparently. I believe they were there from shortly after the Second World War until they died.'

Manthorpe held his freshly filled pipe in the air. 'Yes, that was a few years before I came to Cold Hill, but people were still talking about it. A terrible tragedy, but I suppose it was a blessing in the end, after all those years never leaving the house. You have a lake, right?'

'We do, yes. The one where Harry Walters drowned.'

'As I heard it, there was a particularly hard winter one year. Lady Rothberg was very fond of animals and she had some quite rare ducks she had bred on the lake. I seem to remember an island in the middle?'

Ollie nodded. 'We call it Duck Island.'

'Lady Rothberg trained the ducks to live on the island, to keep them safe from foxes, by putting some kind of duck feed – corn, I think – for them on it. She used to row over to it every few days with a sack of food to top up the supply.

One morning the whole lake was frozen over. Instead of rowing she decided the ice was thick enough to walk on. She got halfway across with the sack of feed when the ice gave way and she fell in. Her husband tried to rescue her, and did apparently get the poor woman out, but because of her time underwater, starved of oxygen, she suffered severe brain damage, and spent the rest of her life confined to bed in a room in the house, in a persistent vegetative state. Then to compound the tragedy, the following year, on the day of his fortieth birthday, Lord Rothberg was apparently hosting a shooting party and there was a terrible accident – I believe the young son of a guest accidently discharged both barrels at Lord Rothberg, blowing away most of his face and part of his neck, blinding him and paralysing him.'

'I'd no idea. How terrible.' Ollie looked at him in silence for some moments. 'Has anybody actually lived out their natural lifespan, without tragedy, at Cold Hill House?'

The retired clergyman smiled. 'Oh, I'm sure plenty of people have. You have to understand, all great houses have their fair share of tragedy, as I said.'

'This seems to be more than what I'd call a *fair share*.'

'You need to put it all in the context of the long history of the place. But yes, there have been quite a number of tragic accidents. Hopefully now they're over and done with.'

'That's what concerns me,' Ollie said. 'Which is why I came here to see you. I'm not at all sure they are over and done with. What do you know about the history of the house, before the Second World War?'

'Well, that's all very sketchy from what I can recall. The house was requisitioned by the government during the war, and a number of Canadian soldiers were billeted there. Before that, during the early part of the twentieth century, there was a bit of a mystery.' He sipped his tea. 'A bit of an odd family, I was told by some local gossip. A husband and wife. Can't recall their names. She disappeared, apparently. The husband told his friends she'd left him and gone to live with a sister in New Zealand. But rumour had it he had a mistress and had murdered his wife and buried her somewhere in the grounds. The police became involved, but he died before it was ever resolved.'

'How did he die?'

'That I really can't remember. I'm not sure I ever knew. But, actually, that's reminded me. The very first owner – the chap who had the place built—' He frowned. 'Trying to remember his name. Bronwyn – no – Brangwyn. Sir Brangwyn *something*. Gallops? Bessington? Ah yes, now I remember. Sir Brangwyn De Glossope. There was a bit of a legend about him.'

'Oh?'

'Rather a ne'er-do-well. I think he was in the tea- or spice-importing business. He came from a wealthy landowning family but gambled most of his inheritance away. Well, as I recall, he married a very rich woman – from the aristocracy, or at least landed gentry, and it was her money that paid the bills to have Cold Hill House built.' He paused to relight his pipe, then blew another huge smoke ring, which rose steadily towards the ceiling, slowly dispersing. The retired vicar watched the ring, as if it was some kind of cloud in which his memory was stored. 'If I'm recalling the story correctly, this woman was, not to put too fine a point on it, unfortunate-looking, by all accounts. There were rumours that she was what we might today call a medium – a psychic – or a clairvoyant. But back in those days she'd have been regarded as a witch. There was a persistent rumour in Cold Hill village that she put a spell on De

Glossope to get him to marry her. Although there was another school of thought that he only married her for her money and had intended from the start to get rid of her as soon as convenient. It wasn't long after the house was finished that this fellow, Brangwyn, had the whole place closed down for about three years while he went to India and then the Far East on business. When he returned, his wife wasn't with him. The story he told people was that she had died of a sickness whilst over there.' He puffed on his pipe again and blew another smoke ring, this one less perfectly formed.

'And you don't believe that?' Ollie asked.

'We're talking about something that happened over two hundred and fifty years ago. I have no idea. But there was an old boy in Cold Hill village – he'd be long dead by now – who was a mine of information. He'd unearthed letters and journals and what-have-you from that time, and he used to like sitting in the pub and telling anyone who'd listen that Brangwyn's wife had not been on the outbound ship with him. That he'd left her behind in the house.'

'In the closed-up house?'

Manthorpe shrugged. 'Or buried her somewhere in the grounds. I don't think they had quite the calibre of detection work we have today. If it's true, he went away for long enough, came home, opened up the house and started life over again with a new bride. Rumour had it, apparently, that his wife's spirit was pretty angry.'

'Understandably!'

Manthorpe gave a wry smile. 'And that she didn't like people leaving the house.'

'Yep, well, it's a big place to be on your own.' He smiled, but the vicar looked miles away and did not smile back.

'So she put a curse on the place?' Ollie prompted.

'Yes, that was the story I heard. And her occult powers gave her the ability to do this.' He smiled as if he himself did not believe it.

'No one's ever tried to find the body?' Ollie asked.

'It's a huge property as you know, acres of land. And besides, it's just a rumour.'

Ollie glanced at his watch. He was going to have to leave in a few minutes, to collect Jade. 'Thank you,' he said. 'You've been incredibly helpful.'

'Come and see me again sometime. You're a nice chap. Don't be put off by all that's happened. Remember what I said, the light can only shine in darkness.'

'I'll remember that, thank you,' Ollie said.

'I'll give you a bit of advice though – I'll tell you what I think you should do – I'd have done it myself for you if I'd been a younger man, but I'm too old now.'

Five minutes later, as Ollie drove away, the old clergyman stood by the front door, holding his dog and giving him a strange look that unsettled him.

It was the look of an old man who was seeing something – or *someone* – for what he knew might be the last time.

It made Ollie shiver.

Manthorpe closed the front door feeling deeply shaken. He needed to make an important phone call, and urgently. He looked around and remembered he had left the handset up in his den on the first floor.

The conversation of the past hour with the decent young man had confirmed so much that he already feared. The Harcourts needed help, and he knew the right person to speak to. He began to climb the narrow stairs, his knees aching, his heart pounding. He was out of breath before he'd reached halfway. Soon he was going to have to find the money for one of those stairlift things. Or else move.

With one step to go to the top, a shadow suddenly crossed in front of him, and stopped.

The old man halted in his tracks and stared up. He wasn't afraid, just angry. Very angry. 'What the hell do you want?' he said.

33

Thursday, 17 September

'Mr Simpson, the music teacher, has asked me if I'd like to play a solo in the school concert at the end of term!' Jade said, bubbling with enthusiasm as she climbed up into the car.

'Wow, that's great, lovely! What are you going to play?'

'Well, I'm not sure yet – he's got a few ideas.'

'I'm very proud of you!'

All the way home she told him about her day and about how much she liked her new music teacher. The discussion about ghosts they'd had this morning, when he'd been driving her to school, seemed to be gone from her mind – for now at least.

At a few minutes past 6.00 p.m., as they drove up the drive and the house came into view, looking stunning in the evening sunlight, his spirits lifted. He was cheered and buoyed by Jade's happy innocence and her growing enthusiasm for her new school. And she had added two more new friends, in addition to Charlie and Niamh, to the ones she wanted to invite to her birthday party, she told him.

He saw Caro's black Golf parked outside the house, and then, as they drew closer, he saw she was still in the car, talking on her phone.

He pulled up beside her, and climbed out. Jade jumped down, clutching her guitar and rucksack, and ran happily to the Golf. Moments later, Caro ended her call and emerged, holding her briefcase. Jade hugged her and delivered the same excited news she'd given her father. Then they went inside and Jade disappeared up to her room.

'How was your day, darling?' Ollie asked.

'I need a drink,' she said. 'A large one. Several large ones!'

They went through into the kitchen. Caro plonked her briefcase down on the floor. 'I'm afraid I've got a good hour's work to do,' she said. 'But I really do need a drink first. God!'

Ollie went over to the fridge and took out a bottle of wine, then began to cut away the foil. 'Have you only just arrived home, darling?'

'No, I got here about twenty minutes ago. I was waiting for you to come home. I'm sorry.'

'Sorry?'

'Yes.'

'Sorry about what?'

She shrugged off her jacket and hung it on the back of her chair. 'I was too scared to come in here on my own. I – I didn't want to be alone in the house.'

He turned to look at her. She was hunched over the table, looking deeply vulnerable.

He walked over and put an arm round her. 'Darling, I understand.'

'Do you? Do you really? Do you understand what it's like to be scared to go in the front door of your own sodding home? Aren't you scared? What's going to happen tonight? Tomorrow? It's like something doesn't want us here. What the hell have we done? What have we got ourselves into? Do you think we should move? Ollie, what are we going to do?'

She was wondering whether she should tell him about

the message on her phone that had appeared – then disappeared – whilst she was having lunch with Kingsley Parkin. But she still couldn't be sure if she had simply imagined it. So she said nothing.

'We need to sort this out,' he said. 'Sort the house out. Find out just what the hell is going on. I went to see the previous vicar here, a nice old boy called Bob Manthorpe. He said the house had a bad history but that all old houses have some tragedies in their past.'

'And beds that rotate one hundred and eighty sodding degrees during the night?'

'I still think there's got to be an explanation for that.'

'Good, I'm glad one of us does.'

He returned to the wine. 'It's not physically possible to have rotated – without being dismantled first. I took Bryan Barker up to the room earlier, and he had a good look at it. The nuts and bolts holding it together haven't been touched in years – decades. They're all corroded.'

'I went to see someone too, today.'

'Who?'

'A client. I didn't want to tell you about him because I didn't want to upset you. He came to see me on Monday. He's a new client, a weird guy, an old rocker called Kingsley Parkin – he had one big hit back in the sixties – who says he's psychic.'

'What was the hit?'

'I can't remember – not something I'd heard of. I think he said his band was called Johnny Lonesome and the Travellers – or something like that. Anyway, he started getting messages about the house when he was in my office on Monday – messages from my auntie Marjorie. Marjie. Remember her?'

'Of course.' The cork came out with a loud pop. 'She was lovely, I liked her.'

'She liked you, too. He knew her name, Ollie. Isn't that strange? How did he know her name?'

'What kind of messages – what was she saying?'

'He said she was telling us to leave. To leave while we still could.'

Ollie wiped fragments of cork from the neck of the bottle, thinking. If Caro's mother, despite being a magistrate, was a tad bonkers, her auntie Marjie had been seven miles north of bonkers. He'd genuinely liked her, but she really was wired on a different circuit from everyone else. 'Did your auntie have anyone in mind to buy this place and pay us back all we've sunk into it?'

'I'm being serious, Ollie.'

'So am I.' He filled two wine glasses and carried them over to the table. 'Look, I'm not going to pretend I'm happy about any of this. I can't explain the bed, and I can't explain what you saw in the mirror. But moving here is the biggest thing we've ever done. We can't just walk away because some drug-addled old rocker with a fried brain is getting messages from your dead auntie. Is that what you want?'

'Kingsley Parkin said that if we wanted to stay we should consider asking for an exorcism. But he's offered to come out here himself and see what he picks up.'

Ollie sat down opposite her. 'An exorcism?'

It was along the lines of what Bob Manthorpe had suggested to him earlier, although he had used less dramatic words, a Christian Service of Deliverance, he had called it. And he had told Ollie he knew a good person to do it if they decided to go that route.

'Parkin said we should talk to the current vicar,' continued Caro. 'Apparently there's an exorcist in every diocese in the country. They get called in when things happen that people can't explain. Like they're happening here.'

'Bell, book and candle. All that stuff?'

'I'm willing to give it a go. Do you have a better idea, Ollie? Because if so, tell me. Otherwise I'm getting the hell out of here.'

'Listen, we mustn't panic, that would be ridiculous!'

'Like rotating one hundred and eighty degrees in the night is ridiculous? Like seeing an apparition in my mirror is ridiculous? Sure, I can accept that this move here is a big thing and massively disruptive. But we've moved into a nightmare.'

'The old vicar chap, Manthorpe, was going to have a word with someone – someone in the clergy who's had experience dealing with odd phenomena. But I don't think it was quite as dramatic as an exorcist.'

'Why not have an exorcist?'

'I'm happy to have an exorcist – or whatever he's called – come here. Let's do it. Would that make you feel better?'

'Would it make you feel better?'

'If he can stop whatever's going on here, yes.'

'OK,' she said. 'I'll sort it. I'll call Kingsley Parkin first and see how soon he could come out here. Maybe he can come this evening. Shall I do that?'

All the time they talked, Ollie continually glanced past her at the archway through into the atrium, looking for the spheres he had seen previously. He glanced around for them, with a shiver, every time he entered the atrium. An *exorcist*. He shrugged at the thought. But he had no better solution.

He also had a feeling there was more that Manthorpe might have told him, if he'd pressed, if he'd had more time and not had to leave to go and collect Jade. He suspected the old vicar knew more about the history of the house than he was telling. He would call him tomorrow and try to go and see him again, he decided. 'Sure, call this Parkin chap,' he said to Caro.

'I'll do it now. Let's carry on this conversation later,' she said. 'We'll make beds up on the sofas. But I've got to deal with something urgently for a client.' Caro leaned down, opened her briefcase and pulled a thick plastic file-holder from it.

'I've got something urgent to do too, for sodding Cholmondley,' he said. 'Want me to make supper tonight?'

'That would be great, thanks.'

'Stir-fried prawns? We've got some raw ones in the fridge.'

'Anything.'

He looked at his watch. It was coming up to 6.30 p.m. 'Eat around eight?'

'Fine.'

As he removed the bag of prawns from the fridge, and poured some into a bowl, Ollie heard Caro on the phone leaving a voicemail message for Parkin. He filled the cats' food bowls, called them, then carried his wine glass up to his office, sat at his desk, and switched on the radio to catch the closing news headlines.

Earlier that afternoon Cholmondley had sent him an email which he had only looked at, so far, on his iPhone. It was a photograph of a 1965 Ferrari GTO that had sold at auction in the USA for thirty-five million dollars a couple of years back. Cholmondley had now been offered its sister car with, he claimed, an impeccable provenance. He wanted star treatment for it on the website.

As the screen came to life, to Ollie's surprise all the

normal folders and documents on the desktop had vanished. In their place were the words, in large black capitals:

MANTHORPE'S AN OLD FOOL. DON'T LISTEN TO HIM. YOU'LL NEVER LEAVE.

As he stared at them in shock, they suddenly faded away and all the folders and documents came back into view.

Then he heard Caro scream.

34

With his heart in his mouth, Ollie raced down the stairs, through the atrium and into the kitchen.

Caro was standing, wide-eyed, in the middle of the room. Shards and splinters of glass lay on the table, across her documents, and on the floor. Open-mouthed, she was staring upwards and pointing. He looked up and saw the remains of the light bulb hanging from the ceiling cord directly above the table.

'It exploded,' she said, her voice quavering with fear. 'It just bloody exploded.'

'It happens sometimes.'

'Oh, does it? When? It's never happened to me before.'

'It's probably from the flood – water was dripping down here yesterday. Must have caused a short or something – or leaked into the bulb.' He peered up at it more closely. 'Looks like it was used in the Ark! Probably some water leaked into it.'

She was shaking her head. 'No, Ollie. I don't believe it.'

'Darling, calm down.' He put an arm round her. She was trembling. 'It's OK,' he said.

'It's not OK.'

'There's a perfectly rational explanation.'

'I'm fed up with hearing you say *perfectly rational explanation*, Ollie. What's happening in this house is not *perfectly rational*. We're under sodding siege. Or are you in bloody denial?' She was yelling.

He raised a finger to his mouth. 'Ssshhh, don't let Jade hear, I don't want her freaked out.'

'She's up in her room with her music blasting, she can't hear.' Caro stared up at the light socket then down at the glass on the table and floor.

'I'll get a dustpan and brush and the hoover,' Ollie said.

'I'm calling Kingsley Parkin again,' she said. 'I want him to come here now, tonight.'

Ollie scooped up as much of the glass as he could with the brush, helped by Caro, who picked up the larger pieces in her fingers. He wondered whether it would help the situation to call his mother-in-law. But he was nervous that the woman, however well-intentioned, might only make matters worse. He emptied the pan into the rubbish bin, then went through into the scullery, returned with the Dyson, and plugged it in. He heard Caro leaving a second voicemail for her medium client. When she hung up, he switched the machine on.

It roared, and there were tiny clinking sounds as it sucked up the smaller, almost invisible glass splinters. Then, suddenly, there was a loud *click*. The room darkened as the other lights went out. The vacuum cleaner's motor fell silent.

Caro looked at him, more calmly than he was expecting. 'Great,' she said. 'How great is that?'

Ollie grimaced. 'The electrics are totally fucked. They're working on the rewiring but it's a massive job.'

'I don't even know where the fuse box is,' she said. 'You'd better show me in the unlikely case I'm ever brave enough to be here on my own.'

He led her through into the scullery and showed her the

two new plastic fuse boxes the electrician had fitted this week, up on the wall. He reached up and flipped open their lids, and pointed out the master switch at the end of the lower of the two boxes, which was down. He pressed it up and immediately the lights came back on, and they heard the roar of the Dyson starting up.

'They're very sensitive – the RCD trip is a good safety thing.'

She peered along the rows of individual switches.

'When they've finished the rewiring they're going to label each of them.'

'Could that bulb exploding have caused this?' she asked.

He felt relieved that she was taking a rational view. 'Quite possible, yes, or more likely whatever caused the bulb to blow then caused this. I think we're going to find it was water from the flood seeping into the electrics that caused both.'

'I hope to hell you're right.'

'They're due to start the rewiring down here tomorrow,' he said.

As they walked back into the kitchen, she stared warily around. 'I don't know how much more I can take.'

'I'll go up and fetch my laptop and work in here with you until supper.'

'I'd like that.' She looked up at the wall clock, then at her watch. 'Why hasn't Kingsley Parkin called back?'

'You only rang him half an hour ago. Maybe he's with a client. Or out.'

She sat back at the table and began looking at a document. 'Yes, maybe.' She picked up her phone and dialled the vendor's solicitor's home number.

*

Later, lounging back on a sofa in the drawing room, after their supper of stir-fried prawns, they watched another episode of *Breaking Bad*. Caro was more relaxed now.

She looked, for the moment at least, Ollie thought, as if she had put her immediate worries behind her. She was enjoying the programme – as well as the second bottle of wine they were now well into.

But Ollie couldn't concentrate on the television. One moment his eyes were darting warily around, looking at every shadow. The next he was far away. Thinking. Thinking.

Thinking.

The message on his computer screen that had faded within seconds.

Had he imagined it?

Was it possible for a message to appear like that, randomly, and then vanish, given the sophisticated firewall Chris Webb had installed on his computer?

Any more possible than for a photograph of a bearded old man to appear then disappear?

He felt deeply gloomy and his nerves were on edge. This dream home, which they had moved into barely a fortnight ago, had turned into a nightmare beyond anything he could have imagined.

They had to sort it out. They would. They bloody well would. Once the modernization of the plumbing and wiring was complete, maybe it would all settle down. Somehow he had to convince Caro of that.

Somehow he had to convince himself.

Then Caro's phone rang.

She snatched it up off the old wooden trunk that was serving as a makeshift coffee table and looked at the display. 'It's Parkin!' she said. 'My client, the medium.'

Ollie grabbed the remote and froze the screen.

'Hello, Kingsley,' she answered, with relief.

Ollie watched her as she said, 'Oh, I'm sorry. I wondered if I could speak with your partner, Kingsley. My name's Caro Harcourt – we had lunch today – he—'

She fell silent for some moments, listening. Ollie watched her face tighten, then go pale.

'No,' she said. 'No. Oh my God. No.'

She turned and stared at Ollie, looking shocked, shaking her head, then she folded her body over, pressing the phone even closer to her face. 'Oh my God. Oh my God. I'm so sorry. I – I can't believe it. I mean – he seemed so well. Like – this is such a shock. I'm so sorry – I'm so sorry for you – I don't know what to say. Look – thank you for calling and telling me. I'm just so sorry. So sorry. Yes, yes, of course. It's very good of you to have called me. Can you – can you let me know what the arrangements are, in due course. I'd like – I'd like – yes, thank you. Thank you. I'm so sorry.'

She ended the call and sat, gripping her phone in her hand and staring, white-faced, at Ollie. 'That was Kingsley Parkin's partner – girlfriend – whatever. She said –' her voice was choked – 'she said Kingsley collapsed in the street this afternoon, near the Clock Tower. That must have been just after our lunch. He was rushed to hospital – the Sussex County – but the paramedics couldn't save him. She doesn't know for sure yet, but it seems he had a massive heart attack.'

'He's dead?' Ollie said, shocked too, and aware how feeble that sounded.

'Dead.' She pressed the back of her hand against her eyes, dabbing away tears. 'Shit,' she said. 'Shit. I can't believe it. He was so – so . . .' She raised her arms in despair. 'What the hell are we going to do now?'

Ollie looked at his watch. It was 10.15 p.m. Too late to call now. 'I'll call the retired vicar, Bob Manthorpe, first thing in the morning.'

'It's just so bloody freaky.'

'How old was he?'

'Not that old. I don't know – I think he might have had a bit of work done. Around seventy, I'd guess. But he seemed so full of life.'

'It happens,' Ollie said. 'I'm sure it's a shock, but – that's a fair age. Those old sixties rockers did their bodies in with drugs. Besides, things can happen.'

'Sure. Straight after I had lunch with him. Things can happen all right. Don't we bloody know it?'

'That box of documents from your office, darling, about the house – do you remember how far back they go?'

'They date right back to the early sixteenth century when there was a small monastic commune here, established by a group of Cistercian monks. But they then moved away up to Scotland around the early 1750s, which was when this house was built, using mostly the ruins as foundations. Why do you want to know?'

'It was something the old chap I saw this afternoon suggested.' He shrugged. 'I want to go through them all, but some of them are pretty fragile, I'm worried about damaging them. Could you get some copies made at the office tomorrow?'

'Yes – assuming we make it through the night,' she said. Only very slightly in jest.

35

'Great serve! Wow, Ollie, you're playing like a man possessed!' his opponent at the far end of the indoor tennis court, Bruce Kaplan, called out in grudging admiration.

Kaplan rarely gave compliments. Turning forty this year, like Ollie, with a tangle of curly hair, round, wire-framed spectacles and shorts that were far too long, Kaplan looked every inch the technology boffin he was. But he played a ferocious game, moving around the court like lightning, and hating ever to lose a single point, let alone a game. They were reasonably evenly matched, although Kaplan won most of the time – just – because he was the better player, as he liked to remind Ollie. Modesty was not one of Kaplan's handicaps.

It felt good being back on the court after a two-week absence, Ollie thought. Good to be running around, getting the physical exertion that these needle games with the American professor always became, taking every ounce of energy and concentration out of him. And good to have his mind clear, for this hour and a half on court, of absolutely everything except about where to place the ball, getting to it and firing it back, trying to outwit that arrogant whirling dervish at the far end.

But as the game progressed, he found himself drawn more and more into all the problems going around his mind, despite himself. And he kept wondering if Bob Manthorpe had called him back yet. He'd phoned him first thing this morning and left a message.

As Kaplan and he changed ends, Ollie stopped by his bag to have a swig of water and glance at his phone, on silent. No messages. It was now 1.15 p.m. and the retired vicar had not called him back. Hopefully he would some-time this afternoon.

He kept his concentration focused enough to win the first set, narrowly, on a tie-break. He lost the second 4–6, got whopped 0–6 on the third and was 0–3 down in the fourth when their time was finally up.

Before showering and changing, they went to the bar. Ollie ordered pints of lime and lemonade and some sand-wiches for them. Then they carried them over to a table, sat and caught up on each other's news.

'You were doing really well in the first set,' Kaplan said. 'Then you kind of lost the plot. I guess it was superior play that made you realize you really didn't have a chance, heh-heh.'

Ollie glanced at his phone and saw there was still no returned call from Manthorpe. He grinned, downed a large gulp of his drink, then wiped his mouth with the back of his hand. 'I've just got a shitload of stuff on my mind at the moment,' he said. 'Sorry if my game was rubbish.'

'It's always rubbish.'

'Sod you!'

Kaplan grinned. 'So what's on your mind?'

Kaplan worked in the Artificial Intelligence faculty at Brighton University. He had a number of theories that had always seemed to Ollie to be on the wild side of science, but he never dismissed anything. One of Kaplan's interests, and the topic of a book he had written, which had been published by a respected academic imprint, was whether a computer could ever appreciate the taste of food, laugh at a joke or have an orgasm.

'What's your view on ghosts, Bruce?' he asked him, suddenly.

'Ghosts?' the professor repeated, quizzically.

'Do you believe they exist?'

'Absolutely, why wouldn't they?'

Ollie looked at him, astonished. 'Really?'

'I think you'll find a lot of mathematicians and physicists – like me – believe in them.'

'What's your theory – I mean – what do you think they are?'

'Well, that's the ten-gazillion-dollar question.' He laughed again, the short, nervous, 'heh-heh' laugh he regularly made, like a nervous tic. 'Why are you asking?'

'I think our new house may be haunted.'

'I can't remember – did you say it had a tennis court?'

'No, but there's plenty of room for one.'

'Going to put one in?'

'Maybe. A lot of maybes at the moment.'

'And you have a ghost, you think? A smart or a dumb ghost?'

'There's a difference?' Ollie considered Bruce to be super-intelligent and he liked that the scientist always had an unusual – and often unique – perspective on almost any topic they ever discussed.

'Sure! A big difference. Want to tell me about this ghost?'

Ollie told him about the bed turning round, about the spheres, the apparition that Caro and Jade had seen and all the other strange events that had happened. Kaplan listened, nodding his head constantly. When he had finished, Ollie asked him, 'So what do you make of all that?'

Kaplan removed his towelling headband and held it up. 'Do you know what Einstein said about energy?'

'No.'

'He said energy cannot be created or destroyed, it can only be changed from one form to another.' Making a show of it, he squeezed his headband until droplets fell from it on to the white surface of the table. 'See those droplets? That water's been around since the beginning of time. In one form or another molecules of it might have passed through Attila the Hun's dick when he was taking a piss, or gone over the Niagara Falls, or come out of my mother's steam iron. Heh-heh. Every molecule in them has always existed, and always will. Boil one and it turns to steam and goes into the atmosphere; then it'll return with a bunch of others as mist or rain one day, somewhere; it's never going to leave our atmosphere. No energy will or can – you with me?'

'Yes,' Ollie said, dubiously.

'So if you stick a knife through my heart now, killing me, you can't kill my energy. My body will decay, but my energy will remain behind – it will go somewhere – and reform somewhere.'

'As a ghost?' Ollie asked.

Kaplan shrugged. 'I have theories about memory – I'm doing research into it right now – I think it's a big part of consciousness. Our bodies have memory – keep doing certain movements in certain ways – certain stretches – and our bodies find them increasingly easier, right? Fold a piece of paper and the crease remains – that's the paper's memory. So much of what we do – and the animal kingdom does – is defined by memory. If a person spends a long time in a confined space, maybe the energy has memory, too. There's one of the colleges at Cambridge where a grey lady was regularly seen moving across the dining hall. About fifty years ago they discovered dry rot and had to put a new floor in, raising the level about a foot. The next time the grey lady was seen, she was cut off at the knees. That's what I mean by a *dumb* ghost. It's some kind of memory within the energy that remains after someone dies – and sometimes it retains the form of that person.'

'So what's a *smart* ghost?'

'Heh-heh. Hamlet's father, he's an example of a smart ghost. He was able to talk. *Let not the royal bed of Denmark be a couch for luxury and damned incest. By howsoever thou pursuest this act, taint not thy mind nor let thy soul contrive against thy mother aught. Leave her to heaven.*' He grinned at Ollie. 'Yeah?'

'So a smart ghost is basically a *sentient* ghost?'

'Sentient, yes. Capable of thinking.'

'Then the next step would be a ghost capable of actually doing something physical? Do you think that's possible?'

'Sure.'

Ollie stared hard at him. 'I thought scientists like you were meant to be rational.'

'We are.'

'But you're not talking about the rational, are you?'

'You know what I really think?' Kaplan said. 'We humans are still at a very early stage in our evolution – and I'm not sure we're smart enough to get much beyond where we are now before we destroy ourselves. But there's a whole bunch of stuff waiting for us out there in the distant future if we succeed. All kinds of levels – planes – of existence we don't even yet know how to access. Take a simple ultrasonic dog whistle as an example. Dogs can hear it but we can't. What else is going on around us that we're not aware of?'

'What do you think is?'

'I don't know, but I want to live long enough to find out,

heh-heh. Maybe ghosts aren't ghosts at all, and it's to do with our understanding of time. We live in *linear* time, right? We go from A to B to C. We wake up in the morning, get out of bed, have coffee, go to work, and so on. That's how we perceive every day. But what if our perception is wrong? What if linear time is just a construct of our brains that we use to try to make sense of what's going on? What if everything that ever was, still is – the past, the present and the future – and we're trapped in one tiny part of the space–time continuum? That sometimes we get glimpses, through a twitch of the curtain, into the past, and sometimes into the future?' He shrugged. 'Who knows?'

Ollie frowned, trying to get his head round his friend's argument. 'So are you saying that the ghost in our house isn't really a ghost at all? That we're seeing something – or someone – in the past, who's still there?'

'Or maybe someone in the future. Heh-heh.'

Ollie grinned, shaking his head. 'Jesus, you are confusing me.'

'Go with it – sounds like you are on an amazing ride.'

'Tell Caro that – she's scared out of her wits. If you want to know the truth, so am I.'

'None of us like being out of our comfort zone.'

'We are way out of that, right now.'

Kaplan was silent for some moments. 'This bed that you're convinced rotated – in a space that made it impossible – yes?'

'Yes. Either Caro and I are going mental, or the bed defied the laws of physics of the universe.'

The professor reached over and grabbed half a cheese and pickle sandwich, and bit into it hungrily. He spoke as he chewed. 'No, there's a much simpler explanation.'

'Which is?'

'It was a poltergeist.' He grabbed the other half of the sandwich and crammed much of that into his mouth.

'Poltergeist?'

'Yeah. You know how poltergeists work?'

'I've no idea.'

Kaplan tapped the surface of the table at which they were sitting. 'This table's solid, right?'

Ollie nodded.

Kaplan tapped the china plate. 'This is solid, too?'

'Yes.'

'Wrong on both. Solid objects are an illusion. This plate and this table are held together by billions and billions of electrically charged sub-atomic particles all moving in different directions. They're being bombarded, just as you and I are, by neutrino particles that pass straight through them. If something happened to change the magnetic field for an instant and, say, all the particles in the plate moved in the same direction, for just a fraction of a second, that plate would fly off the table. The same could happen to the table, making it fly off the floor.'

'Like the *Star Trek* transporter?'

'Yeah, kind of thing, heh-heh!'

'And that's your theory for how the bed turned round?'

'Like I said, Ollie, we understand so little still. Go with it and accept it.'

'Easy for you to say – you weren't the one sleeping in the room. Want to come and spend a night in there?'

'No thanks!' He laughed again.

36

Ollie stayed talking to Bruce Kaplan at the Falmer Sports Centre, then drove straight to Jade's school to collect her at 3.30 p.m.

She came out with a group of girls, chatting animatedly, and he was happy to see her looking so settled now. As she climbed into the car and kissed him, she waved her good-byes out of the window to the rest of the group and said, 'Dad, is it OK that I invited Laura, Becky and Edie to come to my party as well?'

'Of course.'

As they headed off he asked, 'So how was your day?'

'It was OK,' she said, brightly. 'We had English. Our homework is to write a story. I'm going to write a ghost story!'

He gave her a sideways look. 'A ghost story?'

'I'm going to write about a girl who moves into a new house, and is on, like, FaceTime with her friend, and her friend sees a strange old lady standing behind her!'

'OK,' he said. 'And what does this strange old lady do in your story?'

'Well, I haven't decided yet.'

'Is she a nice ghost or a nasty one?'

'Well, I think she frightens everyone. But they shouldn't

really be frightened because she's not nasty, she can't help being a ghost.'

He grinned, loving her sweet innocence, and relieved about how she was still so unaffected by what had happened in the house. If only he and Caro could feel the same levity. 'Is that what you really think?' he asked.

She nodded. 'I mean, a ghost is just like coloured air, right?'

'That's a good way of describing it!' He was thinking back a few years, to when Jade was about six. She'd had an imaginary friend called Kelly who she played with. Back then she talked about Kelly to himself and Caro constantly. She told them that Kelly lived in her cupboard. He remembered one time asking Jade what her friend looked like and she'd replied that Kelly didn't have a face.

It had spooked them both. Caro had talked about it to a friend who was a child psychologist, who had said it was something quite common. Rather than worry about it, they should relax and show an interest. Eventually she would grow out of it. So they had shown an interest, regularly asking about her. By the time she was eight, Kelly was long forgotten.

'Do you remember Kelly?' he asked.

'Kelly?'

'Your imaginary friend, when you were younger?'

'Oh, Kelly, yes.' She fell silent.

'Is this woman that Phoebe's seen anything like her?'

She shook her head. 'No. Do you like my idea for the story, Dad?'

'Yup. I'd love to see it when you've written it.'

'Maybe!' she said with a mischievous grin.

When they arrived home ten minutes later, there was a large, brown cardboard Amazon box, addressed to Ms Jade

Harcourt, sitting on the hall table, which one of the work-men must have signed for.

Ollie moved to pick it up. 'Looks like a birthday present – I'll take it upstairs and put it with your other presents!'

She shook her head vigorously. 'No, no, no, no, nooooo! I know what that is! I got Mum to order it for me, for my party!' She grabbed it possessively, then ran upstairs, clutching it.

Ollie went into the kitchen; three electricians were at work, and there were reels of cable everywhere. He then climbed the stairs and went into their bedroom. There were dust sheets on the floor, and a solitary workman on a step-ladder was pushing a paint roller across the last segment of unpainted new ceiling. The television was back in place on its mountings on the wall.

'Almost done, Mr Harcourt!' he called down.

'You're a total star!' Ollie replied.

He went back down to the kitchen, and then into the cellar. There was no sign of Bryan, Chris, or any of the other workmen. But several steel Acrow props were in place. As he went back up the stairs into the scullery, Barker appeared.

'Well, the good news is that your house won't fall down this weekend, Ollie,' he said.

'Glad to hear it!'

'This is the bad news.' He handed him an envelope. 'I'm afraid it's the bill. If you don't mind paying it next week, I'd appreciate it – I've paid the engineer out of my own pocket.'

Ollie opened the envelope and stared at it in dismay. It was over three thousand pounds. 'Sure,' he said, thinking about his rapidly diminishing bank balance, and hoping to hell Cholmondley would pay promptly. He planned to invoice him this weekend. 'Of course. I'll do a bank transfer.'

'I'm afraid I've got another bill for you – an interim one from myself – we've had to purchase a lot of materials. I'll pop it in on Monday.'

'Of course,' Ollie said, his gloom deepening.

He made himself a mug of tea and carried it up to his office. There were more bills on his desk from the electrician and the plumber, as well as his annual renewal for the Falmer Sports Centre, a reminder that the car tax was due on Caro's Golf, a second reminder from Caffyns garage that the Range Rover was overdue for a service, and more paperwork that he didn't even want to look at right now.

Bob Manthorpe had still not called him back. He dialled the retired vicar's number again, and once more it went to voicemail. He left another message. Then he checked his emails.

There was an enthusiastic one from Bhattacharya of The Chattri House chain, accepting his quote and confirming he would now like Ollie to extend his brief to include all twelve of his restaurants and his wholesale business. There was also an encouraging one from another classic car dealer, from his visit to the Goodwood Revival, who said Cholmondley had spoken well of Ollie, and asking for a quote for an extensive website. His new business was at least starting to get some traction, he thought, with relief.

He began work on his invoice for the car dealer, detailing the hours spent. But he was finding it hard to concentrate. He kept thinking back to his conversation with Bruce Kaplan, earlier. Energy. There had been a lot about that subject in the *Sunday Times* article. Also Caro had said that her medium client – the now-dead Kingsley Parkin – had talked about energy. In particular, *bad energy*.

Could everything that was going on here be put down

to energy? If they could understand more, they could deal with it, surely?

Out of the window he saw Caro's car approaching. It was just after 5.30 p.m., and pelting with rain. He went down to greet her.

She arrived at the front door holding her briefcase in one hand and a heavy City Books carrier bag in the other. She gave him a kiss then handed him the bag. 'These are the copies of all the deeds that you wanted. My secretary blew some of the older ones up because she said they're not that easy to read – they didn't start typing deeds until after the First World War – before that they're all handwritten. And they are pretty verbose and long-winded. In those days lawyers got paid by the folio, so why use two words when you can be paid for using twenty-two . . . What do you fancy for supper tonight?'

'You!' he said.

'That is always going to be the right answer!' She kissed him again. 'I really fancy a curry. A client who lives near here told me there's a great place that does takeaways in Henfield and another good one in Hurstpierpoint. Shall I see if I can find their menus online?'

'That,' he said, 'is the best plan I've heard all day.'

'It's a beautiful evening in Brighton – I was hoping we'd take a walk around the grounds but look at the rain! Amazing how the weather can be so different here – we're only a few miles away, on the other side of the Downs, and it can be like a different climate sometimes.'

'Glass of wine?'

'I'll wait, I've got some work to do first.'

'OK.' Ollie carried the bag up to his office, pulled out the heavy stack of photocopied documents held together by a thick elastic band, removed the band and placed the sheaf of contents on his desk. He began to read through them. As he went back much further than the O'Hare family, as Caro had said, the deeds became increasingly wordy and hard to decipher. Some were written in copperplate, and others in a variety of semi-illegible handwriting.

He started from the top. The O'Hares, who had bought this place on 25 October 1983, had died on 26 October of that same year.

Before them the owners were Lord and Lady Rothberg, who had bought Cold Hill House on 7 May 1947. Prior to them were a couple called Adam and Ruth Pelham-Rees-Carr. They had bought the property on 7 July 1933. The next previous owners were a Sir Richard and Lady Antonia Cadwalliston, who had bought it in 1927. Before them – and the name stopped him, momentarily, in his tracks – were a Wilfred and Hermione Cholmondley.

With such an unusual surname, were they relatives of his client, he wondered? He would ask him – it would be a lovely coincidence if so.

He wrote down their names and the date of their purchase, 11 November 1911. As he did so, his phone rang. He answered it, expecting it to be Bob Manthorpe. But it was Caro and she was sounding strange.

'Darling, there are two policemen – detectives – here downstairs – who want to talk to you.'

'Police – detectives? What about?'

Detectives. He felt a sudden chill. What had happened, had there been an accident? His parents? Brother or sister?

He went downstairs and saw a tall, thin, unsmiling man in his thirties, in a sharp suit, and a smartly dressed woman in her late twenties, he guessed.

'Good evening,' Ollie said.

The man held up a warrant card. 'Detective Constable

Robinson of Eastbourne CID and this is my colleague Detective Constable Louise Ryman. Mr Oliver Harcourt?'

'Yes.' His mind was whirring. Police always made him nervous.

'We're sorry to intrude on your evening, would you mind if we had a quick word?'

'Not at all – come through.' He led them into the kitchen and ushered them to chairs at the table then, joined by Caro, sat opposite them, moving her laptop and briefcase and the papers she had been working on aside.

'So,' he asked. 'What's the reason for your visit?'

'Would it be correct that you've been in contact with the Reverend Robert Manthorpe of number two, Farm Cottages, Beddingham, recently?' asked DC Robinson, producing a notebook.

'Yes – I – went to see him yesterday.'

'And what time would that be, sir, and what was the reason for your visit?'

'It was mid-afternoon, before I picked my daughter up from school.'

The detective constable made a note in his book.

'Why are you asking?' Ollie looked at the female detective. She stared back at him stonily. DC Robinson gave nothing away, either.

'Can I ask you why you're here? I really would like to know what this is about.'

'If you could just finish answering my question, sir?'

'Maybe you'd like to answer mine?'

'Ols,' Caro cautioned.

'Would you prefer that we arrested you, Mr Harcourt, and brought you in to Eastbourne police station? Or would you like to cooperate?'

Caro interjected. 'As a solicitor I know you have no

grounds to arrest my husband and we are within our rights to ask you to leave.'

'I'll give you one more opportunity to answer my question, Mr Harcourt,' the DC said, blankly and unemotionally.

'I went to see him at the suggestion of our local vicar, the Reverend Roland Fortinbrass,' Ollie replied sullenly.

'May I ask why?'

Ollie hesitated, intensely disliking the officious tone of the man, and the hostile stare of his sidekick. 'Because we are having problems with this house, and I wanted to know if he had heard of any problems here when he was the vicar of this parish.'

'I see,' the detective constable said, writing it all down and flipping over to a new page in his notebook. 'Exactly what kind of problems?'

'We think this house may be haunted.'

Ollie watched him as he wrote this down, interminably slowly, lip-reading as the DC mouthed every word he wrote.

Then Robinson looked back up at him. 'Is anyone able to verify the time you arrived and left the Reverend Manthorpe's house, Mr Harcourt?'

'I picked up my daughter, Jade, from school in Burgess Hill at five thirty that afternoon,' Ollie said.

Again he had to wait while Robinson wrote this down.

'Can you tell us what this is about?' Caro asked. 'Has something happened to the Reverend Manthorpe?'

'Yes,' DC Louise Ryman said. 'Something has.'

37

Caro blanched. Her eyes half closed and Ollie thought for a moment she was going to faint.

Both detectives were staring at her, uncertainly.

'Is he all right?' Caro's eyes darted to each of them in turn, almost feral with desperation.

The detectives shot each other a glance. 'The Reverend Manthorpe's neighbour was disturbed by his dog barking all through the night,' Robinson said, his tone less hostile now. 'When it didn't stop this morning, the gentleman became concerned, as his neighbour always walked it first thing, and he called the police. The Reverend Manthorpe was subsequently found dead in his house, and we're trying to establish who the last person was to see him alive.'

Caro grabbed Ollie's arm to steady herself. 'God. Dead? Not another. I don't think there's much more I can take.'

Both police officers looked at her, curiously.

'My wife's very upset,' Ollie explained. 'Someone she knows dropped dead yesterday – and now this.'

'The Reverend Manthorpe's neighbour is the local Neighbourhood Watch coordinator,' DC Ryman said, also more pleasantly now. 'And he had made a note of a Range Rover car that was parked outside the house the previous afternoon, which we established was registered in your name, sir, although at an address in Carlisle Road, Hove.

We understand from the occupants that you've recently moved?'

'Yes, I meant to update the DVLA – sorry.'

'That is technically an offence, sir, but we'll ignore that. I'm sure that's in process?'

'Yes, I'll get on to it, thank you. Can you tell me anything about how he died?'

'I'm afraid not at this stage, no,' DC Robinson said. 'How did the Reverend Manthorpe seem when you saw him?'

'Fine. Elderly and a bit frail, and he told me his memory wasn't too good, although it seemed pin-sharp to me. I was asking him about his time here in Cold Hill as vicar. He was a very nice old boy. The dog sat on the sofa with me for most of the time. *Jasper.*'

Robinson made some further notes, then he said, 'We won't keep you any more tonight. If we need you to make a statement, could you come into Lewes police station sometime?'

'Yes, of course,' Ollie answered. 'I'm sorry. I'm really very shaken by this. We both are. Please let me know what you find out about – how he died.'

He saw the two detectives to the door and watched them hurry through the rain, climb into a small grey Ford, and drive off. When he returned to the kitchen Caro was still sitting at the table, her face drained of colour, shaking her head.

'What the hell's happening, Ollie?'

He stood behind her, put his arms round her, bent over and kissed her on the forehead, smelling the fragrant scent of her shampoo. 'Just a horrible coincidence. Horrible.'

He kissed her again, went over to the fridge, pulled out a bottle of Sauvignon Blanc and opened it. Then he took two clean glasses out of the dishwasher, poured wine into them and carried one over to Caro. 'Want me to bring my stuff down here and be with you?'

She shook her head and sniffed. 'I'll be OK.'

'Did you find any curry menus?'

'No – if I give you their names, could you have a look and order for me? I've got to get this document done and off.'

'Sure.'

She scrawled the names down on the corner of a sheet of paper, tore it off and handed it to Ollie.

He climbed the stairs up to the first floor, heavy-hearted, carrying his glass of wine. It was just a coincidence, as he'd said. Just a bloody awful coincidence and shit timing. And those bloody detectives, did they need to be so officious?

He heard music pounding from Jade's room at the far end of the landing. Wasn't she supposed to be getting on with her homework? He shrugged. It was Friday night, she had the weekend ahead, but she wasn't likely to get much done with Phoebe staying over. Let it be. He carried on up to his office.

As he went in, he stared at all the boxes he had still to unpack. He would make that his weekend project, he decided. To get the whole sodding room straight, ready for the week ahead. A week of working on The Chattri House and of hard-selling. He stared out of the windows, at the pelting rain and rapidly failing light – 7.30 p.m. and it would soon be dark. Winter was approaching. He looked forward to clear frosty days, and perhaps some snow. To blazing logs in the huge inglenook fireplace in the drawing room. They would put all this shit behind them, they really would.

He sat down at his desk, put the glass down beside him, tapped his keyboard to bring his computer screen to life and entered his password. Moments later all his files appeared, against the plain sky-blue background he had chosen years ago.

Suddenly, the temperature in the room dropped.

He sensed someone standing behind him.

The temperature seemed to drop even further.

He spun round in his chair. But there was no one behind him; no one in the room. The door was closed.

He turned back to the screen, and as he looked at it, all the files once again suddenly disappeared. They were replaced by a message in large black letters.

KINGSLEY PARKIN. THE REVEREND BOB MANTHORPE. WHO'S NEXT? JADE? CARO? YOU?

An instant later the words vanished. Then his normal icons came back into view.

His skin crawled. It felt as if someone was very definitely in this room with him.

Someone.

Or some*thing*.

He could feel he was being stared at. By unseen eyes.

He leaped out of his chair, looking wildly all around him. Up at the ceiling. At the closed door. Around at the walls.

Shivering, he stared back at the screen.

All the file names were there. At the top right was the Macintosh HD icon. Below it, Charles Cholmondley Classics. Below that, Chattri House.

Normality.

He had not imagined it.

'WHO ARE YOU?' he called out. 'WHAT DO YOU WANT?'

Shiver after shiver ripped through him. Then he felt

perspiration running down his face. From being freezing, he was suddenly too hot. He went over to a window and opened it. Felt the cool, damp air on his face. Breathed in the sweet smell of wet grass. His heart was pounding.

There *was* something in here.

He stared up again at the ceiling. At the two bare light bulbs hanging from their cords. He broke out in goose pimples.

He shook his head. *Get a fucking grip!* he said, silently, to himself, thinking back on his conversation with Bruce Kaplan. Energy. Was there some energy thing going on?

Go with it and accept it, the professor had said.

Yeah, right, easier said than done.

There was a *click*. The room darkened and the computer screen went blank. He stared up. Both bulbs had gone out.

Another sodding fuse, he thought.

Hoped.

The goose pimples were spreading and hardening.

He grabbed his wine glass and left the room, slamming the door behind him, and hurried down the stairs to the first-floor landing. When he reached it, he looked back up. The lights elsewhere in the house were on, fine.

He was letting it get to him, and he mustn't, he knew. He had to be strong. The last thing Caro needed was for him to start freaking out.

WHO'S NEXT? JADE? CARO? YOU?

His mind playing tricks on him. That's all it was.

That's all it was.

He carried on downstairs. Totally unconvinced.

38

Graham Norton was strutting around on the television screen, in an outrageous checked jacket of the kind a 1930s racetrack bookie might have worn. He cracked a joke about one of his guests, Nicole Kidman, who they could see in the green room, waiting to come on, and Caro laughed. Seated next to the actress was a young hunk Ollie did not recognize.

He was just pleased to hear Caro laugh. Neither of them seemed to have done much laughing recently.

Their bedroom, reeking of fresh paint and new plaster, was dark, the curtains drawn, the overhead light off. He felt desperately tired, drained. Caro was tired, too. Just a few minutes ago she had dozed off, but now she was awake again, watching the show. He had always loved their Friday nights in, with the whole weekend stretching out ahead of them. A time to unwind with frivolous television. Past favourites had been *Have I Got News For You* and *Peep Show* and now this.

After a few more minutes he found himself drifting off, then woke up with a start, some while later. Graham Norton was teasing an American actor whom Ollie recognized, but could not remember his name.

'Who's that guy?' he asked Caro.

He turned towards her and saw she was asleep again.

'Guy?' she murmured.

'It's OK, doesn't matter. Go back to sleep, babes.'

She blinked, staring at the screen. '*Nightcrawler*. We liked that film.'

'Jake Gyllenhaal,' he said.

'Yes. Shlake Shillenhaal.' Her eyes closed again.

He picked up the remote and turned the television off. Then he reached out and pressed the switch on his bedside light.

As the room became almost pitch dark he rolled over, slipped an arm under Caro's pillow, then nestled up to her and kissed her on the cheek. 'Night, my darling.'

'Love you,' she said.

'Love you so much.'

He lay, holding her, for some minutes, then rolled onto his back. As he did so he heard a faint click, somewhere close by.

Something sent another ripple of shivers through him. He thought back to the message on his screen up in his office, earlier. The feeling that something had been in the room with him.

He had that same feeling now.

Goose pimples spread down his body; hard, icy, sharp as pins.

Right in front of the bed a green light was moving towards them.

Moving closer.

Closer.

Human height. An ethereal human form.

He was gripped with terror.

Closer still.

Closer.

'GO, GO, GO!' he yelled.

'Wasser?' Caro stirred, then she screamed, too, a deep, almost preternatural terror in her voice.

'OLLIE! OLLIE!'

Closer still.

'OLLIE!'

He flung his arm out for the light and sent the lamp, his glass of water and his clock radio crashing to the floor. 'WHO ARE YOU?' he yelled. 'WHAT DO YOU WANT? GO AWAY!'

Then he heard a small voice: 'Wooooooo, wooooo, wooooo! I am the ghost of Cold Hill House!'

Jade's voice, he realized.

Then she said, 'Chill, Dad! Mum! GOTYA!'

An instant later the overhead light came on. He saw Jade holding up a torch inside a transparent green outfit of some kind draped over her head, standing by the door.

'Christ, Jade!' Ollie said.

Jade pulled the robe up and off, revealing her face, and stood there, grinning.

Caro lay still, too stunned to speak.

'That is really, really, really not funny, darling,' Ollie gasped.

Jade jigged up and down. 'I'm the phantom of Cold Hill!'

Ollie moved to get out of bed, then realized he was stark naked. 'Joke over, OK!' he said sternly.

'You scared me,' Caro said. 'You scared the hell out of me, darling.'

'I thought I'd wear this at my party. What do you think?'

'I think you should go to bed, NOW!' Ollie said.

'But do you like it, though, Dad?'

'Go to bed. I'll tell you what I think in the morning.'

'I did scare you, though, didn't I? A bit?'

'Just go to bed, OK?'

'Wooooo, woooooo wooooo!' She pulled the robe over her head again. 'Wooooooo, I am the ghost of Cold Hill House. Woooooooooooo!'

She danced out the room, closing the door behind her.

Ollie turned to look at Caro. She was staring, wide-eyed, up at the ceiling. 'Well,' he said. 'Maybe that's her way of dealing with it. At least she's cool with all that's been happening.'

'Lucky her,' Caro said.

39

Ollie barely slept a wink for the rest of the night. Caro tossed and turned beside him, awake much of the time also. He was thinking. Thinking. Churning everything over.

WHO'S NEXT? JADE? CARO? YOU?

Those words on his screen – where had they come from? He toyed with the possibility that it was another prank by Jade, but dismissed it. There had been something in his office, something dark and malevolent. Something watching him with unseen eyes. Some energy force?

He shivered. He was feeling it again now. That there was something here in this room, up on the ceiling looking down at them. Mocking them.

Hating them.

Or was he just losing the plot?

He took several deep breaths to try to calm himself – and to convince himself that this was all in his mind. He wanted to turn the light on, and go to sleep with it on, something he'd not done since he was a small child. But he did not want to disturb Caro any more than she had been already. And at this moment she seemed to be asleep.

He stared constantly at the green digits on his clock radio: 12.20; 12.50; 1.25; 2.12; 2.45; 3.15.

He had a headache that was becoming increasingly insistent.

Bob Manthorpe.

Dead.

The old cleric had seemed so alive, enjoying retirement. Could there possibly be any link between his visit and the man's death?

Ridiculous. It was just coincidence. Unlucky timing.

He got up, went to the bathroom and swallowed two paracetamol. As he returned to bed, Caro asked him, her voice sharp, clear and wide awake, 'Are you OK?'

'Just a bit of a headache.'

'Me too.'

He felt the bed move as she climbed out, heard her cross the floor, then the bathroom door close. He heard the toilet flush. The sound of running water. Then her footsteps approaching. Then the faint *boing* of a spring beneath them and the bed rocked a little. Sheets rustled.

Some moments later she asked, her voice quavering, 'Ollie, what are we going to do? We can't live like this.'

He reached across, took her hand and held it tight. 'We're going to deal with it. We're going to get it sorted. Trust me. I know what we have to do.'

'I'm scared. I'm scared for Jade, I'm scared for us.'

He swallowed, not wanting to tell her that he was scared too. He had to be strong for her.

And for himself.

3.38; 3.59; 5.03.

The room was filling with a very faint grey light. From outside Ollie could hear the sporadic birdsong of the dawn chorus. Looking at the clock again, he realized he had actually slept for over an hour. He could just make out the ceiling now; the shape of Caro's dressing table; the chaise longue beneath the window, strewn with their clothes. Dawn. A new day.

He felt calmer now. Caro was asleep, breathing deeply. Then, suddenly, he was back in his parents' house in Yorkshire. But on the walls of every small room he entered was written, in thick black letters,

WHO'S NEXT? JADE? CARO? YOU?

Ollie's mother was admonishing him, saying, 'You've brought this on us all. You and your stupid ambitions.'

'Told you so,' his father kept saying, repeating it over and over and over.

In sudden panic Ollie remembered he'd left his laptop, with all the Cholmondley website information to be uploaded, in the garage. He rushed through the door, but the garage was empty. His father followed him and lowered his voice. 'Cholmondley's a crook, you know that, son, don't you? You don't want to get involved with a man like that. Get yourself a proper job. Do something decent.'

'Where's my laptop, Dad, what have you done with it?' Ollie shouted at him. 'Where is it?'

'I've sent it away to have some adjustments made. The truth will set you free!'

Ollie woke with a start, drenched in perspiration. Then relief flooded through him as he began realizing it had just been a dream. He rolled over and looked at the clock.

8.11.

But his sense of relief was short-lived, turning rapidly into gloom as everything started to come back to him. He lay still, trying to think clearly. Remembering the conversation he'd had with the retired vicar on Thursday. Remembering his advice.

Slipping out of bed as quietly as he could, he walked across to the window, opened the curtains a chink and peered out, his eyes raw with tiredness. Tendrils of mist were rising from the lake, and several ducks were moving serenely across the surface, looking purposeful but unhurried. The grass had grown since last weekend and he would need to spend some of today on the ride-on mower, and with the strimmer. But before that, he had other tasks.

He went out and along the corridor to the airing cupboard, changed into his jogging kit, then went downstairs. As he entered the kitchen, he smelled curry. The remnants of last night's meal lay on their unwashed plates, along with the takeaway cartons from the curry house on the draining board. Bombay and Sapphire were standing by their food bowls, meowing. He topped them up, changed their water, cleared away the dishes and cartons, then went through to the scullery, unlocked the back door and stepped out into the cool, fresh morning air. It was a fine, still morning, with an almost cloudless sky, full of the promise of those glorious late summer days that occurred so frequently during September.

He did a few half-hearted stretches then jogged down to the lake, stopping to watch the ducks for some moments. Then he ran round to the far side, through the gate into the paddock, and traversed it, making a trail through the tall, sopping grass. At the far end he let himself out of the gate, then tackled the hill.

He ran some way up it, through a large field, until he had to stop to get his breath back. He gulped down air and then, feeling too exhausted to go on for a moment, he sat down on the wet grass. A bunch of sheep stood some distance away, a few looking at him with mild curiosity, one of them bleating. Ridiculous, he thought. Normally he'd have run all the way up a hill like this with no problem. Maybe the move and all that had been going on in the house had sapped his energy.

He hauled himself to his feet, walked further up the hill and then tried to run, but only managed a few steps before he had to walk again, panting hard up the final steep hundred yards to the summit. The soft contours of the South Downs stretched out for miles on either side of him, to Winchester, eighty miles away to the west, and to Eastbourne, twenty miles to the east. He and Caro had been planning to hike the South Downs Way for years, a week-long trek, and now it was literally on their back doorstep, they had no excuse.

Still breathing hard, his heart racing, he turned and looked back down at the house, directly below him, and at Cold Hill village over to the left. He stared across the rooftops, the gardens, the church spire, the black ribbon of road. The cricket pitch. He saw a large Victorian-looking house, with a swimming pool and tennis court, some distance back from the village, with a long driveway. That must be the Old Rectory that Annie Porter had mentioned, where there were children around Jade's age.

It was so beautiful. So peaceful. It could be paradise here.

If . . .

The morning was very quiet. He heard another bleat, the caw of a crow, the faint, distant drone of a microlight, as he gazed down at the lake, at the green rectangle of the empty swimming pool, the outbuildings, the red-brick walls of their house, the round tower.

Were Caro and Jade still asleep in there?

What the hell else was in there, too?

Thirty minutes later, standing in the shower, half-listening to his favourite radio show of the week, *Saturday Live*, he was feeling a lot better and much more positive. Bruce Kaplan was a smart guy. *Energy*. There was just a load of weird energy in this house, that's all it was. All of it. Energy had to be harnessed, and Bob Manthorpe, on Thursday, had told him something. He hadn't used the word *energy*, but that, Ollie was certain, was what he had meant. He was going to take the old man's advice.

As he walked back out of the bathroom, with a towel round his waist, he saw Caro was awake, lying in bed, checking her messages on her phone.

'Hi, darling,' he said.

'Did you get some sleep?'

'A little, finally.'

'I think we ate too late, I had indigestion,' she said.

'Me too,' he lied, thinking it was better she put their lack of sleep down to something tangible, rather than anything else. He heard a rasping sound.

'I think that's your phone,' she said. 'It vibrated earlier while you were out and woke me.'

'I'm sorry.' He went over to his bedside table and picked the phone up. He always left it on silent at night. Glancing at the display, he could see it was Cholmondley.

He frowned. This was early for his client to be calling – and at the weekend.

He answered, breezily. 'Charles, good morning!'

There was a brief silence from the other end, followed, rapidly, by an explosion of anger.

'Just what the hell do you think you are playing at, Mr Harcourt?'

'I'm sorry?' Ollie replied. 'Playing at?'

'You'll be hearing from my lawyers first thing on Monday, if not sooner. How bloody dare you?'

His heart sinking, and completely confused, Ollie said, 'I'm sorry, Charles – has something happened? I don't understand?'

'You don't understand? Just what the hell do you mean by this – this – outrage? These slurs? Have you taken leave of your senses? What's your game? What's your bloody game?'

Ollie stood, stunned. The towel loosened and began to slip away, but he barely noticed. 'I'm sorry, Charles, please – can you explain?'

He turned away from Caro's curious gaze, and stepped out of the room, the towel falling away completely as he did so, closing the door behind him. 'Explain?' Cholmondley said. 'I think you're the one who'd better explain.'

'I honestly don't know what you're talking about.'

'No? Is this your way of having a laugh? When you get drunk perhaps and start insulting your clients?'

'I can assure you I've done nothing of the sort. Please tell me what you mean?'

'And telling the whole world at the same time? Our arrangement is terminated. You'll be hearing from my lawyers on Monday.'

'Charles, please,' Ollie said, desperately. 'I'm really sorry – what's happened? Please tell me, I'm totally in the dark.'

'In which case you must be suffering short-term memory loss.'

'Memory loss?'

'You're either mental or you have a very strange sense of humour, Mr Harcourt.'

Ollie heard the beeping of an incoming call. He ignored it. 'Look, I'm sorry, I really don't know what you are talking about, or why you are upset.'

'No? Well try imagining how you might feel if I'd sent you an email like that – and copied it to all your rival companies. Eh?'

The phone went dead. As Ollie pressed the button to finish the call his end, utterly baffled and reeling, he heard another voice on the line that he recognized. The cultured Indian accent of Anup Bhattacharya.

'Mr Harcourt?'

'Anup, good morning!' Ollie said, uneasily.

'Just what exactly is the meaning of this?'

If Cholmondley had sounded incandescent, Bhattacharya's tone, although reserved, contained even deeper anger.

'I'm sorry – the meaning of what?'

'I'm just calling to let you know that our business relationship is over, Mr Harcourt. Goodbye.'

The line went dead.

His head spinning, and now even more bewildered, Ollie knelt down, pulled the towel back round his midriff, then hurried along the corridor and up the stairs to his office. *If I'd sent you an email like that . . .*

What the hell was Cholmondley talking about? From time to time his mate Rob Kempson would send him crude or risqué emails containing sexual and sometimes politically incorrect jokes. Occasionally he would forward them on to other friends. Had he forwarded one to Cholmondley and Bhattacharya, by mistake, that had offended them?

He was certain he hadn't. He'd not heard from Rob in over a week or so.

Had he been hacked?

He sat down in front of his computer and logged on. He went straight to his mail box, and then to Sent Mail.

And could not believe his eyes.

There was an email from him, dated *today*, timed at 3.50 a.m., to Cholmondley. It was also openly copied to each of the other classic car dealers whom he had met at the Goodwood Revival last Sunday, whose business cards he had brought back and entered into the computer.

Dear Charles,

Forgive the directness of this email, but I'm a man who has always maintained strict moral principles in all of my business dealings. When you commissioned me to create a new website for your business, I knew you were a bit of a wanker, but not a fraudster as well.

I've now learned that most of the cars that you are advertising on this site do not have the provenance you are claiming. You specialize in cloning exotic cars, providing them with a fraudulent history, and trying to get away with it through your veneer of respectability. What has prompted this email is that you have now asked me to put up an advertisement for the sister car of a 1965 Ferrari GTO that was sold in the USA recently for $35m. You told me this 'sister' car has impeccable provenance. If 'provenance' comes from cannibalizing a couple of written-off Ferraris and manufacturing new 'old' parts in a workshop in Coventry, faking a newspaper article on how this vehicle had been found in a barn, where it had been under a dust sheet for 35 years, and faking its serial numbers and logbook, then fine, this car does indeed have 'provenance'. The provenance of a master shyster who should long ago have been drummed out of the motor trade and put behind bars.

Ollie could not believe his eyes. Who the hell had written this? A disgruntled former employee of Cholmondley? Someone with computer skills who had hacked his computer here? And this person had somehow found a way in through the website?

He looked again at the Sent box, and saw another email, this one to Bhattacharya.

He clicked to open it.

Hey, Anup, you old fraud, you! You put yourself out as a Brahmin in your caste system, but we all know that really you are an Untouchable. From just how many different, honest, hard-working Indians have you stolen the recipes for your restaurants? How many people have bought from your online 'deli' – or should that read, 'Delhi belly'??? – your amazing Prawn Tikka, or Prawn Dhansak, or Prawn Korma, not knowing that those little curly things are not prawns at all, but monkfish cast-offs?

Oh and you have conveniently omitted that your Nottingham restaurant was shut down for three weeks by the Food Safety Officer and you were fined three thousand pounds after a dead rat was found beneath one of your kitchen fridges.

Ollie sat back in his chair. These were emails sent from this computer, no question about that. But who the hell had written them?

His first thought was Jade. But he dismissed that, rapidly. She might have been able to log in – his password, Bombay7, wasn't that difficult to crack. But she could not possibly have known the technical details about the Ferrari.

Neither could she have known stuff about Bhattacharya, true or otherwise.

He phoned Chris Webb and asked his computer guru if it was technically possible for an outsider to have hacked into his computer and sent these emails.

'Well, yes. Not easily, but it could be done.'

Webb asked him to fire up the TeamViewer application, then give him the code and password. Moments later Webb had control of his computer and Ollie saw the cursor moving around the screen.

'I could send any email I wanted, as you, right now,' Webb said. 'So which are the two emails you wanted me to see?'

Ollie temporarily took back control and directed him to them.

For the next few minutes, as he stayed on the phone, Ollie watched the cursor shoot up to the toolbar, then move to System Preferences, and then begin drilling down through the options.

Finally, Webb said, 'I can't find any evidence that you've been hacked – but then again someone good enough to do that would know how to hide their tracks. You sure you didn't get pissed last night and just not remember sending these?'

Ollie thought back to his weird dream during the night. The one where his laptop went missing. Was it possible he could have sleepwalked and sent these emails, composing them from deep inside his unconscious mind? But why on earth would he have done? That made absolutely no sense.

'Chris,' he said, 'why would I want to insult these clients and self-destruct my business?'

'You sure you're OK at the moment, Ollie? You've been seeming pretty stressed these past few weeks.'

'I'm stressed because I'm trying to build my business – and deal with all the work and stuff going on here. But I'm coping with it.'

'I'm sorry, mate, I just don't have any other explanation.'

After ending the call, Ollie sat in silence and read through both of the emails again. So who had done this?

Had the *energy* here driven him to do it?

Had stress?

Without any recollection the next day?

Had he been hacked by a rival?

Cholmondley owed him thousands, and the contract for The Chattri House could have been worth thousands more – money he was depending on.

He had to recover them both.

Somehow.

Somehow he had to come up with a credible explanation – and an apology they would accept.

40

Ollie was surprised to find Jade already up and dressed so early on a Saturday, as he went downstairs, deep in troubled thought, to organize breakfast. The round metal clock, designed to look like it had once adorned the wall of a nineteenth-century Paris cafe, read 10.07. He noticed it was at a slightly wonky angle.

Looking a little chastened, his daughter asked, 'Which pod would you like today, Dad?' She spun the Nespresso capsule dispenser, which she had racked out with a wide variety. Not only was she in charge of making the coffee, she had long taken charge of keeping the dispenser topped up as well.

'The strongest,' he replied. He went to the front door, collected the newspapers, carried them through into the kitchen and laid them neatly on the refectory table. Then he lugged a chair over to the wall, climbed on to it, and reached to straighten the clock.

Jade held up a black pod. 'Kazaar?'

'Perfect.'

'Long or short?'

'Short, and could you make it a double?'

'You'll be flying, Dad!'

He climbed down from the chair, stood back and studied the clock. It was still not completely straight. He climbed back on to the chair again. 'Yep, well I need a major shot of something – I didn't sleep too well last night. Nor did your mum. We had this strange little ghost that came in the room and freaked us out.'

Jade giggled. 'I did fool you, did I? Was my costume quite realistic?'

'It was *very* realistic. And not funny, OK.'

'I thought it was a screeeeaaaaam!!!'

He shook his head, her impish grin making it hard for him to be angry with her. 'And how did you sleep?'

Jade nodded, inserting the pod in the coffee machine, then flipping down the lid. 'OK. You haven't forgotten about Phoebe coming for a sleepover, have you, Dad?'

'And your boyfriend coming tomorrow, too. How is Ruari?'

She shrugged. 'Yep. Fine.'

'Are you still sweet on him?'

She blushed and looked away. 'It's sort of not really like that, Dad.'

'Sort of not really like what?'

'You know – romantic stuff.'

Ollie grinned; his daughter was lifting his gloom, however momentarily. 'So you don't kiss him?'

'Yuk, snog? Yechhhh!'

He adjusted the clock again then stepped back down. The Nespresso machine was rumbling and he smelled the delicious aroma of fresh coffee. Caro came into the kitchen in her dressing gown, yawned, then went over to Jade, glaring at her.

'That was seriously not funny, last night, OK?'

For a moment Jade looked like she was going to answer back. Then, seeing the anger in her mother's face, she bowed her head and said, meekly, 'Sorry.'

'Scrambled eggs, anyone?' Ollie asked. It was one of two things he could cook well. French toast, which Jade loved, was the other.

'Meeeee!' Jade raised her arm in the air. 'Or French toast? Could I have French toast? And will you make that tomorrow, too, for Phebes and me?'

Ollie looked at Caro.

'Just scrambled eggs. A tiny amount.' Then she said, 'Is everything OK? What was that phone call earlier?'

'It was just Charles Cholmondley – he wanted me to add some things urgently to his website.'

'Has something gone wrong?'

'No, it's fine.'

'He owes you a lot of money, doesn't he?'

'Yes, I'm invoicing him for it.'

She gave him a dubious look. 'You told me you thought he was dodgy – is he trying anything on you?'

'No, he's fine.'

Ollie cooked the eggs, but his mind was all over the place. He burned them. Then he burned the French toast, too.

As soon as breakfast was over he hurried back up to his office, then sat down at his computer and logged on apprehensively, ready to screenshot any message that might appear. An instant later everything vanished from his screen, then the words appeared:

**BURNT EGGS. BURNT TOAST.
WE'RE IN A BAD WAY, AREN'T WE, OLLIE?**

His door slammed shut behind him, as if someone had stormed into the room.

He spun round.

There was no one.

All the windows were shut, but in any case, there was no wind. He shivered. He could feel a presence in the room with him. Something above him, staring down.

Then he turned back to the screen. The letters had vanished and all his files were back. He had missed his chance to take a screenshot.

He felt a swirl of cold air around his neck. He looked up, then around. Then he leaned forward and buried his face in his hands for some moments, thinking. Was he losing his bloody mind?

He opened his eyes and stared at the deeds laid out on his desk, and the list of names that he had written down, going right back into the eighteenth century. But he was too distracted by worry to concentrate on them. The more pressing thought was how the hell he was going to recover the situation with Cholmondley and Bhattacharya. He pulled his phone out of his pocket and laid it on his desk. Through the window he saw two rabbits playing on the lawn. What a simple life those creatures had, he thought.

What a bloody mess his own was right now. God, what a mess. Then he looked up at the ceiling, another ripple of shivers going down his back. 'Who the hell are you? What do you want?' he said aloud.

Then he googled *The Reverend Roland Fortinbrass, Vicar of Cold Hill*.

Moments later he saw the man's name and the address and phone number of the vicarage. He dialled it.

The vicar answered promptly. 'Ah, Oliver! How nice to hear from you. You were on my mind – I was thinking of popping up to see you – would this morning be convenient?'

'Please,' Ollie said. 'It would be very convenient. I need to speak to you. I need to ask you something. How soon could you come?'

'Well, in about an hour? Eleven thirty?'

'Perfect, thank you,' Ollie said.

Then the vicar sounded hesitant. 'Is everything all right?'

'Yes – thank you – well – the truth is – no, no, it's not. Everything's not all right.'

41

After he ended the call, Ollie returned to the deeds, trying to decipher the increasingly illegible handwriting as they went back in time, steadily adding more names to the list of past owners of Cold Hill House. But all the time his mind was focusing on what he could say to his two major clients to recover the situation. He would have just one shot with each of them. It was going to need to be good. And so far he was still at a loss about what to say.

If he blamed being hacked he knew, in his current mood, that Cholmondley would blame him for having insufficient firewalls. So would Bhattacharya.

Suddenly he heard the click of the door and spun round. He was becoming scared of his own shadow, he realized. Caro came in, dressed in jeans, cardigan, sleeveless puffa and designer trainers. 'I'm going off to Waitrose in Burgess Hill. Anything you can think of that we need?'

He wondered whether to tell her to wait for the vicar. But then decided it might be better, initially, for him to chat to the man on his own. 'I'll have a think – I'll text you.'

'And anything you fancy for supper tonight?'

He pointed his finger at her. 'You!'

It had been a sign of affection between them, in answer to that question, ever since they had been together. But instead of her usual grin in response, she gave him a wan smile.

'We've got Phoebe with us tonight, and all day tomorrow, too, as well as Ruari for lunch.'

'Avocado and prawns for sups, and some grilled fish if you see something nice and not crazy money in the wet fish department? What about the kids?'

'Jade's said she wants pizza. I'll pick some up. And I have a very specific chocolate ice cream order from her, too. For lunch tomorrow I thought I'd do a roast. Jade says she doesn't want lamb – she's been looking at the sheep on the hill. Beef or pork or chicken?'

'Maybe pork?'

She nodded. Then she walked over and put her arms round his neck. 'What was that conversation with Cholmondley about, darling? If there's a problem it's better if you share it with me.'

Maybe he should tell her, he thought. But she looked so strung out as it was. The vicar was coming shortly and she would be out. He'd seemed a wise man. Perhaps he could talk everything through with him, quietly, on their own. Man to man.

'Everything's OK, darling. We need more eggs, and we're getting low on milk.'

She nodded. 'They're on my list.'

Five minutes later he saw her Golf head off down the drive, and was feeling bad for not telling her the truth. He read again the two emails that had gone to Cholmondley and Bhattacharya.

What the hell could he say to them?

Was something in here, looking down at him, having a laugh?

He returned to the deeds, and twenty minutes later had

completed his search through them. Eighteen people had owned Cold Hill House since it was built, in the 1750s. Next he googled death registry websites, and signed up to one, for a fourteen-day free trial, called DeadArchives.com/uk.

Then he began the laborious task of entering each name in turn, from the bottom up. The information he got back was scant. It gave him the name, address and date of birth and death of each person, though little else. But it was sufficient.

He worked feverishly, speeding up even more as 11.30 approached. He was just looking at the names of the first owner in the nineteenth century when he saw a small, boxy-looking purple Kia coming up the drive.

He logged off then hurried downstairs, along the hall, and opened the front door, in time to see the vicar closing the door of his car, then carefully locking it. The vicar turned to see Ollie standing in the porch, and gave him a wave.

'Would you like a drink?' Ollie asked. 'Tea, coffee?'

'Builder's tea would be very nice – milk, no sugar, thank you.'

Five minutes later they sat in the drawing room, facing each other on sofas. Fortinbrass, in jeans, a sweater with his dog collar beneath it, and stout brogues, sipped the mug of tea Ollie handed him. Ollie gestured to the plate of Penguins he'd laid out on the coffee table between them.

'I'm tempted but I mustn't, thanks – putting on a few too many pounds at the moment.' Fortinbrass smiled. 'This is such a very beautiful house,' he said, looking up at the ornate cornicing moulding around the ceiling, and the grand marble fireplace.

'It will be if we ever get the place finished!'

'Well, I'm sure you will. It reminds me of the house I

grew up in. My father was a vicar, also, and until I was fifteen we lived in a very grand rectory in Shropshire. I say very grand but it was a nightmare in winter because my father couldn't afford to put the central heating on. I'm afraid we're not paid very much in the clergy. We spent the winters of my childhood living in the kitchen, sitting as close to the Aga as we could get.' He sipped his tea, then eyed the plate again, clearly wavering. 'So tell me how you and your family are settling in here? You said on the phone that things were not all right?'

'Yes – I – well, I thought it would be good to have a chat with you on my own.'

The vicar nodded, his face giving nothing away.

'I went to see your predecessor, the Reverend Bob Manthorpe, as you suggested,' Ollie said.

'Good! And how is he?'

'You didn't hear?'

'No – hear what?'

Ollie gave him the news.

'Good Lord, that is so very sad. I only met him a few times. He seemed a very dedicated man – he—'

The vicar stopped in mid-sentence, looking distracted, staring at the doorway into the hall.

Ollie followed his gaze. He could see a shadow moving, very faintly, as if someone was hovering outside the door.

'Do you have someone else living here, in addition to your wife and your daughter – I think you said daughter?'

'Jade, yes, she's twelve. No one else living here.'

Fortinbrass was staring again at the doorway, his face troubled. Ollie could still see the shadow, moving very slightly. He jumped up, strode out of the door and into the hall.

There was no one.

'Very strange,' Ollie said, walking back into the drawing room. Then he stopped in his tracks, and stared.

The vicar wasn't there.

42

Ollie stared around at the empty room. Where the hell could the vicar have gone? There was no way he had gone out of the door. And the windows were closed.

But then he saw the plate of Penguins wasn't on the coffee table either. Nor were their two mugs. The room felt still, as if no one had been in here all morning. He could smell furniture polish and new fabric. The curtains hung motionless.

He frowned. He'd only been gone a few seconds, into the hall. He ran across to one of the bay windows and stared out at the driveway. The vicar's little purple Kia was not there, either. What – what —

He was startled by a patter behind him.

He turned and saw Sapphire walk in, her back arched, looking around as if something was bothering her.

'Hey, girl!' Ollie knelt to stroke her, but before he could touch the cat it let out a meow and shot back out of the room.

Then he heard the sound of a car arriving. Through the window he could see a purple Kia heading up the drive towards the house. He watched in astonishment as it pulled up, then the vicar climbed out, locked the door carefully, and strode towards the front door.

Had he imagined it? Ollie wondered. Was he having a Groundhog Day moment?

Feeling dazed, he walked through into the hall, and opened the front door.

Fortinbrass, dressed just as he had seen him only minutes ago, in jeans, a sweater with his dog collar beneath it and stout brogues, gave him a wave as he came towards him.

'Good morning, Oliver!' he said, giving him a firm handshake. 'Very nice to see you again.'

'Yes,' Ollie said, hesitantly, staring at the man's face for any sign that he was being hoodwinked in some way. But all he saw was a pleasant, open smile.

'Would you like a drink?' Ollie asked. 'Tea, coffee?'

'Builder's tea would be very nice – milk, no sugar, thank you.'

Exactly the words the vicar had just used only minutes ago.

'Righty ho!' He showed Fortinbrass through into the drawing room, then went into the kitchen, still dazed. What the hell was going on inside his head, he wondered? Was he actually going mad?

He opened a cupboard where the biscuits were kept and looked in. There was an unopened family pack of Penguins. He studied the cellophane wrapping, then opened them and placed several on a plate.

Five minutes later he was seated, as before, on the sofa opposite the vicar, with a mug in his hand. Ollie gestured to him to help himself from the biscuits he'd placed on the table between them.

'I'm tempted but I mustn't, thanks – putting on a few too many pounds at the moment.' He smiled and patted his stomach. 'This is such a very beautiful house,' he said, looking up at the ornate cornicing moulding around the ceiling, and the grand marble fireplace.

This was so weird, Ollie was thinking. This was exactly the conversation they'd just had, surely? 'It will be if we ever get the place finished!' he said.

'Well, I'm sure you will. It reminds me of the house I grew up in. My father was a vicar, also, and until I was fifteen we lived in a very grand rectory in Shropshire. I say very grand but it was a nightmare in winter because my father couldn't afford to put the central heating on. I'm afraid we're not paid very much in the clergy. We spent the winters of my childhood living in the kitchen, sitting as close to the Aga as we could get.' He sipped his tea, then eyed the plate again, clearly wavering. 'So tell me how you and your family are settling in here? You said on the phone that things were not all right?'

'Yes,' Ollie finding this extremely weird. '– I – well, I thought it would be good to have a chat with you on my own.'

The vicar nodded, his face giving nothing away.

'I went to see the Reverend Bob Manthorpe, as you suggested,' Ollie said, for the second time in – how many – minutes?

'Good! And how is he?'

'You didn't hear?'

His demeanour darkened. 'No – hear what?'

Ollie gave him the news, again.

'Good Lord, that is so very sad. I only met him a few times. He seemed a very dedicated man – he—'

The vicar stopped in mid-sentence, looking distracted, staring at the doorway into the hall.

Ollie saw the shadow moving again, as if someone was

hovering outside the door. His skin crawled with goose pimples.

Still staring at the door, Fortinbrass asked, 'Do you have someone else living here, in addition to your wife and your daughter – I think you said daughter?'

'Jade, yes, she's twelve. No, no one else living here.'

Ollie could still see the shadow, moving very slightly. He jumped up, strode out of the door and into the hall again.

There was no one.

'Very strange,' he said, walking back into the drawing room. To his relief the vicar was still there, and reaching for a Penguin.

'Can't resist these, I'm afraid,' he said. 'What was it Oscar Wilde said about temptation?'

'I can resist everything except temptation,' Ollie prompted.

'Yes, so true.' The vicar unwrapped the end of his biscuit and bit a small piece off. 'These always remind me of my childhood,' he said after he had swallowed.

'Me too.'

Ollie was feeling slightly disassociated, as if he wasn't actually fully in his body, but was floating somewhere above it.

Suddenly the words of Bruce Kaplan, after their tennis game yesterday, came back to him.

'*Maybe ghosts aren't ghosts at all, and it's to do with our understanding of time . . . What if everything that ever was still is – the past, the present and the future – and we're trapped in one tiny part of the space–time continuum? That sometimes we get glimpses, through a twitch of the curtain, into the past, and sometimes into the future?*'

But they were in the present now, weren't they? The vicar took another bite of his chocolate biscuit. Then another. Ollie stared back at the doorway. The shadow was there again, just as if someone was hovering outside.

'Who's that out there, Oliver? Is there someone who wants to join us?'

'There's no one there.'

Both men stood up and walked to the doorway. Fortinbrass stepped out, followed by Ollie. The hall was empty.

They returned to their seats.

'It's why I called you,' Ollie said, and glanced out of the window, hoping Caro would not return until they'd finished this conversation. She would be an age, he knew – it would take her a good couple of hours to finish her shopping. But nevertheless he worried.

'Please feel free to speak openly. Tell me anything that's on your mind.'

'OK, thank you. When I went to see Bob Manthorpe on Thursday, he told me some quite disturbing rumours about this house. He said that every county in England has a diocesan exorcist – or Minister of Deliverance, I believe you call them? Someone to whom clergymen can turn when something happens within their parish that they cannot explain. Is that correct?'

Fortinbrass nodded, pensively. 'Well, broadly, yes. You want me to see if I can arrange someone to come here?'

Ollie watched the vicar's eyes move back to the doorway. The shadow was still there, lurking.

'Tell me something, you seem a very rational man to me, Ollie. Are you sure you want to open yourself up to this? Might it not be preferable to close yourselves to whatever is bothering you, ignore it and wait for it to go away?'

'You've seen that shadow out there, right, Vicar – Roland – Reverend?' He pointed at the doorway. There was nothing now.

Fortinbrass smiled, amiably. 'It could just be a trick of the light. A bush moving outside in the wind.'

'There is no wind today.'

Fortinbrass cradled his mug and looked thoughtful.

'I'm an atheist, Roland. I had religion drummed into me so much at school. All that Old Testament stuff about a vengeful, sadistic, egotistical God who would kill you if you didn't swear undying love to him? What was that about?'

The vicar studied him for some moments. 'How God presents himself in the Old Testament can indeed challenge all of us, I can't deny that. But I think we need to look to the New Testament to find the true balance.'

Ollie stared hard back at him. 'Right now I'm prepared to accept anything. We're living a nightmare here. I feel like we're under siege from something malign.' He glanced up, warily, at the ceiling, then his eyes darted around at the walls, the doorway. He shivered.

Fortinbrass set his mug down on the table and placed the Penguin wrapper next to it. 'I'm here to try to help you, not to judge you. Would you like to tell me exactly what has been happening?'

Ollie listed everything he could remember that had happened. His mother-in-law's first sighting of the ghost. His father-in-law's encounter with her. Caro's sighting of her. Jade's friend's sighting. The spheres he had seen. The bed rotating during the night. The taps. The photograph of Harry Walters. Parkin then Manthorpe being found dead. The computer messages. The emails to his clients. He omitted only the curious déjà vu he had experienced over the vicar's arrival this morning.

When he had finished he sat back on the sofa and stared, quizzically, at the clergyman. 'It sounds mad, I know. But, believe me, it's true. All of it. Am I insane? Are all of us?'

Fortinbrass looked deeply troubled. 'Look,' he said, 'I believe you.'

'Thank God,' Ollie said, feeling a sense of deep relief.

'I'll put in a request. I'm not sure of the formalities, but I will ask.'

'There must be something the church can do,' Ollie implored. 'We can't go on like this. And we can't leave – if we could, we'd be out of here like a shot. But there must be something – something you can do to help us, surely?'

An hour later, as Ollie stood in the front porch watching the vicar's car heading away, Caro's Golf appeared.

'Hi, darling,' she said, as he opened her car door for her. 'Who was that?'

'The vicar,' he said.

'And – what did you tell him?'

'Pretty much everything.'

She walked round to the rear of the car and opened the tailgate. The boot was crammed with white and green Waitrose carrier bags.

'I'll help you in with everything,' he said.

'So what did the vicar say? Was he sceptical or helpful?'

Ollie hefted out four heavy bags. 'He saw something himself, while he was here.'

Following him into the house, holding a clutch of grocery bags herself, she said, 'Did he have a view on it?'

'He took it seriously.'

'Great,' she said, sarcastically. 'That makes me feel a whole lot better.'

They dumped the bags on the refectory table. Ollie took

her in his arms. 'We'll get this sorted, darling, I promise you. In a year's time we'll be looking back on all of this and laughing.'

'I'm laughing right now,' she said. 'I was laughing all the way down the supermarket aisles. Just how much fun has our life become, eh?'

43

Early that afternoon Ollie glanced out of the tower window to the north, and for some moments watched Jade and her friend, Phoebe, standing at the edge of the lake looking playful and happy, throwing something – bread perhaps – to the ducks.

Throughout his own childhood, which had not been particularly happy, he had longed to be an adult and get away from the dull and stultifying negativity of home. But right now he envied them the innocence of childhood. Envied them for not having to deal with arrogant shits like Cholmondley. He knew childhood and growing up were fraught with their own traumas, but with everything that was bombarding him right now, he'd trade places in an instant.

What had the vicar's first appearance been about? He'd seen him, he'd spoken to him, and yet – suddenly he was gone. Then reappeared. He thought back again to his conversation after tennis with Bruce Kaplan, trying to make sense of his theory. *'We live in* linear *time, right? We go from A to B to C. We wake up in the morning, get out of bed, have coffee, go to work, and so on. That's how we perceive every day. But what if our perception is wrong? What if linear time is just a construct of our brains that we use to try to make sense of what's going on? What if everything that ever was, still is – the past, the present and the future – and we're trapped in one tiny part of the space–time continuum? That sometimes we get glimpses, through a twitch of the curtain, into the past, and sometimes into the future?'*

Had he been through some kind of time-slip earlier on? Or was his mind playing tricks on him, somehow reversing time inside his head?

Or was he cracking under the stress of everything?

Suddenly there was static crackle from the radio, which he had on in the background for company, and he heard the unmistakeable, deep, sonorous voice of Sir Winston Churchill.

'Upon this battle depends the survival of Christian civilization. Upon it depends our own British life, and the long continuity of our institutions and our Empire. The whole fury and might of the enemy must very soon be turned on us. Hitler knows that he will have to break us in this island or lose the war. If we can stand up to him, all Europe may be freed and the life of the world may move forward into broad, sunlit uplands.' The static increased steadily in volume, drowning out some of Churchill's words.

Shit, Ollie thought. Was he now inside some weird time loop?

Then he heard the voice of a radio presenter. 'Well, Bill, can you think of any UK politician today, in any party, who would have that same quality of leadership that Churchill displayed? Anyone with those powers of oratory?'

Ollie switched the radio off then turned back to his desk and his most pressing problem. Cholmondley and Bhattacharya must know, like everyone, surely, that there were some weird and nasty people out there on the internet. Trolls. Facebook bullies. Malicious hackers. Did a disgruntled customer have a grudge against Cholmondley? Was a rival jealous of Bhattacharya's success?

Or was it someone with a grudge against himself?

Who?

He really could not think of any enemies. Everyone had been happy with the sale of the website business. He was treating all the tradesmen at the house decently. He'd never screwed anyone over. Why would someone want to do this?

He stared, gloomily, at the screen. On it was the screen-saver image of a close-up of Caro and Jade's smiling faces pressed together, cheek to cheek. Normally, seeing it always made him smile, but at this moment he could find nothing to smile about.

His door opened behind him and Caro stuck her head in.

'I'm just off to pick up Jade and then collect Phoebe,' she said. 'Be back in about an hour. Anything you need while I'm out?'

'Pick up Jade?' he said, puzzled. 'What do you mean? And Phoebe?'

'Yes, picking Jade up from her riding lesson – then we're going into Brighton to collect Phoebe from her parents.'

'*Riding lesson?*'

'Yes.'

He shot a glance through the window towards the lake. There was no sign of Jade or Phoebe.

'You're taking Jade or you're *picking her up*?'

'I'm picking her up.' She gave him a strange look. 'Are you all right, Ols?'

'All right? I – yes – about as all right as it's possible to be at the moment. Why?'

'We talked about it a couple of days ago – I told you I

was going to try to book her into a riding school in Clayton, just a few miles away.'

He swivelled his chair to the left and looked out of the window again towards the lake. Jade and Phoebe had been playing there just a couple of minutes ago, he'd been watching them. Was this the start of a nervous breakdown? Or something even worse?

'When – when did you take Jade to the riding place?'

Caro looked at her watch. 'Over an hour ago. I'm going to have to rush, I'm late.'

'Drive safely,' he said, lamely. 'You're picking up Phoebe, too?'

'Yes, that's what I said.'

'She's not – already – sort of here or anything?'

Caro frowned. 'Have you been drinking?'

'No!'

'You're behaving very oddly. I'll see you in a bit, OK?'

He was staring back out through the window at the vast lawn, which he would have to mow tomorrow, and at the ducks on the lake. There was no sign of Jade or Phoebe. No children. No humans. Nothing.

He'd imagined the vicar this morning. Now his daughter and her friend?

His computer made a barely audible ping. An incoming email.

He hit the keyboard and instantly held his breath as he saw the name. It was from Cholmondley. Perhaps, he thought, with hope momentarily rising, the classic car dealer had found out the source of the toxic email sent to him earlier, and was writing now to apologize for his outburst? After all, he was a businessman, and however angry he might have been, Cholmondley would know he had to keep his website up and running – and for that he needed him.

Then, as he opened the email, his heart sank even lower.

There was a short message from Cholmondley at the top, with a longer one from himself beneath, sent from his personal email address, with his electronic signature, and timed and dated just over thirty minutes ago.

Sent from this computer.

Cholmondley

I imagine you've been waiting all day for a grovelling apology. Well, so sorry not to oblige, dear boy, but I just wanted to let you know that I stand by every word in my earlier email. I despise you, you arrogant little shit, with your natty bow tie. Just found out about your criminal record, too. Tut, tut, tut! You kept that one a secret, didn't you? My oh my, you are a dark horse! Bad boy, you got caught turning the odometers back on second-hand cars. Made to sit on the Naughty Step for that one, weren't you? Eighteen months in Ford Prison. I'm afraid I cannot take the reputational risk of dealing with someone of your background.

I have sent you in a separate email all the codes and files you will need for someone else to take over the management of your website in a smooth – quite seamless – transition.

Oliver Harcourt,

CEO, Harcourt Digital Solutions Ltd

Once again, he saw to his horror that it was copied to the same wide number of Cholmondley's rival dealers. And all the files for the website, which would have been the only leverage he had to get paid by the man, had been handed

over. So now he had no hold over him. And reading Cholmondley's reply, it was even clearer than this morning that
he would never see one penny of the money he was owed.

Dear Mr Harcourt

This email is outrageous. I will hold you personally liable
for any sales I lose through your vile and deeply libellous
communications today. For the record I've never been
charged with, or convicted of, any of the offences you
allege. I have no criminal record and I've never been to
jail. You'll be hearing from my lawyers on Monday and
you will be a very sorry man.

C. Cholmondley

44

Ollie sat, stunned, staring at the email. He was utterly bewildered and feeling sick deep inside. And close to tears. Just what the hell was happening? He had imagined the vicar; he had imagined Jade and her friend in the garden. Was he now sending emails that he had no recollection of? Should he go and see a doctor?

Another email pinged in, and his spirits sank even lower still when he saw it was from Bhattacharya.

He could scarcely bring himself to open it. His hands hovered over the keypad, his fingers trembling. His whole body was shaking. Normally when he was stressed he'd go for a run or a bike ride. But he felt too sapped right now to do anything other than sit and think and stare.

Chris Webb would be able to find out where the emails had really come from, wouldn't he? That would be the solution. Get him to show they were being sent from someone outside, who was using this address, and then he could go back to Cholmondley and Bhattacharya.

Unless.

But he didn't want to go there. Not down that line of thought.

He did not want to entertain the possibility that he might have been the sender.

Or someone or some*thing* here in his office with him.

He looked up at the ceiling with a start, as if he again sensed something there, looking down, mocking him.

Then he opened the Indian restaurateur's email. It was every bit as bad as he expected. A litany of food hygiene regulations each of his restaurants had allegedly broken. And a livid reply from Bhattacharya.

For a moment he thought he was going to throw up at his desk. He closed his eyes and took several deep breaths, trying to think clearly. Then he dialled Chris Webb.

'Chris, I have an absolute emergency here. There have been more emails to those same two clients, and they've been copied to other potential clients. You've got to help me, we have to do something – my business is being destroyed.'

'More emails?'

Ollie could hear a roar in the background, as if Webb was watching a football or perhaps rugby match on television. 'Yes, in the past hour – while I've been sitting in front of my bloody computer. I just don't know what's going on. You've got to help me, please, could you come over?'

'OK.'

'I'd really appreciate that. How soon can you come?'

'I'll be with you in about forty-five minutes. Meantime, what I suggest you do is disconnect from the internet – or, even better, switch it off completely until I get there. Can you do that?'

'Yes, right away, thank you.'

Ollie stared at the keyboard, then at the screen, as if scared something new might have appeared while he'd been talking to the computer guru. He did as instructed, selected Shut Down from the Apple menu and clicked on it.

He waited until the screen was dark and the machine was silent, then stood up, went downstairs and out into the garden, feeling desperately in need of some fresh air to try to clear his head. The sun in the clear blue sky barely registered, nor the warmth of the air, or anything around him as he walked down towards the lake, his heart like a massive weight inside his chest. He felt as if all the energy had been sucked out of him and he was just a dark, discarded husk.

He stood and stared bleakly at two mallards, a male and female, paddling seemingly aimlessly across the water. Just what the hell was happening to them all? Had they made a terrible mistake moving here – not just taking on more than they could cope with financially, but coming into some unfathomable darkness?

Should they just move out and put the place on the market? It was something he had considered several times in the past few days. And yet, it seemed absurd to give in, and give all this up, just because of – if Bruce Kaplan was right – some energy at large in the place. Both Bob Manthorpe and Caro's strange client who had died, had advised requesting the diocesan exorcist – Minister of Deliverance – to come and clear the house. Maybe that was all it needed. And everything would be OK after that. The vicar had said this morning he would put in a request to the Sussex Minister of Deliverance and get back to him as quickly as he could.

His phone vibrated in his trouser pocket and began ringing. He pulled it out and saw a mobile number on the display he did not recognize.

'Hello?' he answered.

'Ah, Oliver, is this a good moment?'

It was Roland Fortinbrass.

'Yes, it is, thank you.'

'Well,' he said. 'I've got some good news and some bad news.'

45

An hour and a half later Chris Webb was seated in Ollie's office, in front of his computer. Ollie hovered anxiously behind him, peering over his shoulder at the screen. It was filled with a maze of rows and columns of numbers and letters that were meaningless to Ollie, but Webb was studying them with fierce concentration, emitting a string of comments out loud as he did so.

'What the—? Oh, I see . . . But how the hell did you get there? What? What's this?'

'What's what?' Ollie asked.

'I mean, that just shouldn't be there!'

'What shouldn't be?'

'Have you been in here changing any settings?'

'No, why would I?'

'Someone has,' Webb said.

'Someone? That's not possible, Chris – I'm the only person who would ever touch this computer.'

Webb grimaced. 'Could just be a Mac glitch – I've got a few clients where something similar's happened recently on the latest operating system – settings changing of their own accord.'

'Or could this be evidence of the hacker?'

Webb lifted the large mug of coffee Ollie had brought him, and drank some. 'Well, this wouldn't give anyone a pathway in. I think it's more of an operating system glitch. Jade wouldn't have been on this?'

'Absolutely not. I'm certain.'

'You see, I can't find any footprints at all. I can see the tracks I left earlier, when I connected through TeamViewer, but there's no sign at all of any unauthorized user having been here.'

Distracted by movement through the window to his right, Ollie saw Caro coming up the drive in her Golf, with Jade beside her and a figure, presumably Phoebe, on the back seat.

'It's a mystery,' Webb said. 'I'm sorry, I'm baffled. I don't know what to suggest. We could put in an extra firewall and see if that stops it.'

'Chris, I've got to do something to salvage the situation. I can't afford to lose these clients.'

'Of course.'

'OK, I've had an idea,' Ollie said, suddenly brightening up a little. 'Cholmondley and Bhattacharya aren't aware of each other. So, how about you write an email to each of them, explaining that you are my IT manager and that these emails have been sent from some malicious hacker who must have a grudge against them?'

Webb looked dubious.

'I'll compose it and give you the wording. All you have to do is just sign as yourself, as my IT manager. Then I can follow it up by phoning them, when hopefully they've calmed down.'

'OK, sure. But—'

'But?'

'I'll write it, sign it, whatever, but I'm not sure it's going to be the end of it.'

'What do you mean?' Ollie asked.

'What I mean is I don't think you've been hacked, mate.' He stared at Ollie.

'So who do you think wrote these?'

'Someone in this house.' Webb raised his arms. 'Look, I know that sounds crazy to you, but I really don't think you've been hacked. Unless it's by someone a lot cleverer than me – and that, of course, is always a possibility!'

'Chris,' said Ollie, becoming impatient with the man's intransigence about hacking, 'those last two were sent while I was sitting here at my desk. Jade was out at a riding lesson and Caro sure as hell didn't come in and start typing under my nose without my seeing her.'

'All right, emails can be programmed to be sent at a scheduled time. Perhaps someone typed these during the night, when you were asleep, scheduling them to go at a specific time. Either by accessing this computer or by hacking it.'

Ollie shook his head. 'Who the hell would do that, Chris?'

'I don't know. Have you made any enemies?'

'No.'

Could it possibly be Jade, Ollie wondered, lapsing into thought? Sleepwalking and now sleep-typing? She was pretty computer savvy, it wasn't impossible. Yet the language in those emails, the technical information about the Ferrari, the information about the restaurants, she couldn't possibly have known all that. But who had? And equally importantly, why had these emails been sent? By someone out to destroy him, that was evident. But who, he thought again? Who the hell could it be – and why?

'I honestly can't think of anyone I've upset. This is just a complete mystery.'

Webb gave him a sideways look. 'Maybe it's that pesky ghost of yours again!'

Ollie did not smile.

46

'So what did the vicar say, Ols?' Caro asked, perching on the edge of the battered leather armchair in which Ollie liked to sit and read. At the moment, like almost every other inch of space in his office, it was covered in files he'd not yet put away into the cabinets, and framed pictures he'd not had the time to hang.

Chris Webb had just left, and the fresh emails to Cholmondley and Bhattacharya, bearing his signature as IT Manager, had been sent. Hopefully, when Ollie followed them up, perhaps later today – or maybe leaving it until tomorrow – they would listen and accept his explanation. It was credible. If he used all his powers of persuasion and charm, they would surely believe him.

They must.

'The vicar's spoken with the Minister of Deliverance for Sussex, and they're both going to come here on Monday around six, after you're back from work, darling,' he replied.

'Good,' she said, and seemed a little relieved. 'What's this Minister of Deliverance – exorcist – man going to do? Walk around the house swinging a smoking censer full of incense, muttering incantations?'

Ollie smiled, glad that despite everything she'd not lost her sense of humour. 'I didn't get the impression it would be quite that dramatic. He wants to come and have a talk to us so he can get an idea of what's going on, and how to deal with it. From what the vicar told me, he sounds a bright and very grounded guy. And not in any way a sanctimonious "Holy Joe" type. Apparently he's highly educated, an Oxbridge double first, with a background in psychology before becoming ordained.'

'How did the vicar – what's his name – Rosencrantz?'

'Fortinbrass. Roland Fortinbrass.'

'I knew it was something out of *Hamlet*. How did he sound? Is he confident this minister will be able to deal with everything here?'

'Yes.'

'What did Fortinbrass say – I mean, did he have a view himself?'

Ollie did not reply immediately. Fortinbrass had said quite a lot on the phone earlier. Delivering the good news and the bad. The good news was that the Minister of Deliverance had agreed to come. The bad was how much Fortinbrass had found out about this house's very long history of disturbances. Ollie remembered the former vicar, Bob Manthorpe, mentioning it, but quite dismissively.

'*Yes. I'm afraid the house has had a few tragedies. But don't be put off. Some of the older folk in the village used to talk a lot of rubbish about the place being cursed or damned. But the reality is any house of that historic age is more than likely to have had its fair share of deaths.*'

Had Manthorpe just been trying to reassure him, and hide what he really knew? Fortinbrass had certainly not minced his words earlier, as he related the salient points of his conversation with the Minister of Deliverance to Ollie.

There had been exorcisms carried out here by the church in the distant past, with records from the Bishop of Chichester's office, under which diocese it fell, going back to the late eighteenth century. Back in Victorian times, it seemed, Cold Hill House was known to locals as the *Death House*. Many believed it was cursed and many would not go near the place. It was also rumoured that some clergymen during the previous two centuries had refused to go and help when requests for assistance had been made. Of course, the small rural community rumour mill was bound to have exaggerated everything.

But, Ollie knew, rumours always began from some foundation, some grain of truth, however small. And at this moment he didn't need a rumour mill to tell him things were not right in this house.

Still, there was nothing to be gained from telling Caro what Fortinbrass had said. That would just worry her even more over the weekend. The visit from the two clergymen on Monday evening would, hopefully, be the turning point here. But what disturbed him most was that there had been such a history of past exorcisms. Why? What had happened to set all this off?

He felt a fool for not having found out any of this history before going ahead with the purchase of the house. It had never occurred to him. Yet even if it had, how could he have found out any of this dark past? He'd tried googling *Cold Hill House* before their first viewing, but nothing significant came up. There were several entries for the house, giving its postcode, the last purchase price paid for it, a listing under Zoopla and one under Rightmove, but nothing of significance about its past. No history of any gruesome events.

'No,' Ollie replied, finally. 'Fortinbrass didn't have a view. But he said he was confident this man – minister – would sort the house out for us. Whatever that means.'

Caro shrugged. 'What about contacting a medium? Perhaps a psychic, someone like poor Kingsley Parkin, could tell us what's going on?'

'I've thought about that too, but I'm not sure it's a good idea to – I don't know – dabble ourselves. Not until we've talked to this clergyman.'

'What's his name – this Super-Cleric Ghostbuster?'

He grinned. 'Benedict Cutler.'

'Benedict. Sounds the perfect name for a man of the cloth,' she said. 'I'll go down and cook the pizza for the girls. I've bought a load of Yolande's yummy cupcakes at Jade's request to put on a nice display for Ruari tomorrow. Want me to bring anything up?'

'I'm fine, thanks, I had some tea earlier when Chris Webb was here.' He pointed at the two empty mugs.

She scooped them up, then kissed him. 'We're going to be all right, Ols, aren't we?'

'Of course we are.'

He watched her leave the room. Then, as she closed the door behind her, he heard the ping of an incoming text, and looked at his iPhone. And froze as he stared at the words.

OH NO YOU'RE NOT!

47

Instantly the words disappeared. Ollie checked his phone, but there was no new message. There was no trace of the words.

Where had it come from?

He glanced, warily, up at the ceiling, his eyes jumping around. How much else had he imagined today?

He wondered whether to call Chris Webb and tell him what had happened and to see if he could find the source of the words. But he felt that Webb's patience was wearing thin. He could tell from the man's attitude that he was starting to have doubts about what was going on. Doubts about Ollie's sanity? Yet Webb had seen the photograph of the old man, before it had disappeared, hadn't he?

Hopefully, on Monday evening, Fortinbrass and the Minister of Deliverance would be able to help them.

To try to distract himself he turned his attention back to his task of working through the deeds, sometimes having to use a magnifying glass to decipher the handwriting, which was badly faded on some documents, listing each of the previous owners of the property.

What he was coming up with was not looking good. And over the course of the next hour, it looked even worse.

He doggedly continued typing each past owner's name into Google, but there were no matches of any significance

– just several links to various relatives, and one to an arts foundation in the Gambia. It surprised him a little, as this was such a substantial property and several of the owners had grand names.

An hour later he reached the final name on the list: the first owner of this house, Sir Brangwyn De Glossope. The name that the old vicar, Bob Manthorpe, had struggled to remember.

He entered that into Google, and moments later he was staring at a small sepia photograph of the front of Cold Hill House. It was beneath a listing on a website of a book titled *Sussex Mysteries*, which had been published by a small press in 1931 and was written by an author called Martin Pemberton. Ollie read the two brief paragraphs beneath.

Cold Hill House built to the order of Sir Brangwyn De Glossope, on the site of monastic ruins, during the 1750s. His first wife, Matilda, daughter and heiress from the rich Sussex landowning family the Warre-Spences, disappeared, childless, a year after they moved into the property. It was her money that had funded the building of the house – De Glossope being near penniless at the time of their marriage.

It was rumoured that De Glossope murdered her and disposed of her body, to free him to travel abroad with his mistress, Evelyne Tyler, a former housemaid in their previous home, who subsequently bore him three children, each of whom died in infancy. Evelyne subsequently fell to her death from the roof of the house. Did she fall or was she pushed? We'll never know. De Glossope was trampled to death by his own horse only weeks after.

Ollie found himself looking up at the ceiling again, uneasily. *Evelyne Tyler.* Was it her ghost that was causing all this mischief? Angry at what had happened? Or Matilda De Glossope – formerly Warre-Spence?

He googled the names further. There were several entries about the Warre-Spence family, but all of them referring to relatively recent events. Nothing more on the history.

Next on the internet he searched for the lifespan of human beings in the eighteenth, nineteenth and twentieth centuries. In the eighteenth century, he read, although life expectancy was only forty years old, if people survived childhood and their teens, they had a good chance of living into their fifties or sixties, or even older. For his purposes at the moment, that was not good news. Life expectancy steadily increased through the twentieth century, to the current level in the UK of seventy-seven for a man and eighty-one for a woman.

Then he looked back down at his desk. At the stack of deeds, and the list of names he had written on the A4 pad beside them. And the dates he had obtained from DeadArchives.com/uk. The dates of their births and their deaths.

Sir Brangwyn De Glossope had died at the age of thirty-nine. Not one of the past owners of this house, subsequently, had ever reached their fortieth birthday, except for the Rothbergs, neither of whose lives had been much worth living past it.

Shit. He felt cold suddenly, and shivered. He would be forty himself, in just over a week's time.

He stared out of the window. All the warmth and colour seemed to have faded from this glorious afternoon, like a photograph that had been left in direct sunlight for too many years. Then, as he looked down towards the lake, he saw Jade and Phoebe standing at the edge of the water, looking playful and happy, throwing something – bread perhaps – to the ducks.

Exactly as he had seen them earlier, when Jade had been out having her riding lesson and Phoebe had been at home with her parents.

48

'I found some interesting stuff on the internet about ley lines, Ols,' Caro said, out of the blue. Having put the roast in the oven, they were strolling around the lake, watching two ducks waddling across the little island, through the fronds of the willow tree. A solitary coot, with its shiny black body, white beak and ungainly legs like hinged stilts, hurried urgently through the long grass in front of them and into the murky water, as if it was late for a meeting.

Ollie's arm was round her waist. It was late Sunday morning and the weather was on the turn. The sky was overcast and heavy rain was forecast for the afternoon; gales were expected over-night. The Indian summer had come to an abrupt end and there was a chill in the air. Autumn was arriving today. A flock of migrating birds winged by, high overhead.

'Ley lines?' Ollie replied, distractedly. He was finding it hard to think clearly about anything. He'd barely slept during the night, fretting about Cholmondley and Bhattacharya, his mental state and the mounting costs of making this place habitable. He'd gambled on building his new business sufficiently during the course of the next twelve months to be able to cope with the bills.

Another thing was worrying him, too. He'd gone for an early-morning run up to the top of the hill again, and this time he'd only got a very short distance up it before having to sit down to get his breath back. What the hell had happened to his fitness and stamina – had the house sapped that, too? It had taken every ounce of his strength and determination to get to the summit, where he'd had to sit down again, gasping, struggling to find the energy to make it back to the house.

'A client a few weeks ago asked me about them,' Caro replied. 'I just remembered last night. He was buying a cottage and I had to do a search to make sure it wasn't on any ley lines.'

'Remind me what they are?'

'Historic lines of alignment – dead straight lines criss-crossing the whole country. A lot of ancient monuments, like churches, are built along them. No one knows exactly what they are – there are theories about them being underground water passages or metal seams. There's been a ton of stuff written about them – and apparently where there are two intersecting ley lines you can get all kinds of electro-magnetic disturbances. In what I've read so far, quite a few supposedly haunted houses have been built on these intersections.'

'What about this place?' Ollie asked.

'I've been googling maps of Sussex. It looks like we might be, but I can't be sure, I'd need to do some more research.'

'And if it turns out we are, what do we do – jack the house up on wheels and move it?'

She smiled, thinly. 'Apparently there are ways of dispersing the energy by lancing the ley lines, literally sticking some rods along them – a bit like acupuncture on a huge scale.'

Ollie shrugged. 'Sounds weird, but I'm happy to try anything.'

'Have a read up about them.'

'I will.'

As they walked back towards the house, music was pounding out of Jade's bedroom window. They could see figures jumping up and down. Jade, Phoebe and Ruari.

'What are they doing?' Ollie said. 'Aerobics?'

'She's making another music video – she wants to project it on the wall at her party next week. But . . .' Caro hesitated.

'But?' he quizzed.

'I don't know, Ols. Should we risk having a party with all that's happening at the moment? I've been feeling uneasy as it is about having had Phoebe staying overnight, and even Ruari coming today. I'm not sure we should have any visitors until we sort out whatever's going on here. I think we ought to go out to dinner on your fortieth rather than invite people to the house.'

He fell silent for some moments at the mention of his fortieth. Remembering what he had read and discovered yesterday.

'We can't start living in fear, darling, w—'

'We can't *start* living in fear? I've got news for you – I *am* living in bloody fear. I used to love leaving work because that meant I'd soon be seeing you, seeing your face, spending the evening with you. Now I'm scared. Every mile I cover in the car takes me nearer this house and sometimes I just want to turn round and go straight back into Brighton.'

'Tomorrow night it's going to get sorted, darling. Whatever stuff is going on here, we'll get it cleared.'

'By ghostbuster Benedict Cutler. Bell, book and candle,

eh? Just so long as he doesn't make Jade's head rotate three hundred and sixty degrees like in *The Exorcist*. Because that's what he is really, isn't he? An exorcist?'

Ollie smiled. 'From the sound of him that's not a title he'd want to use.'

'But it's what we need here, in reality, isn't it? To make this place safe, normal. A *ghostbuster*.'

The two of them had always had an open and frank relationship. No secrets. They always told each other everything. Ollie felt bad, now, keeping back what he'd found out about the past history of Cold Hill House. The exorcisms that had failed to work. The clergymen who'd refused to come to the house.

Almost none of the past occupants reaching their fortieth birthdays.

A sudden movement caught his eye in an upstairs window.

Caro looked at him in panic. 'Did you see that?'

'Not clearly – what was it?' He stared at the window. 'What did you see?'

'People – people up there looking at us.' She pointed up at the tiny window just below the eaves that he'd hardly noticed before, above which was a strip of rusted, broken guttering.

'Probably the kids.'

Her face a mask of unease, Caro pointed up at Jade's bedroom. All three children were jumping up, arms crossed in the air, doing a crazy dance to some music. 'They're all in there, Ols. There's people in the house.'

'Stay here,' he said. 'Keep watching.' He sprinted to the house, went in through the atrium without removing his wellingtons, then clumped up the stairs to the landing, looking wildly up and down it. He went into the blue bedroom, but it was empty, and then into the yellow bedroom and through into the bathroom.

No one.

And, he realized, the windows in both the yellow and blue room were much bigger than the one Caro had been pointing at.

So which was it?

He could see her down on the lawn, still looking up, and hurried back down to her.

'Did you see anyone?' she asked.

'No. Where exactly was it you saw them?'

She pointed again at the tiny window. 'There,' she said. 'I saw them there.'

'Can you describe them?'

'I could see faces, but not clearly, and I only saw them for a second.'

'What faces? Male, female?'

She was still staring up, as if transfixed. Her voice sounded remote, almost trance-like. 'It looked like a male and a female and a child. They were sort of there but not there.'

She continued to stare.

Her words resonated through him, chilling him. He looked up again at the tiny window, higher up than the sash windows on either side of it, right beneath the eaves of the roof, trying to get his bearings on where exactly it was. 'Which room is that?' he said. 'I can't work it out.'

'Isn't it the one next to our bathroom?'

'No.' He pointed with his finger, moving from left to right on the first floor. 'That's Jade's room; next is the *yellow* room and next is the window of its en suite. Then next to that is the *blue* room.' They'd named these two spare rooms, as well as Jade's room, after the colour of their wallpaper.

'Those two at the end are our bathroom window and then our bedroom.'

She followed his finger, concentrating hard. Then she looked back at the one below the broken guttering, where she had just seen the figures. 'So what's that window? Which room is that?'

'I really don't know. I'm not sure but—'

He froze in mid-sentence.

Both of them saw them now. It looked like a whole family, parents and a child in silhouette, peering out in turn, one after the other, through the small square of glass, before they disappeared.

'It could be Jade, darling,' he said. 'Trying to spook us again.'

Her voice trembling, Caro said, 'No, Ollie, I don't think so. They're all still in her room.'

'They've rigged something up, the little bastards!' He ran back to the atrium door, opened it, went inside again and sprinted up the stairs, followed by Caro. He turned left when he reached the landing, then opened the door to the room where he thought they had seen the faces. But there was no sign of anyone having been in here. Just the large, empty spare bedroom, with ancient, peeling, blue and white floral wallpaper, and a sash window. It had an old, stained washbasin, several floorboards missing and clusters of black mould on one wall. An empty light fitting dangled at the end of a brown cord from a ceiling rose. The room felt cold and smelled musty.

He shut the door then opened the next one along and peered in. It was another empty room, with yellow wallpaper curling at the edges in places. The bathroom was in a similar state of neglect, with a large sash window that did not look as if it had been opened in years.

Followed by Caro, he strode down to Jade's room and opened the door, to be greeted by a blast of music and the sight of Jade, Ruari – with his pop-star hair and big smile – and Phoebe, each swivelling round in turn, holding up a placard on which the word *YES!* was written on one side, and *NO!* on the other.

Seeing her father, Jade stepped forward and stopped the music, then looked at him. 'Dad!' she said, reproachfully.

'Were any of you just in the room next to this one?' he asked.

'You're interrupting, Dad, this is really important!' Jade said.

'Have you been in either of the empty bedrooms in the past few minutes, Jade, Phoebe, Ruari?' he asked, ignoring her protest.

'Dad, this is soooo awkward. We're busy, OK? We've not been anywhere.' Phoebe and Ruari nodded in concurrence.

Ollie stared hard at the window. As he closed the door he was so preoccupied he barely heard the music start up again. Caro gave him a quizzical look.

'It's not them,' he said. 'But there's something I can't work out. We've got Jade's room, then there's this spare room.' He opened the door, entered the yellow room, pointed at the window then went through into the decrepit adjacent bathroom. 'Here's the next window.'

Back out on the landing they opened the next door along, and peered into the blue room. 'OK, there's this window. Then next door along to the left is our bathroom, and on our right is the yellow bathroom, correct?'

She nodded, doing her own calculations.

'Which mean's we've got an extra window.'

'An extra window? That's not possible,' she said.

He walked slowly along between the doors to the blue and yellow rooms, tapping the wall all the way, but there was no change in the sound. They both went back outside into the rear garden. Ollie took a photograph with his phone, told Caro to stay where she was, then strode back into the house and upstairs. He went through into the blue room, walked over to the window and tried to open it. But the sash cords were broken on either side and he struggled to lift it more than a few inches. He kneeled and called down to Caro through the gap. 'OK, darling, I'm in the *blue* room and I'm now going into the *yellow* room's bathroom, which should be the next window along.'

He went into the yellow room and through to the bathroom. It was also a sash window, smaller than the ones in both bedrooms, but equally busted. He struggled hard to lift it six inches. Below him he could see Caro looking baffled.

'OK, darling?' he called down. 'Is this the next window?'

Her eyes widened in shock. She was staring up at the house, a short way to his left.

'Darling?' he said again, louder. 'Darling? Is this the next window?'

'No,' she said. 'No, it's not, Ollie. There's a window in between. And there's people in there.'

49

Ollie raced out of the yellow room and back again into the blue room. It was deserted and icy, the temperature seeming to have dropped since he'd last been in it, only a couple of minutes ago. It was like entering a walk-in deep freeze. He went over to the window and called down. 'Caro, are you sure? This is the next window!'

She shook her head vigorously. 'No, there's a small one in between. They're not there any more. But they were, Ols.'

He struggled as hard as he could to lift the broken window enough to get his head out and look properly, but it would not budge. How the hell could there be an extra window, he wondered? Had there originally been another room, and the window left in place when it was knocked through? He had seen plans of the house a few months ago, before making an offer on the place, when he was discussing work that needed to be done with the surveyor. But he couldn't remember at this moment where they were.

'Wait there, Caro!' he said.

He went downstairs and out of the front door, where several metal ladders belonging to the builders lay on the ground. He selected the longest, lugged it round to the rear of the house, and propped it up against the wall beneath the tiny window with the broken guttering. The ladder didn't quite reach, but it would at least enable him to see in, he calculated. The base was resting on the mossy flagstones of the rear patio.

'Be careful, Ols.'

'If you hold it to stop it slipping, darling.'

She grabbed the vibrating ladder as he began to climb, jamming her feet against both legs, watching him anxiously.

Ollie climbed slowly and carefully. He'd always been scared of heights, and even a short distance above the ground made him uneasy. And as he neared the top he realized he was short of breath again. He stopped for a moment, feeling giddy, his head swimming.

'Ols, darling, are you all right?' Caro called out, anxiously.

'Yes.' The word came out as a gasp. He carried on until his hands reached the top rung, where he was still not high enough to see in the window. Another couple of feet. Very slowly, still holding the top rung, he raised his feet up one rung, then the next.

'Ols, please be careful!' Caro said, her voice irritating him now.

'I am being sodding careful, OK?'

Placing his hands against the rough brick wall for balance, he slowly raised his body up, inches at a time, until he was able to grab the sill with its flaking white paint. But as his fingers gripped the wood it crumbled like papier mâché.

'Jesus!' he cried out, almost toppling over backwards.

'Ollie!' Caro screamed.

He just managed to grab the top of the ladder with one hand, and then leaned forward, steadying himself, gulping air.

'Come down!' she commanded. 'Come down, we'll get one of the builders to go up – this evening if we can.'

Ollie hesitated. But his head was swimming again, he realized. This was not smart. Slowly and very carefully, he descended. When he climbed off the last rung, relieved to have his feet back on terra firma, he was sweating heavily.

Caro looked at him, anxiously. 'Are you feeling OK?'

'Yes,' he fibbed. His heart was pounding and, strangely, he had toothache. The garden seemed to be swaying in front of his eyes, as if he had just stepped off a boat and hadn't yet got back his equilibrium. He wiped his brow with the back of his hand; his T-shirt beneath his jumper felt sodden. 'Yes, I'm fine.'

'You've gone a horrible colour.'

'Really, I'm fine, darling. I'll phone Bryan Barker and see if he can get someone over right now.'

With her help, he lowered the ladder then carried it back and laid it down with the other, shorter ladders. When he stood back up, he was again panting, his heart racing. He was coming down with a bug, he realized. Flu. But he had no time for that.

'You don't look right, Ols,' Caro said.

'Ley lines,' he replied. 'I'll go and call Bryan and then check them out on my computer.'

'I'll come up and show you the sites I've been looking at,' she said, still staring at him, concerned.

He climbed up the two flights of stairs to his office, hauling himself on the handrail much of the way, then had to stop for a moment when he entered the room to get his breath back.

'You should go to bed,' Caro said. 'You need to be right for tomorrow evening.'

'I'm fine,' he said, sitting down in front of his screen.

'I'm fine. I feel like bashing that wall down, but with a houseful of kids we can't do that. I don't want to freak them out.'

Barker's phone went to voicemail and he left a message, asking him to call back urgently.

They spent the next ten minutes scanning and studying segments of websites on ley lines. Then Caro looked at her watch. 'I'd better go down and see to lunch.' She looked at him anxiously once more. 'Are you sure you shouldn't be in bed?'

He stood up and put his arms round her, holding her tightly. 'I'm fine,' he said. 'Really. I guess I'm just all wound up about everything.'

'That makes two of us,' she said. 'And we're both going to be like this until we find out just who the hell else we're sharing this house with.'

'We will,' he said. 'And we'll get rid of any unwanted guest we have, OK? The vicar and this Minister of Deliverance, Benedict Cutler, will sort it out tomorrow. They will, darling.'

She smiled, thinly. 'I hope so.'

'We *will* get this sorted out,' he said, adamantly. 'I promise you.'

She kissed him on the forehead then went out of the room and headed downstairs. He sat back down, turned to the computer screen, and froze. There was another message in large black letters.

IN YOUR FUCKING DREAMS.

50

As he stared, rooted to the spot, feeling as if his stomach had turned into a block of ice, the words faded. An instant later there was a tearing sound above him like someone ripping up a sheet of stiff paper or cardboard.

His eyes shot to the ceiling. A spider's web of cracks was appearing, spreading out in front of his eyes. Moments later, a small chunk of plaster, accompanied by a shower of dust, fell down on his head and on to the keyboard.

He looked up again, shivers rippling through him, at the tiny area of exposed rafter.

As suddenly as it had started, it stopped. The cracks did not grow any bigger. No more dust fell.

He stared up again, shaking uncontrollably, thinking, thinking, thinking.

Jesus, what the hell was happening?

He went down to the first-floor landing, where he could smell the aroma of roasting meat from the kitchen and hear the music pounding out of Jade's room, then walked along to the yellow room, and back into the en-suite bathroom. He looked at the old-fashioned enamel bathtub, with brown stains below the big old taps and around the plughole. Then he stared at the tiled walls. He went through into the blue room next door, and over to the wall which should adjoin the bathroom, and rapped hard on it, to see if it was hollow.

But it was solid.

What the hell was behind that tiny window? What room? Who was in there?

As he went back out onto the landing someone barged into him, sending him flying forward, crashing down onto the threadbare carpet.

'Hey!' he said angrily, thinking for a moment it must be Ruari.

Then, as he looked around, he realized there was no one there.

'Lunch!' Caro shouted out from downstairs. 'Lunch!'

'OK, darling!' he called back, his voice shaky, hauling himself up onto his knees.

'Tell Jade, Phoebe and Ruari to come down,' she called back.

He stood up, looking around and up at the ceiling. 'Yes, OK, I'll get them.'

'It's on the table!'

Jade was full of excitement, at lunch, about the music video, showing them all a clip on her phone and talking about her party next week, and the labradoodle puppy they were going to go and see. Ruari, whom Ollie and Caro liked a lot, was his usual chatty self, talking about football and in particular Brighton's bitter rivals, Crystal Palace. Ollie and Ruari both agreed that Crystal Palace looked like they were going to struggle to avoid relegation from the Premier League this season.

'Jade says you've got a ghost here,' Ruari said suddenly, with a grin. 'That's pretty cool.'

'I think most old houses have ghosts of some kind,' Ollie replied. His plate of food sat on the refectory table in front of him, virtually untouched. Roast pork and crackling was one of his favourite dishes, but right now he had no appetite.

'Epic,' Ruari said, nodding his head. 'Just epic.'

Then Ollie saw a shadow moving in the doorway to the atrium. Hovering. Just as it had hovered before when he'd been in the drawing room yesterday morning with the vicar.

'Excuse me a second.' Ollie stood up abruptly and strode over to the door and out, across the atrium and into the hall. The hairs rose on the nape of his neck. A short distance along, at the foot of the stairs, facing away from him, stood the translucent silhouettes of a woman and girl. From behind they looked like Caro and Jade. He ran towards them and, as he reached them, they vanished. There was nothing there. He stood, shivering, looking all around and up the stairs.

Nothing.

Shaking all over, wondering again just what was going on in his head, he went back into the kitchen and saw Caro frowning at him. Jade, Phoebe and Ruari were giggling over some private joke.

'Thought I heard a car,' he said, lamely.

As soon as lunch was over, Ollie excused himself and went back up to his office, glancing around nervously with every step he took. Then, as he entered the tower room and looked up at the ceiling, he stopped and stood still in disbelief.

The cracks had gone. The ceiling was intact, as it always had been.

He sat down at his desk and buried his face in his

hands. *Oh God*, he thought, again. *Oh God, what's happening to me?*

Then he looked at his keyboard, turned it upside down and shook it. Dust fell out.

Dust from the ceiling earlier? Or had it been there for a while?

He listened for some moments to the sound of rain pattering against the window. Then, opening his eyes, he saw on the display of his mobile phone that he had a missed call and a voicemail from Cholmondley.

He snatched it up and listened to it.

Cholmondley's voice was terse and the message brief. 'This is Charles Cholmondley, Mr Harcourt. One twenty, Sunday. Will you please call me and explain just what the hell's going on now?'

He took several deep breaths, then pressed the button. The phone was answered after just one ring, as if his client had been sitting with it in his hand, waiting.

'Charles!' he said, as disarmingly as he could. 'Just got your message.'

'Perhaps you'd like to explain?'

'You got the email from my IT manager?'

'I've got an email from a Mr Chris Webb, signing himself as your IT manager, intended for someone else, I believe.'

'Pardon? Someone else?'

'Is your organization so inept – or should I say your IT manager – that you can't even address an email to the correct recipient?'

'I'm sorry?' Ollie said, totally confused. 'He emailed you to explain the problems we've been experiencing. You see—'

'My name is Charles Cholmondley, Mr Harcourt. The

email your man has sent me was written to a Mr Anup Bhattacharya.'

It took several moments for his words to sink in. Ollie shook his head. *No. No. They couldn't have done. They'd been so careful, so incredibly careful.*

'He's been receiving malicious emails, apparently, this Mr Bhattacharya. Someone who has a grudge against him, and has hacked your system to attack him. Was there some other reason why Mr Webb sent it to me?'

Shit! Ollie thought. *Shit, shit, shit.* So much for his carefully constructed plan to calm the man down. How the hell did he dig himself out of this one?

'Perhaps you should be more careful who you are sending emails to, Mr Harcourt.'

'Let me try to explain, Charles, please.'

A few minutes after he ended the call, he saw an email had come in from Bhattacharya. It was the one Webb had sent to Cholmondley. There was a curt message from his Indian client at the top.

Wrong recipient.

Ollie checked his Sent Messages box. Both the messages, to Bhattacharya and to Cholmondley, had been sent correctly. So how the hell had the wrong one ended up with each of them?

He phoned Chris Webb and told him what had just happened.

'No way,' Chris replied. 'I double-checked, knowing how sensitive this was. There's no way those emails went to the wrong people. It's just not possible.'

'I checked too. It may not be possible, Chris, but it's happened. OK?'

'I'm telling you, it's not possible. Hold on a sec, will you?'

Ollie listened to the putter of a keyboard. Then Webb came back on the line.

'You there?'

'Yes,' Ollie replied.

'I'd blind-copied myself on both emails, Oliver. They've both come through. The one to your client, Cholmondley, was sent to Cholmondley's address. The other one to Bhattacharya – that was sent to his address. There is no way each could have received the other's email.'

'Well, they have, Chris. How do you explain that?'

'I can't. I don't have an explanation. Maybe there's some problem with your address book. Or . . .'

'Or?'

'You know what I'm going to say, don't you?'

51

The green digits on Ollie's clock radio showed 3.10 a.m. He had barely slept. Apart from just now, when he'd woken from a dream in which he'd been in the retired vicar Bob Manthorpe's house. A gale was raging outside, rattling the windows, and a cold draught blew on his face. The Sunday papers lay on the floor by his bed, unread. He'd been unable to concentrate on anything during the evening. He just kept thinking about the figures by the stairs he had seen at lunchtime, and the ones he and Caro had seen behind the mystery window.

The window where there was no room. Or no way into it – or out.

In the dream he had been in the vicar's sitting room, watching a rising smoke ring. They were having the same conversation they'd had on Thursday – just three days ago – three days that felt like a month.

'*He'd unearthed letters and journals and what-have-you from that time, and he used to like sitting in the pub and telling anyone who'd listen that Brangwyn's wife had not been on the outbound ship with him. That he'd left her behind in the house.*'

'*In the closed-up house?*'

'*Or buried her somewhere in the grounds. I don't think they had quite the calibre of detection work we have today.*

If it's true, he went away for long enough, came home, opened up the house and started life over again with a new bride. Rumour had it, apparently, that his wife's spirit was pretty angry . . . And that she didn't like people leaving the house.'

Ollie could hear his heart pounding in his chest. A slightly uneven *boomph . . . boomph . . . boomph* like a boxing glove striking a punchbag. Unease shimmied through him. This room, this secret room – was Matilda De Glossope – formerly Matilda Warre-Spence – in there?

Suddenly there was a loud cracking sound. An instant later something smelling damp and musty fell on the bed, covering his face and dripping foul-smelling water on him.

He sat up, yelling, pushing it away with his hands, but it kept falling back onto him.

'Ols, what's happening, what's happening, what's happening?' Caro was trying to push it away, too.

It felt like paper. Sodden paper. He rolled sideways out of the bed and crashed to the floor. Caro was still wrestling with it, shouting. He stood up, found the wall light switch and pressed it. And saw the writhing mound of Caro on the bed, struggling to find her way out from under a huge sheet of red flock wallpaper that had come away from the wall behind the headboard and fallen across the bed, leaving a bare brown strip of exposed wall, like a wound.

He stepped forward, grabbed an edge of wallpaper and pulled it free.

Caro sat up, wide-eyed, shaking her head. 'Jesus!' she said. 'What – what the hell?'

As she looked fearfully around there was another cracking sound. The top section of a full-length strip of wallpaper on the left side of the room suddenly detached itself from the wall. Ollie ran over to it and tried to push it back into place. It was sodden, he realized. Then as he looked around the walls, fear and confusion shimmying through him, he saw they were all glistening with damp.

Then another strip came partially free, folding over on itself.

Caro screamed and threw herself out of bed; she ran over to Ollie and clutched him. Her eyes darted about, wild with terror. 'What's happening, Ollie, what the hell is happening?'

'Must be another water leak,' he said, feeling utterly useless and helpless.

Caro looked at him in terror. 'Another this, another that. I was nearly electrocuted by the bloody shower. Now I'm being smothered by wallpaper. This place is a sodding health hazard. What's going to happen next?'

'We'll get on top of it all, darling.'

'I can't cope with this, Ols. I just can't cope with this—'

She was interrupted by another loud crackle.

Ollie could not see where it came from. Christ, he wondered, were all the rest of the strips about to start peeling away from the walls, too?

'We can't sleep here,' she said. 'I'm scared more's going to come down. God, and I've got such a load of meetings tomorrow . . .'

'Maybe we should go downstairs, sleep on the sofas again tonight?' Ollie said. 'I've got an important day, too, we've got to get some sleep.'

But ten minutes later, lying under a duvet on the sofa that was a little too short for him, he was wide awake, thinking once more about the emails.

There was absolutely no way they'd sent them to the wrong recipients.

The more he turned it over in his mind, the more

certain he was they'd not made a mistake. But at the same time, less certain. What kind of tricks was his mind playing on him? It seemed that since moving here someone else had taken control of it, similar to the way Chris Webb, thirty miles away, could take control of his computer through that simple bit of software, TeamViewer.

Was someone – or some*thing* – controlling his mind? Controlling it remotely? Making him see messages on the screen that weren't there? Messing around with time inside his head? Making him see cracks on the ceiling that magically repaired themselves?

Making wallpaper fall off?

Caro sounded as if she was asleep, finally. He lay very still, not wanting to disturb her, trying to sleep too, but he was thinking, now, about tomorrow. Much to his surprise, Cholmondley had agreed to meet him – at his north London showroom. He would head off there straight after dropping Jade at school.

He had a headache. His scalp was pulling tightly round his skull, as if it was several sizes too small. He felt a vice-like grip in his chest, and his teeth were all hurting. And just like when he was a small child, he was keeping his eyes closed, scared of what he might see if he opened them.

This house, which he had thought would be paradise for the three of them, had turned into a nightmare he could not wake from.

And a nightmare that would not let him go to sleep.

It was all his fault, he was well aware. Caro would have been happy to have lived in a modest house in Brighton all her life, as her parents had. He was the one with the big ambition, the hubris, who had persuaded her to take the gamble and move here.

Now he was no longer sure about anything and, least of all, his sanity.

Shadows that moved; vicars who appeared before they had arrived; girls who were not there feeding ducks; faces in windows; cracks in ceilings that sealed themselves; a window with no room behind it.

And himself, who had always been fit, now out of breath at the slightest exercise.

That scared him more than anything. Maybe he should have a check-up. Could he have a brain tumour?

Occasionally he opened his eyes to check his clock radio. Time was passing slowly, incredibly slowly.

4.17.

4.22.

4.41.

He heard a click and stiffened.

Then Jade's whispering, anxious voice.

'Mum? Dad?'

'What is it, lovely?' he said, as quietly as he could.

'There's a man in my room. He keeps saying he's my dad.'

Ollie snapped on the lamp on the side table at the end of the sofa, and saw his daughter, in a long cream T-shirt, looking gaunt.

'Uh?' Caro said.

'It's OK, darling,' he whispered.

'He says he's my dad. He's really scary. I can't sleep, Dad.'

Ollie stood up, in his boxers and T-shirt, and hugged her. 'Tell you what, lovely, stay down here with us – you can sleep on the sofa with your mum. Tell me about this man in your room?'

'He comes in every night.'

'Every night?'

She nodded. 'But normally he doesn't speak.'

'Why didn't you tell me? What does he look like?'

'Like you, Dad. I thought it was you. He said we should all have left, but it's too late now.'

He hugged her again. 'Is that how you feel?'

Jade shook her head. 'I like it here now. This is where we belong.'

'We do, don't we?'

'We do,' she nodded, then moments later was fast asleep, standing up in his arms.

Gently, he eased her onto the sofa, beside Caro, who sleepily pulled the duvet over her daughter and put a protective arm round her.

Ollie lay down again on the other sofa, with the light on, listening to his wife and his daughter sleeping. Thinking again, as he had earlier. Full of guilt for bringing them into this.

What a sodding mess.

Ghosts.

Bruce Kaplan had no problem with ghosts.

Hopefully, after tomorrow, he would not either. There would be no ghosts here any more. Benedict Cutler would deal with them.

Lay Lady Matilda finally to rest.

And then they could get on with their lives.

It was going to be fine. Really it was. Exorcisms here might not have worked in the past, but hey, the past was another country, wasn't that what they said? This was today, 2015. Peeps felt different about stuff, as Jade might say.

And this was their dream home. You had to try to live your dreams. Too many people went to their graves with their dreams still inside them. And that was not going to happen to him. Life presented you, constantly, with idiots. But, just very occasionally, if you opened yourself up to the opportunities, life presented you with magic, too.

They mustn't lose the dream. He would make this house safe and happy for Jade and Caro. Somehow. They'd find a way. It would begin tomorrow. This house was magic. He listened to his daughter and his wife breathing. The two people who meant more to him than anything else on earth.

The two people on this planet he would die for.

52

The Monday-morning traffic into London was shit, with the M25 and then the Edgware Road clogged, and it was almost midday when Ollie finally arrived at the swanky Maida Vale premises of Charles Cholmondley Classic Motors.

As he pulled into one of the velvet-roped visitor parking bays, he stared, covetously, at the array of cars behind the tall glass wall of the showroom. A 1970s Ferrari, a Bugatti Veyron, a 1950s Bentley Continental Fastback, a 1960s Aston Martin DB4 Volante and a 1960s Rolls-Royce Silver Cloud. All of them gleamed, as spotless and immaculate as if they'd spent all their years wrapped in cotton wool and had not yet been exposed to a road.

On the way here he had managed to speak to his builder's foreman, frustrated that his calls yesterday hadn't been returned, and asked him, urgently, to have someone climb in through the tiny window to see what was there between the blue and yellow bedrooms, and left another voicemail for his plumber to investigate the sudden dampness of the walls in their bedroom. Then he spent twenty minutes on the phone trying to pacify Bhattacharya. He wasn't sure he had succeeded, although the restaurateur had at least accepted the possibility of a malicious hacker – albeit one malicious to Ollie, not to himself. Someone with a grievance against Ollie, he told him. Very unfortunate, but was he willing to take the risk of someone whom Ollie had upset damaging his own business? He told Ollie he would think about it.

Seated in Cholmondley's oak-panelled office, which was adorned with silver models of classic cars and framed photographs of exotic car advertisements from decades ago, overlooking the showroom floor, the discussion did not go so well. The car dealer himself was the very model of unctuous charm. He gave a reasoned explanation as to why he was not going to pay his bill, accompanied by expansive arm movements, and periodic flashes of his starched white double cuffs and gold links. However, he told Ollie, if he was prepared to waive this bill, in lieu of damages caused, he would be prepared to consider retaining his services going forward.

Leaving Maida Vale shortly after 1.00 p.m., having been offered neither tea, coffee nor water, Ollie was parched and starving. He'd barely eaten a thing yesterday, and he'd only managed to swallow a couple of mouthfuls of cereal for breakfast today. His nerves were jangling, his stomach felt like it was full of writhing snakes, and he was feeling light-headed from lack of sugar.

He pulled onto a garage forecourt, filled up with diesel, then bought himself a ham sandwich, a KitKat, and a Coke. He returned to his car and sat, listening to the news on the radio, while he ate.

The traffic was better than earlier but still heavy, the rain not helping, and it would be touch and go whether he made it to Jade's school in time to pick her up. He decided to ignore the route the satnav was suggesting, which would put him outside the school ten minutes late, and shortcut his way down through Little Venice, White City and then Hammersmith, and cross the Thames there.

Suddenly his phone rang. He saw it was Bryan Barker. 'Hi, Ollie, sorry I didn't call you back yesterday, we'd gone over to my sister in Kent and I left my phone behind. How was your weekend?'

'I've had better.'

'Wish I could give you some good news now to cheer you up, but I'm afraid every time we look behind anything at the house, we find another problem.'

'So what's the latest doom and gloom?'

'There are some nasty-looking cracks around the base of the tower, below your office – we've only found them since chipping away some of the rendering.'

'What's causing them?'

'Well, it could just be slight movements of the earth – changes in the water table, the soil beneath drying out. Or it could be subsidence.'

'Subsidence?' Ollie said, knowing full well what that would entail. Cripplingly expensive underpinning. 'Why didn't this show up on the survey?'

'Well, I'm looking at the relevant section of the survey now. It warned of possible movement but inspection wasn't possible without removing some of the rendering. It says they brought this to your attention and you told them to leave it.'

'Great!' Ollie said, gloomily. 'Just one thing after another after another.'

'Should have bought yourselves a nice little brand-new bungalow if you wanted an easy life!' Barker said.

'Yeah, great.' Ollie concentrated on the road for a second. He used to know this part of London well – his first job was for a small IT company down the skanky end of Ladbroke Grove, on the fringe of Notting Hill – and he cycled everywhere then. He drove along with the canal on his right.

'Oh, and another thing,' Barker said. 'That window you asked us to take a look through – there's a bit of a problem.'

'What?'

'I climbed up this morning – we put two ladders together – but I couldn't see in – there are metal bars blocking out the light.'

'Metal bars? Like a prison cell?'

'Exactly.'

'So is it a room?'

'I don't know – we'd either have to cut away the bars or go in through a wall.'

'How long are you going to be there today, Bryan?'

'I've got to leave early today – I've got a site visit to make, and it's Jasmin's birthday – I'll be in big trouble if I'm late!'

'I've asked the plumber, but if you have time could you also take a look in our bedroom? I think we may have a serious damp problem there.'

'OK – and you'll be at the house in the morning?'

'Yes, I'll be working from home all day.'

Ollie ended the call and drove on, immersed in his thoughts. At least he had a resolution, of a kind, with Cholmondley. He was going to have to accept the bastard's deal, he knew, because it was still a gateway to other classic car dealers. And he had a lot of damage limitation ahead with the other dealers who'd been copied in on the vile email that had gone to Cholmondley. With luck, Bhattacharya could be salvaged. And tonight the vicar and Benedict Cutler were coming.

He had a good feeling about that.

Fortinbrass seemed a very human man, concerned and interested. He and Benedict Cutler would help them clear whatever malevolence was in the house. It was 2015, for God's sake. Ghosts might have terrified people in past centuries, but not any more. This evening was high noon for any spectral guests at Cold Hill House.

The thought made him smile. He was nearing Gatwick airport on the M23, in heavy rain, and was only about twenty-five minutes now from Jade's school. He would get there with a good ten minutes or more to spare. He leaned forward and switched channels to Radio Sussex. He liked listening to the Alison Ferns afternoon show.

The three o'clock news came on and he turned the volume up a little. The announcer, in his sombre, clear, unemotional BBC voice, stated there was more controversy over the wildcat French industrial action in Calais causing further Eurostar cancellations. There were fresh airstrikes against an ISIS stronghold. A family doctor was questioning the effectiveness of flu vaccinations. Then, suddenly, Ollie stiffened as he heard:

'Two people who died today when their Volkswagen Golf was in a head-on collision with a lorry, on the B2112 Haywards Heath to Ardingly road, were named as Brighton solicitor Caroline Harcourt and her daughter Jade.'

53

Monday, 21 September

Ollie swerved off onto the hard shoulder and slammed on his brakes, switching on the hazard lights, the wipers clouting away the raindrops. He sat for a moment, drenched in perspiration, his entire body pounding. The Range Rover rocked in the slipstream of a lorry that thundered past, too close, inches away from his wing mirror, as he stabbed Caro's direct line on his speed-dial button.

It rang once, twice, three times.

'Answer, please answer, please, please, please, darling.'

Then, with an immense surge of relief, he heard her voice, the professional tone she always adopted when at work. 'Hi, Ols, I'm with a client at the moment – can I call you back in a while?'

'You're OK?' he gasped.

'Yes, thank you very much. I'll be about half an hour.'

'Jade's not with you?'

'I thought you were picking her up from school?'

'Yes – yes – yes, I am. Call me when you can.'

Another lorry rocked the car.

Had he imagined it?

He must have. Unless, he thought with growing terror, it was another time-slip. Something he had seen that had not yet happened? More evidence that he was going insane?

But he wouldn't let Caro drive the Golf, nor take Jade anywhere, not for a few days, not until he was absolutely certain he'd just imagined this.

He checked his mirror, accelerated and pulled out onto the inside lane. He was still shaking uncontrollably, perspiration running down the back of his neck.

He didn't calm down until he saw Jade trotting out of the school gates, rucksack on her back, cheerily chatting with a group of friends. She headed over towards him and climbed up into the car.

'How was your day, lovely?'

She shrugged, pulling on her seat belt. 'Mr Simpson was really annoying.'

'Your music teacher? I thought you liked him.'

She shrugged again. 'I do, but he can be sooooooo annoying!'

He smiled. But, inside him, a storm was still raging.

When they arrived home shortly before 4.00 p.m., the rain had eased to a light drizzle. The only trade vehicle parked outside the house was the plumber's black van. As Jade went up to her room, Michael Maguire came out of the kitchen, his face grimy.

'Ah, Lord Harcourt!' he greeted him.

'What did you discover about the bedroom walls, Mike?'

Maguire shook his head. 'A mystery.'

'But they're damp, right? Where's it coming from – upstairs again?'

'They're hardly damp – a tiny bit, I suppose – enough to loosen the old wallpaper paste.'

'A *tiny* bit? They were sopping wet last night. We had to move down to the drawing room and sleep on the sofas.'

The plumber shook his head again, looking baffled. 'We'll go up there, if you like?'

Ollie followed him up the stairs, and into their bedroom. He went over to each wall in turn, laying the palm of his hand flat against the paper, and across to where the strips had fallen. Maguire was right. The walls felt almost bone dry. 'I don't understand – they were sopping in the middle of the night. They can't just have dried out, it's been raining all day.'

'I spoke to Bryan Barker earlier,' Maguire said. 'He's got a meter for measuring damp, and we'll do some checks tomorrow if I get time. Got a busy day – the new boiler's arriving first thing. You won't have any hot water for a few hours, but I'll make sure it's all up and running by the evening.'

'Do you have a sledgehammer?' Ollie asked, suddenly.

'A *sledgehammer*?' Maguire looked surprised.

'Yes.'

'Planning to crack a nut, are you?'

'Something like that.' Ollie gave him a weak smile.

'I've seen one lying around . . .' The plumber frowned, pensively. 'I think there's one down in the cellar.'

'Great, thanks.'

Ollie stared around at the two bare patches of wall which the paper had fallen from, and several other places where it had begun to peel. He walked around the room as he had done in the middle of the night, placing the palm of his hand against the wall.

Maguire was right. The dampness of the middle of the night had gone.

How?

But he had a bigger worry at this moment. He perched on the edge of the bed, pulled out his phone and went to the *Argus* online, which carried the latest Sussex newsfeeds. He searched down through them for Traffic. There was a three-car accident on the A27 at Southwick which had happened an hour ago. A pedestrian was in critical condition after being struck by a van near the Clock Tower in central Brighton at midday. An elderly man had been cut out of an overturned car at the Gatwick intersection of the A23 earlier in the day.

No fatalities.

No mother and daughter in a collision with a lorry.

His mind playing with him again?

Or a deadly timeslip?

The two cats, Bombay and Sapphire, came into the room, and both in turn nuzzled against him.

He stroked them for some moments, changed out of his business suit into jeans, a sweatshirt and trainers, then went back downstairs and into the kitchen, feeling badly in need of a drink.

He had always tried to make it a rule, apart from the occasional glass with lunch, never to have a drink before 6.00 p.m. But today he grabbed a bottle of Famous Grouse from the kitchen shelf, twisted off the cap, and necked a gulp straight from the bottle. Its fiery warmth sliding down his throat and into his belly instantly made him feel a little more positive. He took a second swig, replaced the cap and put the bottle back on the shelf. Then he went down into the cellar.

Barker's workers had been busy here. Huge chunks of wall had been knocked out, exposing raw red brick, supported in several places by steel Acrow props. Lying by one wall was a large metal tool box, next to which was an angle grinder, a power drill, and, on the floor, a sledgehammer with a long wooden handle.

He lifted the heavy tool and carried it up, through the kitchen, and on up to the first-floor landing. Music was, as ever, coming out of Jade's bedroom door.

Good, he thought. Hopefully, she wouldn't hear him – or would assume it was the builders.

He entered the blue bedroom, walked straight over to the right-hand wall, and swung the sledgehammer hard against it. It struck with a dull thud, making a tiny indent, and throwing up a small shower of plaster. He swung it again in the same place. Then again. Again. The indent slowly grew larger.

Suddenly the head of the hammer embedded itself into the wall. He pulled it back and swung it again, exposing raw red brick. As he did so, he became aware of someone standing behind him in the room.

He turned.

There was no one.

'Just fuck off!' he shouted, then swung again, again, again, the hole in the wall steadily getting larger, more and more pieces of brick crumbling and falling onto the floor.

Finally, after ten minutes, sodden with perspiration, and out of breath again, another chunk of the wall fell away, and the hole was just about big enough to crawl through.

He stepped closer to it, his heart thudding, knelt and peered through. There was a stale smell, of old wood and damp. But the light was so dim he could barely see anything. He switched on the torch app on his phone and shone the beam inside.

A shiver ripped through him.

It was a tiny room, no more than six feet wide. Another spare bedroom – once?

Except it was completely bare.

Apart from what was on the far wall.

More shivers rippled through him.

Shit. No. No.

A pair of manacles, on the end of short lengths of rusty chain, were bolted to the wall. Protruding from each manacle were bones – part of what once would have been a hand and wrist. Several fingers were held together by black sinews, but most were missing.

And he could see where they were.

They lay scattered on the floor, along with the skull and all the other bones of the person who had once been imprisoned here. Also on the floor were the decayed remains of a blue dress, other strips of clothing, a pair of yellow silk slippers with tarnished gold buckles and a dusty fan.

He stared, shaking with shock, unsteady on his legs. Stared at the skull. At the scattered bones. He could make out legs, arms, ribcage. He stared at the grinning skull again.

He felt as if a current of electricity was running through him. It seemed as if every hair on his body was standing on end, and that a hundred tiny, ragged fingernails were plucking at his skin.

Then he felt a sharp prod in the small of his back.

54

'SHIT!' he screamed, cracking his head on the top of the hole as he jumped backwards.

And saw his daughter right behind him.

'Sheesh! You scared the hell out of me, Jade!'

'What are you doing, Dad?'

'I'm – I'm – just tracing the wiring in the house.'

'Can I have a look?'

'There's nothing there. Go back to your homework, lovely. I'm sorry if I disturbed you.' He put an arm round her and hugged her tiny frame. After the shock he'd had driving this afternoon it felt so good to feel her, smell her, hear her sweet, innocent voice.

Just to know she was alive.

'I'm doing some geography stuff, Dad. What do you know about tectonic plates?'

'Probably less than you do! Why?'

'Stuff I have to do.'

'They shift, apparently.'

'Can we go to Iceland? You can see a join there! You can walk along it, I was reading about it and saw some cool pictures!'

'Iceland? Sure. When do you want to go – in half an hour?'

'You know, Dad, sometimes you're just so – so – so annoying.'

Ollie waited until she had gone back out of the room. Shaking again, it took him several minutes before he plucked up the courage to look back through the hole. He shone the beam down on the skull. Was this Lady De Glossope – formerly Matilda Warre-Spence?

Had he finally cracked the mystery of her disappearance two and a half centuries ago?

Had her husband done this to her? Used her money, manacled her to this wall, then bricked in the entrance and left her to die and rot, while he went gallivanting off across the world with his mistress?

Was this the reason why Sir Brangwyn De Glossope had shut the house down for three years? To give time for the stench of her decomposing body to fade? To give time for the rats to feast on her and conveniently dispose of her remains?

Was it her ghost, or spirit, or whatever it was, that was so angry, and causing all the problems here? Had she cursed this place?

He felt the sensation of an electric current running through him again. His skin felt as if it were being pinched in, then released, again and again. He sensed the presence of someone behind him, and spun round. Stared at the empty room. Felt someone grinning at him. He staggered away from the hole, reeling with shock. *Jesus*, he thought. *Jesus*. This had been in the house with them all the time.

What the hell was he going to say to Caro? How on earth could he tell her this?

Hopefully, in less than two hours, when the clergymen arrived, they would find out just what was really going on here.

He should call the police, he knew, but after their last visit, that worried him.

He went out onto the landing and slammed the door shut, then stood there for some moments, trembling. *Oh shit, oh shit, oh shit.*

He went down into the kitchen, sat at the refectory table and shaking uncontrollably, began flicking through the glossy pages of *Sussex Life* magazine, which must have arrived with the morning's papers, to try to calm himself down.

He looked at some pages of estate agency particulars of grand country houses – each one described with estate agency hyperbole. Descriptions that could apply to Cold Hill House.

A very well-presented period property in need of some modernization.

A beautiful, detached family house on the periphery of a village in stunning countryside.

A spectacular country home, boasting a wealth of exposed timbers.

A striking Georgian manor.

Did they all have ghosts, too?

Spectral residents on a mission to screw up the lives of their occupants?

A shadow moved in front of him.

He looked up, startled. Then his eyes widened in relief. It was Caro.

'Darling!' he said, jumping up. 'You're home early!'

'Didn't you get my message?'

'Message?'

'I phoned you back but you didn't answer. And I texted you. My last client of the day cancelled, so I thought I'd come home early.' She gave him a vulnerable smile. 'You know, get ready for our visitors. Tidy up a bit, get some nice biscuits out. So how did your meeting go?'

'Yes, OK,' he said.

'Worth the journey?'

'Apart from coming back with car-envy. You should see his showroom – it's incredible. I was drooling at some of the cars in there.'

'I'm afraid you're going to have to keep drooling for a while yet. How's everything here?'

'Oh, you know, fine.' He was thinking how to break the news about the skeleton upstairs – without totally freaking her out.

'I'll go up and see Jade – how was her day at school?'

'OK. But not very happy with her music teacher today.'

'I thought she really liked him.'

'So did I.'

Caro paused for a moment, then she said, 'So where are we going to meet Mr Ghostbuster and his mate? In here or in the drawing room?'

'I think in here,' Ollie replied. 'It's warmer for a start – unless you want me to light a fire?'

'Here's fine,' she said. Then she peered at him. 'You're covered in dust – what have you been doing?'

'Oh – I was down in the basement earlier with the build-ers,' he said.

'Are you feeling OK, Ols?'

'OK?'

'Yes.'

'I'm fine.'

'You don't look OK.'

Nor would you if you'd just hacked through a wall and found a manacled skeleton, he nearly said. Instead he replied, 'I'm just looking forward to these guys coming.

I've got a good feeling about them.' He was thinking that perhaps he could use them to help soften the shock of the skeleton to Caro.

'I wish I shared your optimism,' she said bleakly. 'I don't have a good feeling about anything at this moment. I'm going to change. I think you should too, you look like you've just come off a building site.'

'I have!'

'Yes, well, I think it might be respectful to look a little smarter, OK?'

'It's all going to be fine, darling. It will be.'

Caro said nothing for some moments then she said, 'I don't think we should stay here for a bit, Ols. Mum said we could stay there until the damp and stuff is sorted. Why don't we do that? We can't go on like this here.'

Ollie had memories of staying with his in-laws for several months, five years ago, while renovation work was happening to their Carlisle Road house. After about three days he had been ready to murder his father-in-law and after five days his mother-in-law, too.

'Things are being sorted, Caro.'

'Good, well, when they are sorted, we can move back in.'

'I need to be here on site to manage all the workmen.'

'Fine, you can commute. We can stay in Mum and Dad's basement – Jade can have her own room. At least we'll be safe – and dry.'

And insane, Ollie thought. 'Shall we see how we feel after the vicar and the minister have been?'

'OK,' she said, reluctantly. 'But I'm not totally convinced. They might be able to clear ghosts, but I doubt they'll know much about putting in damp-proof courses and stopping wallpaper from falling down.'

'Well, if God can part the Red Sea, I wouldn't have thought a spot of damp would cause Him too much of a problem,' Ollie said and grinned.

She gave a faint smile. 'Let's see.'

Feeling a little more confident with Caro home, Ollie went upstairs, washed the dust off his face and brushed it out of his hair, and changed into clean clothes. Then he went up to his office to deal with his emails until the two clergymen turned up – they were due in an hour and a half. He sat down at his computer and logged on, worried about what he was going to find next.

Suddenly his iPhone pinged with a text message. He looked down and saw the words:

TWEEDLEDUM AND TWEEDLEDEE ARE ON THEIR WAY! THAT'S WHAT YOU THINK. THEY'RE DEAD. YOU ALL ARE.

And, as before, a second later the words vanished.

55

Ollie sat and stared at his phone, where moments earlier the message had been, in desperation.

Yes, Fortinbrass and the minister were on their way and they were going to clear the shit out of this place. But how the hell did whoever was doing this know? He was aware hackers could access phones as well as computers – was that the source of this and all the previous taunts?

Desperate for them to arrive, and feeling powerless, he attempted to turn his focus back to the urgent task of sending apologetic, damage-limitation emails out to all the other classic car dealers to whom the unfortunate Cholmondley email had also been copied. After that he sent a holding response to a query from a criminal law firm in Brighton who were looking for a new website design – the recommendation had come via one of Caro's partners in her firm. He couldn't deal with it properly now, his mind was all over the place, and his hands were shaking so much he was struggling to type.

Shortly after 6.00 p.m. Ollie heard a deep metallic boom, some distance away, like two giant dustbins that had been swung into each other. Then, after another quarter of an hour, he was again distracted from his emails by another sound, this time the wail of a siren in the far distance. When they had lived in Brighton these sounds were part of the ambient noise of the city. But out here, they were rare.

It was getting louder. Closer. Then it stopped, abruptly, only a short distance away. He glanced through the tower window overlooking the drive, and looked down towards the lane. Although it was only a quarter past six, it was already growing dark – there was perhaps another hour of daylight left, if that. He could hear another siren now, then a third one as well. A few moments later Ollie saw slivers of blue light moving fast, glinting through the trees. Then they all halted.

Although he couldn't actually see all the way to the end of the drive from here, he estimated, with deepening dread, that it was roughly where the emergency vehicles had stopped. His office door opened behind him. He swivelled round and saw Caro, looking anxious. At the same time, he heard yet another siren.

'Ols, something's going on. I hope there's not a fire or . . .'

He nodded. 'Shall I go and take a look?'

'It sounds really close – like on the road outside. Whatever's happening might be stopping the vicar and this minister from getting here. They were due fifteen minutes ago, weren't they?'

He glanced at his watch and saw she was right. 'I'll jump on my bike and go down and take a look,' he said.

The wail of yet another siren added to the din.

'Be careful, Ols.'

He hurried downstairs, out through the atrium door and strode towards the shed where his bike was kept. As he pedalled down past the field of alpacas, careful not to let the flapping legs of his jeans catch in the chain, misty drizzle stung his eyes and he regretted not having put on a baseball cap. Nearing the gates, he saw a blaze of strobing blue lights directly outside them.

He braked and dismounted, his heart in his mouth.

Ten yards or so down the hill a tractor was halted, at an odd angle. Beneath it he could see the remains of a small purple car. It looked as if the tractor had T-boned the car, ploughing straight across the passenger compartment, which was almost crushed flat. A crimson ribbon of blood, widening as he looked, was spreading across the wet tarmac.

It was the same tractor he had seen before on a number of occasions, belonging to the local farmer, Albert Fears. He saw several police cars, two ambulances with masked-out windows, a slab-sided Fire and Rescue truck, and a group of police officers in white caps, two of whom were kneeling beside the purple car.

The car he recognized. It was the one he had seen, twice, on Saturday.

The Reverend Roland Fortinbrass's Kia.

'Please stand back, sir,' a woman police officer said to him.

'I – I live just up there,' Ollie said, lamely, unable to take his eyes from the carnage. 'I'm expecting visitors,' he added, looking at the car again, and unsure why he said that.

'They'll have to park and walk, sir, we're closing the road until the Collision Investigation Unit have been.'

Ollie saw the figure of the farmer, Albert Fears, sitting hunched and forlorn in the back of one of the police cars.

Fortinbrass and the Minister of Deliverance, Benedict Cutler, were in that purple car. He knew it. And he could see from the way the passenger compartment had been flattened, like a sardine tin that had been stamped on, that no one in there could be alive.

That asshole farmer Fears, he thought, feeling sick. Staring at the blood again, he thought for a moment he was going to throw up.

He shivered.

TWEEDLEDUM AND TWEEDLEDEE ARE ON THEIR WAY! THAT'S WHAT YOU THINK. THEY'RE DEAD. YOU ALL ARE.

He shivered again at the memory of those words, just a short while ago.

God, what the hell was happening? Was he responsible for this somehow? Was his mind somehow controlling events?

He tried to rationalize. It was clear what had happened. Fortinbrass had been driving up the hill and turning right into Cold Hill House. Albert Fears had been thundering down, recklessly as usual, in his tractor. Either Fortinbrass had misjudged the farmer's speed, or he'd stalled the engine. Whatever.

He felt deep, black despair seeping through every cell in his body. What was he to do now? Ride back up to the house and tell Caro that their big hope had just been snatched away? She needed help. They all did, but Caro most of all right now. Who could give it to her? Her mother? Her mother would be best.

Or what about Annie Porter, he wondered?

His kindly neighbour would understand Caro's shock. She would probably be seriously shocked herself, and he was surprised, with all the commotion, that Annie hadn't come out to see what was going on. Especially remembering how angry she was about the reckless speed at which the farmer, Albert Fears, always drove his tractor.

'May I come past?' he asked the officer.

She escorted Ollie hurriedly past the crash site. As he wheeled the bike he glanced back at the scene in horror. His view of the wreckage was partially blocked by fire officers, one wielding a hydraulic cutting device, like giant bolt-cutters, and paramedics who were kneeling, peering in through the windows. There were shouted instructions, intermittent static crackle and bursts of voices from radios.

Bile rose in his throat. Swallowing hard, he jumped back in the saddle and freewheeled a short distance down the lane, swinging across and stopping by the front gate of Garden Cottage. As he dismounted again he noticed, to his surprise, that the gate had been painted – a brilliant white. He wondered when she had done that – must have been over the weekend, he decided.

He leaned his bike against the fence carefully, and noticed that, in addition to the new paint, the gate was no longer sagging and had new hinges as well. As he walked up the short garden path to the front door he saw it was also newly painted, a gloss navy blue. There was a small, shiny brass lion's-head knocker, where before there had just been two empty clasps. She'd really had a makeover on the cottage, he thought, rapping hard, hoping this did not mean she was sprucing the place up to sell it and move away. He liked her a lot.

A few moments later the door was opened by a pleasant but weary-looking woman in her twenties, holding a grizzling, puce-faced baby in a spotted babygro. A male voice called out from another room, above the sound of a television, 'Who is it, Mel?'

Ollie suddenly realized the interior looked quite different. Annie Porter's antique furniture and her framed nautical pictures and photographs on the walls had gone.

Instead there was a gilded mirror and three watercolours of cricket scenes on newly decorated walls. It all looked so completely different from when he had last been here, just days ago, that he wondered, for a moment, if in his confusion he had come to the wrong house.

But that was impossible: this was the only cottage for a good three or four hundred yards.

Wasn't it?

'Yes?' the woman said, sounding mildly irritated, and he realized he had just been standing there, looking around. Was she Annie Porter's daughter, or perhaps niece, he wondered? Were she and her husband doing a makeover of the place for the old lady?

'I just popped in to have a word with Annie – is she in?' he asked.

'Annie?'

Now he was really wondering if he had come to the wrong house. 'Yes, Annie Porter.'

She was pensive for a moment. 'Annie Porter? You mean the old lady who used to live here?'

Ollie felt a strange sensation, as if the ground was moving very slightly beneath him. '*Used* to live here? This is Garden Cottage, isn't it?'

The young woman was staring at him very strangely. 'Yes, this is Garden Cottage. But we've been here almost a year. We bought this as an executor sale, after Mrs Porter died. You didn't know she'd died?'

'Died? That's not possible!'

'I think she's buried in the village churchyard.'

The cottage seemed to sway even more. He felt the ground rising beneath his feet, tilting him. He touched the door frame to support himself. 'I'm Oliver Harcourt – my wife and I live just up the lane – in Cold Hill House. I

saw Annie here only a few days ago. I don't understand – I
– I—'

The young woman continued to stare at him very
strangely. 'Kev!' she called out, suddenly, with slight panic
in her voice. 'Kev!'

A harried-looking man in his late twenties, in a grey
T-shirt and tracksuit bottoms, came out into the hall. 'What
is it, Mel?'

She pointed at Ollie. 'Kev, this man doesn't believe me
that we've been here for months.'

He frowned, tilted his head at her then stared directly at
Ollie, frowning again, and asked her, 'What man?'

56

The woman with the baby turned and went back into the house. As she did so, Ollie heard her say, 'There was a man standing there, Kev, I promise! I saw him! He told me his name – Oliver Harcourt. He said he lived up the lane in that big house, Cold Hill House.'

'Mel, there was no one there,' her husband replied.

'I didn't imagine it!'

'Your postnatal depression. Maybe it's playing tricks on your mind?'

The door closed behind her.

Ollie stood still for some moments. What the hell was going on? Was he trapped in the middle of some elaborate conspiracy to drive him insane? Annie Porter dead?

Impossible.

'*I think she's buried in the village churchyard.*'

He climbed back on his bike. The sirens had all stopped. There was complete almost ethereal silence, just the last twitters of birds as darkness fell. His head spinning, he rode on down into the village. He passed the cottage that always displayed the 'Bed & Breakfast' sign. The sign was gone. Then he braked hard as he reached the smithy. It was no longer a smithy. Instead a large sign outside proclaimed: Ye Olde Tea Shoppe.

When had that happened? It must have been in the past few days, because he'd not seen that earlier in the week.

Moments later, as he pedalled on, something struck him as different about the front of the pub. It had been spruced up, painted a lighter colour that was hard to make out in this light – white or cream – and 'The Crown' pub sign had gone. In its place was a larger sign, in elegant script.

BISTROT TARQUIN

He braked hard, locking up the back wheel, and stared, blinking in confusion. Several smart cars were in the car park; the place looked expensive and rather precious.

He rode on, pedalling urgently to increase his speed, as if trying to ride back into sanity. As he saw the lychgate of the church ahead of him he dismounted and propped the bike up against the flint wall.

Moments later, as went in through the gate, a short, very serious-looking man in a tweed jacket and dog collar came out of the church and headed down the path towards him. As they crossed, Ollie asked him, 'Excuse me, do you know by chance where I can find the grave of a lady called Annie Porter?'

The clergyman walked straight past him without any hint of acknowledgement, as if he had not seen him.

Ollie turned. 'Excuse me!' he called out. 'Excuse me!'

The man went out through the lychgate and turned left towards the vicarage.

Rude bastard, Ollie thought.

The more recent graves were towards the rear, behind the church, he recalled. That was where he had found the O'Hare family, and there had been quite a bit of open ground beyond them, no doubt to accommodate more graves in the future. He hurried up the path, anxiously, and although it was steep, he was pleased that neither the exertion of the cycling, nor of this fast walking, was giving him the breathlessness and tightness in his chest he'd been experiencing just recently.

He reached the grand marble headstone of the O'Hare family, then saw a further row of headstones beyond it that he didn't recall from his previous visit here.

He peered through the gathering dusk at the newer headstones and then stopped, in disbelief, as he read the inscription.

Annie Elizabeth Violet
PORTER
16th March 1934 – 6th January 2016
Beloved Wife of Angus,
Lieutenant Commander,
killed in action.

2016? Ollie thought. This was not – not possible. Somehow, whatever was going on inside his messed-up brain, he was seeing into the future, or at least imagining he was. But suddenly, it no longer seemed to matter. It didn't bother him, he was just mildly curious – as if he had become aware in a dream that he was dreaming. He would wake up in a few moments and everything would be fine. Back to normal.

Out of curiosity he moved along to the next headstone. It was a similar size to Annie Porter's, but it looked more expensive, a fine white marble.

Then, as he read the carved inscriptions, he felt the ground suddenly dropping beneath his feet, as if he was in a plunging elevator.

He stared, rooted to the spot. The twenty-first of September was today.

57

Ollie turned on his heel and sprinted through the church-yard, out through the lychgate, grabbed his bike and, without wasting time to switch on the lights, rode as fast as he could back up through the village.

Then, as he approached the pub, he saw it was back to how it had been before. Slightly gloomy and shabby-looking, the sign, 'The Crown', in need of some maintenance. The smithy was still there, too, as it had been before. And the 'Bed & Breakfast' sign was back.

Normality again.

But he was shaking. He was scared rigid. He wanted to get back to Caro and Jade. Had to stop them from leaving the house. They *must* stay there, be calm, wait, get through the night and into tomorrow. To 22 September. To make sure what he had seen was just a dream, part of the weird stuff that was going on in his head, and not a time-slip into the future.

He was finding the exertion of pedalling hard. A short distance up the hill, he stopped and dismounted, panting hard and sweating profusely. Then as he stood, slowly getting his breath back, a figure loomed out of the darkness, striding down the hill towards him, with a pipe in his mouth. Moments later he could make out the white hair and the goatee beard of Harry Walters.

'Harry!' Ollie said.

Walters strode straight on past him as if, like the clergyman in the graveyard just now, he had not seen him. Then he stopped a short distance along the road and turned his head. 'You should have listened to me. I told you to leave while you could. You stupid bugger.' Then he marched on.

Ollie dropped the bike and sprinted after him. 'Harry! Harry!' Then he stopped. Right in front of his eyes, Harry Walters had vanished into thin air.

An icy slick of fear wormed through him.

He turned and walked back up to his bike. As he stooped to pick it up, he heard the roar of a powerful car coming up the hill, fast. Then he saw its headlights. He stepped to the side of the road to let it past, although with the road closed ahead for the accident, it wasn't going to get very far, he thought.

As it drew alongside, still travelling at speed, too fast for this narrow lane, he saw it was a massive, left-hand-drive 1960s Cadillac Eldorado convertible. The driver's window was partially down and Ollie could hear music blasting out. The Kinks, 'Sunny Afternoon'.

Then, as he watched its huge tail lights disappear round a bend, he smelled a rich waft of cigar smoke in the air.

He remounted and pedalled on, wary of meeting the Cadillac coming back down. It would not get through the police roadblock. Then, after only a couple more minutes' riding, as he drew level with Garden Cottage, he had to stop again for a rest. What the hell was wrong with him, he wondered? Why was he so short of breath?

As he stood panting he was distracted by the cottage gate. It was back to how it had been, shabby and hanging badly from its rusty hinges.

He didn't have the energy to ride any more, so he

pushed the bike on up the hill. He was greeted by the grinding sound of cutting equipment as he rounded the bend. A blue and white 'Police Accident' sign had been placed in the middle of the road, and an officer in a yellow fluorescent jacket and white cap, holding a torch, stood beside it.

As Ollie reached him, panting hard, and staring with a deep chill at the work going on around the crushed car, he said, 'I live just up there – Cold Hill House.'

'OK, you can come through, sir, but I'll have to accompany you.'

'Can you tell me anything about what's happened?' he asked.

'I'm afraid not, sir.'

'I think the people in that car were coming to see my wife and me,' he said.

'Friends of yours, sir?'

'The local vicar and another chap. I recognize the car. That tractor driver – he's a bloody reckless idiot – tears up and down here like it's a racetrack.'

'But you didn't witness the collision, did you, sir?'

'No, I didn't. I think I may have heard it.'

'Thank you, all right, if you could move along please, sir, there's a hoist just coming up the hill.'

'Yes – sure. Er – can you tell me, where did that Cadillac go, just now?'

'Cadillac?'

'Yes, a great big 1960s convertible – it went shooting past me a couple of minutes ago.'

'It didn't come up here, sir, I'd have stopped it. It must have turned off.'

Ollie nodded and said nothing as he pushed his bike,

shivering with shock as he passed the wreckage, and went in through the gates. But he knew.

Knew that from the point where the Cadillac had passed him, to here, there was no turn-off.

58

Two alpacas trotted over through the misty gloom, as Ollie stopped again for a rest, halfway up the drive. He was feeling so exhausted that if he'd had his phone with him, he might have called Caro and asked her to come down and pick him and his bike up in the Range Rover. But in his haste he'd left it up in his study.

He had a bug, clearly. He needed to go to bed when he got home. Maybe he should have gone to bed over the weekend to shake it off.

He was feeling sick and feverish. Images of two crushed bodies, bleeding, maybe some of their internal organs exposed, went round in his mind. Friendly, caring Roland Fortinbrass. Crushed. The Minister of Deliverance whom he had not met. Crushed.

TWEEDLEDUM AND TWEEDLEDEE ARE ON THEIR WAY! THAT'S WHAT YOU THINK. THEY'RE DEAD. YOU ALL ARE.

The house loomed ahead in the starless darkness. He could see the yellow glow of the hall light, and the one up in his office. Drenched in perspiration, he wheeled his bike, treading carefully in the darkness, round to the back of the house. There were more lights on here – the atrium and the kitchen, their bedroom and Jade's room. In the weak glow from the windows he put the bike back in the shed, then went into the atrium.

'Hi, darling!' he called out.

Then he saw the two suitcases in the hall, by the front door.

'Caro?' he shouted.

'I'm up here,' she shouted back.

He climbed the stairs and went along into their bedroom. Two more large suitcases lay on the floor. She was folding clothes into one of them.

'What are you doing?' he said.

'I tried to get hold of you, you weren't answering your phone.'

'I left it up in my office.'

'The old lady from Garden Cottage called me. She told me about the accident – the vicar's car. She said there are two people in it. I think we both know who they are, don't we?'

She turned to face him.

He walked over to her and put his arms round her. 'We're going to get through this, darling.'

'We're leaving. Now. Jade, you, me, Bombay and Sapphire. We're not staying another night here.'

'I don't feel well, I need to go to bed.'

Breaking gently away from his arms, she walked over to the bed and put her hand on it. 'You're going to sleep in this? Touch it, Ollie. Touch it!'

He followed her and touched the counterpane. It was sopping wet. He touched the top pillow and it was sodden.

'Shit,' he said.

'Look at the walls,' she said, pointing with her finger.

They were glistening with moisture.

'We could sleep in the drawing room again.'

'No,' she said. 'All the bedding is sopping wet. Jade's room is the same. We don't even have a dry towel in the house. We need to leave, now.'

She closed up her suitcase. 'Get packing. Just take whatever you need for tomorrow. Mum and Dad are expecting us, she's making some supper.'

'Caro, this is—'

'This is what, Oliver?'

His head was swimming. 'Darling – OK – give me an hour, I've got to get some stuff together up in my office.'

'No, we're going now. I'm taking Jade and the cats. You come on when you're ready. I'll make sure we keep some supper for you.'

There was no point arguing. 'OK,' he said, thinking about the news report he had heard earlier today on his way back from Cholmondley's showroom. 'Take the Range Rover, will you?'

'I don't like driving it, you know I don't, it's too big for me.'

He held her again in his arms and tried to kiss her, but she turned her face away. 'Please, tonight, take it. I'll bring the Golf.'

'Why?'

'Because . . .' He hesitated, not wanting to tell her what he had heard on the radio. 'You can get all the stuff in there more easily.'

She shrugged. 'OK.'

'I'll give you a hand loading it.'

'No, get on with your packing. Jade'll help me. OK?'

'OK,' he said, reluctantly.

He lugged her suitcase down into the hall and placed it by the front door with the other cases. As he turned round he saw his daughter coming towards him holding the two cat baskets.

'OK, my lovely?'

'Are we coming back soon, Dad?'

'Soon.' He kissed her, then climbed back up the stairs. He stopped on the landing to get his breath back, feeling giddy and as if he was about to throw up. He took several deep breaths, then carried on up the tower stairs and into his office.

He walked over to his desk and sat down in his swivel chair in front of his computer, completely exhausted and half-expecting to see another message on the screen.

But there was nothing.

He closed his eyes. It felt like a steel band was tightening round his chest. He sat there for several minutes, dozing fitfully.

A *ping* from his phone startled him.

Down below, he heard the crunch of tyres on gravel, and the sound of a car receding.

He dozed again for a few moments. There was second *ping*.

Only half aware, he reached forward for his iPhone, picked it up and looked at the display. There was a message from Caro.

> **Range Rover has a flat battery. Have taken Golf.**
> **Call RAC and then join us as soon as you can.**
> **Love you. X**

'Nooooooooooooooo!' he yelled, jumping up from his chair with his phone in his hand, and throwing himself down the stairs, along the landing, down into the hall and to the front door. He raced out on to the driveway. 'Caro!' he shouted. 'Caro!'

The Range Rover sat there, dark and silent. Red tail lights were moving away from him, disappearing down the drive, over the brow of the hill.

'Caro!' he screamed. 'Caro!' He ran after her, breaking into a sprint, the tail lights receding further and further into the distance.

The police would stop her at the bottom, he thought. The accident. The road would still be closed. They wouldn't let her pass. Oh God, please don't!

As he ran on down past the field of alpacas he lost sight of the lights. Still he kept going, his chest tight, the steel grip tightening, tightening, tightening. The pain was excruciating.

It worsened.

Worsened.

Like daggers pushing into his chest and then twisting. He could not breathe.

Then, all at once, he felt unseen hands pulling him backwards.

'Noooo! Lemmego!'

It felt as if he was running against an ever-tightening elastic band. Running, fighting for breath.

'Lemmego!'

The faster he ran, the more the band hardened, tightened. The more the daggers twisted.

And suddenly he was treading air as if he was treading water.

The pain stopped.

He was being dragged backwards.

'Noooooooooo!'

He was pedalling air. Floating. Rising skywards.

'Nooooooo! Caro! Caro! Caro!'

Something was pulling him back towards the house. Faster and faster. Accelerating. Accelerating.

He saw the silent Range Rover right below him. He was going to be smashed to pulp against the front of the house.

Then, suddenly, he was in the kitchen. Everything was calm. All the pain around his chest was gone. Caro and Jade were seated at the table looking at him, and smiling. They were bathed in shimmering green light, as if a powerful lamp was shining behind each of them.

'Darling!' Caro said.

'Dad, epic!' Jade greeted him.

'Welcome home!' Caro said.

Jade nodded, enthusiastically.

The television on the wall was switched on. There was an aerial shot of emergency vehicles. A lorry at a skewed angle on a country road he recognized as being on the way to Caro's parents. The remnants of a Volkswagen Golf lay on its side a short distance away.

'See!' Caro said, happily. 'That's us! The dead have no more fears! We're in a good place now, aren't we, Ols?'

'We can stay here forever now, can't we, Dad?' Jade said.

As he looked at them both, they began to fade, the light behind each of them dimming.

'Come back! Come back!' he cried out.

His own voice was becoming weaker.

Then a stranger, a smartly dressed man in his late thirties, with slicked-back fair hair, wearing a grey suit with loud socks and buckled loafers, came into the kitchen, holding a clipboard with a notepad on it, a digital measurer and a camera.

He took several photographs from different angles.

'Excuse me, who are you?' Ollie asked.

The man ignored him, as if he had not seen him. He

began to ping a laser off the walls, measuring the width and length of the room, jotting them down on his pad.

'Hello?' Ollie said. 'Excuse me, hello?'

The man moved on, without responding, through into the scullery.

59

Wednesday, 21 September 2016

'Are we nearly there yet?'

Connor, sitting on the rear seat next to his sister in the Porsche Cayenne hybrid that was loaded to the gunwales with their possessions, had been driving both his parents nuts all the way down from London.

'Just a few minutes now.'

Why the hell couldn't his son be quiet, like his sister, Seb wondered? Leonora was sitting next to Connor with her headphones on, absorbed in the movie playing on the screen set into the rear headrests.

Nicola glanced at the satnav and turned to Connor. 'Five minutes, darling!'

They passed a sign saying COLD HILL – PLEASE DRIVE SLOWLY, then moments later the car, gliding fast and silently on electrical power, almost took off over a humpback bridge.

'Whoops!' Seb said.

'Slow down, darling,' Nicola cautioned him.

'Dad!' Leonora chided.

'Can we do that again, Dad?' Connor asked, excitedly. 'Can we, can we?'

It was a fine, late summer day. The roads from London had been clear all the way and they'd made good time. Seb was excited. He'd been a townie all his life, as had Nicola, but moving to the country had always been his dream. Now the takeover, by an American bank, of the wealth management company he'd been employed by for the past ten years had given him a massive windfall on his share options, enabling them to afford this country pile a few miles north of Brighton.

He shot a glance in the mirror and saw his son's excited face. 'This is where we're going to be living, Connor. We'll have tons of opportunities to do that bridge again!'

'Yeahhh! Coolio!'

'Coolio!' Seb replied.

He had never felt so happy in all his life. They were now minutes away from their new life.

It was going to be incredible!

Cold Hill House.

They'd already had the headed notepaper printed. *Cold Hill House.*

Not bad for a state-school-educated chap, whose dad had been a London postman. Not a bad achievement for a man who had not yet reached his fortieth birthday. Not bad at all, he thought, the grin on his face growing wider by the second.

They drove past a Norman church on their right, with an ornate wooden lychgate, a row of terraced Victorian artisan cottages, then the poshed-up gastropub, Bistrot Tarquin, where, just two months ago, he and Nicola had lunched on Oysters Rockefeller followed by grilled lobster, washed down with a rather fine Pouilly-Fuissé, and made the decision to offer on the house.

They passed a building with a sign, YE OLDE TEA SHOPPE. The road wound steeply uphill, past detached houses and bungalows of various sizes on either side.

The satnav read: *150 yards to destination.* An arrow indicated right.

Seb slowed the car down and flicked the right-turn indicator. 'Here we are!'

On their right, opposite a red postbox, were two stone pillars, topped with savage-looking ornamental wyverns, and with open, rusted, wrought-iron gates. Below the large Richwards 'Sold' board, fixed to the right-hand gatepost, was a smart gold-on-black sign announcing: COLD HILL HOUSE.

A minute later they crested the drive, and the house was directly in front of them. Seb's heart did a little flip at the beauty of the location. 'We're here!' he whooped with joy.

Nicola, peering through the windscreen, said, 'Who's that in the house?'

'Where?'

'I saw some people – there's a man, a woman and a young girl up there – in that window above the front door. The one with the Juliet balcony.'

Seb slowed down and stared up to where she was pointing. 'I can't see anything.'

'I must have imagined it,' she smiled.

'It looks pretty spooky!' Leonora shouted.

'Maybe it's full of ghosts!' Connor shrieked. 'Wooooo . . . wooooo!'

Seb halted the car in front of the porch, and glanced at the house through the windscreen. 'Just as soon as we get the planning permission through, we're going to tear the whole place down and build our dream home here!'

Nicola leaned over and kissed him.

A moment later his phone pinged with an incoming text. He looked at the screen and saw the message on it.

OVER MY DEAD BODY.

ACKNOWLEDGEMENTS

I owe an enormous debt of thanks to the Rance family – Matt, Emma and their daughter, Charlie – for allowing me to use the lovely and smart Charlie as the model for my character Jade Harcourt. She and her parents were massively generous in their help and advice and I could never have conjured such a personality out of thin air.

In addition I'd like to thank others who helped so much with my research, including Gary, Rachel and (superstar!) Bailey Kenchington, Jim Banting, Richard Edmondson (Senior Partner, Woolley Bevis Diplock solicitors), Michael Maguire, Robin and Debbie Sheppard, Jason Tingley, and the Reverend Dominic Walker.

I'm fortunate to have a terrific support group, whom we jokingly call Team James, who all provide vital feedback at various stages of the writing process. A massive thank you to Susan Ansell, Graham Bartlett, Martin and Jane Diplock, Anna-Lisa Hancock, Sarah Middle and Helen Shenston. To my agents Carole Blake, Julian Friedmann, Louise Brice, Melis Dagoglu, and to all the team at my UK publishers, Pan Macmillan – including Wayne Brookes, Geoff Duffield, Anna Bond, Sara Lloyd, Toby Watson, Stuart Dwyer, Charlotte Williams, Rob Cox, Fraser Crichton, and my wonderful publicists, Tony Mulliken, Sophie Ransom, Becky Short and Eve Wersocki of Midas.

I need to single out three people above all others – former Detective Chief Superintendent David Gaylor, my model for Detective Superintendent Roy Grace, who has become my good friend and sometime slave driver(!); my assistant, Linda Buckley, who has an endless capacity for hard work and helping free up my time for writing, as well as a brilliant eye for detail; and lastly, but also first – my beloved Lara, who is such a wise head and brilliant sounding board, and a constant pillar of support in every possible way. And of course no acknowledgements would be complete without a mention of our wonderful canine friends, Oscar, our Lab/Bull Mastiff/Parson Russell cross rescue dog and our recent arrival – our labradoodle puppy, very appropriately named, for this book, Spook!

As ever, thank you, my wonderful readers! I always love to hear from you, either on Twitter, Facebook or Instagram, and your comments give me such constant encouragement.

Peter James
Sussex, England

scary@pavilion.co.uk
www.peterjames.com
(You can also sign up to my regular
Newsletter – the link is on my website.)
www.facebook.com/peterjames.roygrace
www.twitter.com/peterjamesuk
www.instagram.com/peterjamesuk